GW01539824

Mr Brouard's Odyssey

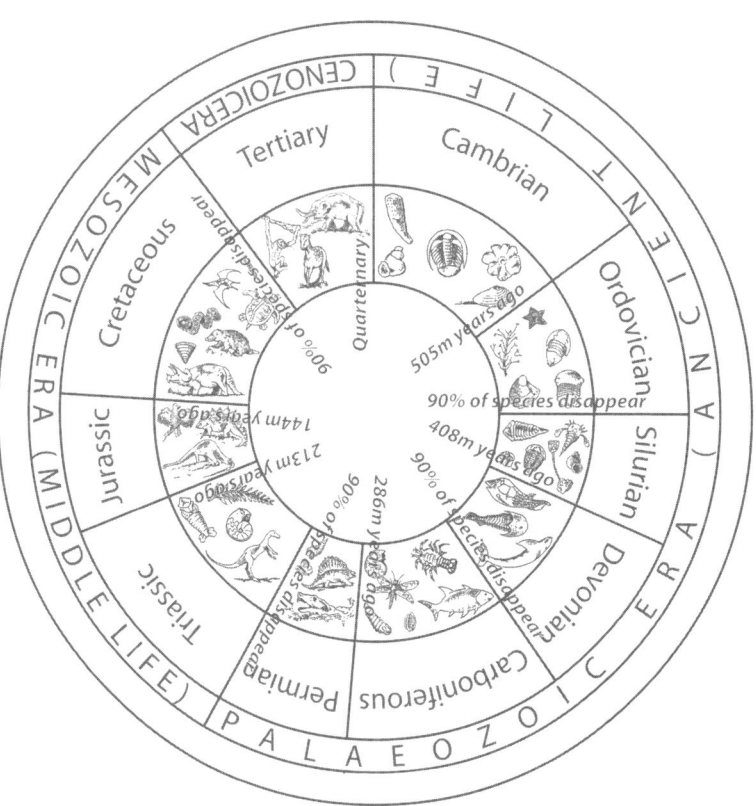

Diana Winsor

To Dad

© Diana Winsor 2004

ISBN 09544233-5-6

Published by
Polperro Heritage Press
Clifton-upon-Teme
Worcestershire WR6 6EN

Cover design by Steve Bowgen

Printed by Orphans Press
Leominster HR6 8JT

CONTENTS

He tipped it out of the bucket on to the white sand of Proof Beach. It was called Proof Beach because it was used for proving ammunition by firing. Behind it were immensely high cliffs to which tall pines clung, draped with lianas. At one end of it was the entrance to the armament depot, where Gurpal Singh guarded the gates set into a high iron perimeter fence. You would not have known that within the fence were vast underground chambers filled with explosives. Stonecutters was then a secret place, one of the last fragments of the old woodland of the Pearl River delta. Kites circled above its canopy of trees and you might meet a cobra on the road that ran along its narrow spine. The Chinese called it Ngon Shun Chau, which means sunk ship island, for that is what it looked like. The British called it Stonecutters because it had once been quarried for granite building stone. In the 1990s it was subsumed into the new Hong Kong airport.

"I could take it to school," I said. "To show Mr Brouard."

Hong Kong was very English in 1957. My father was in charge of the armament depot and we lived in a large white house on the highest peak of Stonecutters Island, with a view across the harbour to Victoria. At night the city lights were a necklace of diamonds beyond the velvety red geraniums that stood in pots along the garden wall. My mother had a part-time job in the governor's office. The junks and sampans still had sails, VC10s still skimmed the Kowloon rooftops as they came into land at Kai Tak Airport and the only Americans were on leave from Korea looking for Suzie Wong. There were red London buses and I went to a British school where we were taught by a man who wore a red handlebar moustache. He had flown Hurricanes in the war. He read *The Odyssey* to us and made us learn a poem every month. He kept a size thirteen gym shoe in his desk for wayward boys. We worshipped him. His name was William Brouard.

"By God," said Mr Brouard. "It is a king crab. Otherwise known as a horseshoe crab. One of the oldest creatures on earth. Leave it with me. I'll find out about it."

We were ten years old but he treated us like adults. It was one of the reasons we worshipped him. Another was that he always kept his promises.

"All right," he said at lunchtime the next day. "I've found out about it."

We gathered round his large desk. Outside the hot Hong Kong sky was like aluminium and the leaves of the banana trees hung motionless in the humid air. Typhoon Vera was predicted.

"Starting to smell a bit," he said, as he placed the crab on a sheet of newspaper. It had lost its shiny wetness: it looked dull, a little rusty, its black bean eyes greyer.

"There isn't much that hasn't changed over six hundred million years," he said. "But the horseshoe crab is one of them. Its shell is an external skeleton which it sheds every now and then as it grows, and it produces a new and larger one. But its eyes are actually part of the shell, so it also has to grow new eyes as well. They are quite complex compound eyes. Any of you know what the world was like six hundred million years ago?"

"Dinosaurs," said Charlie Thomas.

"You're about four hundred million years out," said Mr Brouard. "There wasn't much life at all on the earth six hundred million years ago, except for mosses and lichens and green slime on ponds. No other plants, no animals. The continents were different, too. They were still to come together over hundreds of millions of years to form a single vast land mass, then break up until they formed the world as we know it today. And there weren't any fish in the seas six hundred million years ago. But there were all kinds of worms, molluscs, jellyfish and trilobites – strange little creatures with highly developed eyes. The horseshoe crab is their last surviving relation. That might be because it learned to come out of the sea to lay its eggs, so that all the other creatures couldn't eat them. And it's still doing it. Every year, at the time of the highest spring tide, hundreds of thousands of horseshoe crabs come out of the sea for miles along the sand. Their domed shells shine in the light of the full moon as they move slowly up the beach. The males mate with the females and then the females dig nests in the sand to lay their eggs in. After that they go back into the sea. Sometimes a few get left behind, or get turned over by the waves and can't get back. Like this one."

We looked upon the horseshoe crab with compassion.

"What about the eggs, then?" I said. "I mean, if they hatch

out, then how do the little horseshoe crabs get back into the sea?"

"Well," said Mr Brouard, "that's the clever bit. At first they're just tiny larvae, looking like tiny trilobites, and they manage to make their way down to the wet sand at the tide's edge, and then they spend a year or two living there, burrowing into the sand in the daytime. Quite soon they look like minute horseshoe crabs, and as they grow they shed their shells. And as they get bigger, so they move down into the deep sea, where they live for years until they're old enough to come back to the shore to spawn."

"But how do they know where to come? I mean – if the continents are in different places now?"

"Well, for the horseshoe crab it doesn't really matter. Five or six hundred million years ago Proof Beach was probably somewhere near the South Pole. But the horseshoe crab just follows its instincts and comes back to the place it's always known – now, the coasts of south east Asia and the Atlantic shores of North America, but then, well – anywhere."

For a moment we stood and regarded the horseshoe crab with deep respect. Then Charlie Thomas said: "if that's been around for six hundred million years – how long have we been here, then? I mean us people?"

Mr Brouard leaned back on his swivel armchair. "Well, let's think about time. Even the greatest experts find it hard to imagine such a vast stretch of time as six hundred million years. Picture a clock. An ordinary clock, like that one over the blackboard. If you think of the horseshoe crab appearing on earth at about midnight, and today being twelve noon, then every figure on the clock face represents fifty million years. Every time the minute hand moves, more than eight hundred thousand years pass. You could get some idea of the timescale of events by looking at that clock. The dinosaurs would appear about eight o'clock this morning and disappear about twenty past ten. It's nearly twelve noon now: nearly break time. If I let you off two minutes early by the horseshoe crab's clock, it would mean about a million years. That's when the first human beings may have appeared. The first civilisation was built in Iraq only around six thousand years ago, and some people would say that's when human history began. But that would be a mere half a second on the horseshoe crab's clock. Does that answer your question?"

Charlie looked baffled. "We haven't been here long, then," he said at last.

It was getting dark. The sky was like a great dark bruise. A spatter of wind and rain hit the windows of our classroom.

"Makes you think, don't it?" said Charlie Thomas. "I mean, about where we come from."

"We were apes in Africa," I said. "Once."

"Well, I'm not absolutely certain about that," said Mr Brouard. "Evolution is a complicated subject. It rather depends on what you mean by 'we'. The horseshoe crab hasn't evolved at all: it's almost the same as it was six hundred million years ago, because nothing has made it necessary for it to change. We have: but just what has *made* us change is arguable. At least in my opinion. You've probably got your own opinions about it, but I have my doubts as to whether *Homo sapiens sapiens* evolved from apes in the African savannah".

We tried to look as if we did have our own opinions about evolution, but with some difficulty. Mr Brouard, observing our intelligently blank expressions, gave his jolly laugh and said it was about time we did some work.

He came home with me that evening. He had become friendly with my father and he often came to supper. The wind was still increasing and the journey in the small boat to Stonecutters Island was unusually exciting. The harbour was almost empty. Junks and sampans had all gone to the typhoon shelter at Yau Ma Ti. Except one.

Typhoon Vera struck just before midnight and by morning the garden was littered with broken branches, although the gardener had moved all the pots to safety and secured everything that might be blown away. The banana trees, complete with their fat little bananas that tasted like strawberries and cream, were intact. Even the frangipani tree still stood, its grey skeletal limbs bearing a few waxy perfumed flowers. But from the garden wall I could look down from our hill, beyond a grassy meadow and the tennis court, to the east gate and pier of the armament depot. The grey surrounding sea was still lashing the boulders along the sandy shore. And I could see that a sampan had capsized. It was being carried in on the breakers on the white-marled waves, and clinging to its upturned hull were several figures. All around it, spread in the sea, was the bobbing flotsam of all their possessions. Sampan people seldom went ashore: each small boat was home to two or three generations of a single family.

My father and Mr Brouard were among the first there, both in flapping khaki shorts, launching my father's little clinker-built sailing dinghy kept inside the depot gates. My mother and I followed, as did the Sikh policemen. Once the sampan-dwellers were helped ashore my father and Mr Brouard managed to recover cargoes of pots and pans and sodden bedding, lamps and mats and clothes. And a hen coop with a loudly complaining cockerel. The wind had eased but even so they only had the mainsail up a bit, and several times almost capsized themselves.

The following morning, when the sun had come out again and we had lined up in our two rows outside his classroom ("Not a *muscle* is to move...") Mr Brouard asked me how the sampan people were.

"They've gone," I said. "They stayed with us last night – well, with Ah Chan and Ah Jong in the servants' quarters – but this morning it was just as if they'd never been there at all. They'd taken everything, and the sampan, and just disappeared. Well, except for a plastic bucket with a hole in it."

He looked me in silence for a moment, as if on that Peak in Darien (we did Keats too). Then his blue eyes became even more prominent than usual, his face redder, his voice, when it emerged, louder. "Of course! This is the key to it! They could come ashore – they could use the sampan as shelter, make some sort of home here on land – but they couldn't go back without a boat! They'd have to build one, wouldn't they? And if they did, then the only evidence of their being here at all would be what was left on the land. A blue plastic bucket! And *no* evidence of all those other sampans over there in the typhoon shelter, of the junks in the harbour or the estuary or out at sea. You see – *no one ever considers the sea!*"

I suppose that was the real beginning of my part in his obsession.

2.

Darwin and DNA

The following year I returned to England with my family, and although Mr Brouard had said "keep in touch" in his breezy way, I thought no more of him in the upheaval of departure and arrival. My father had been appointed to Bath, and I had won a scholarship to a girls' direct grant school. Hong Kong was another world. Mine, then, formed an intimate schoolgirl pattern, days of Wordsworth and Shakespeare and Gerard Manley Hopkins, inexplicable maths and the ordeal of asthmatic hockey, each day bound by the final saunter down Lansdown Hill in the sunlight of golden afternoons. Few of Bath's buildings had been cleaned in those days, and its pale porous stone was smudged with a century of soot, but it was still beautiful. People fought, then, to save the simple vernacular of Georgian terrace and cottage from the planners' destruction. Much was lost. Such was the certainty of progress: modern architecture must be an improvement on the eighteenth century, concrete on oolitic limestone.

Yet I never quite forgot Mr Brouard, or the horseshoe crab. Despite my other preoccupations with exams and ponies and giggling over Cliff Richard, my interest in boats and prehistory gradually increased, like an idle stream meandering through watermeadows. And there was a good deal of watery exploration going during that time. Wilfred Thesiger had been living with and chronicling the life of the Marsh Arabs in southern Iraq, Thor Heyerdahl had sailed his raft Kon-Tiki across the Pacific, and the oldest boat in the world had been discovered beneath the Great Pyramid of Giza in Egypt. It had been buried at the same time as King Cheops about four and a half thousand years ago. Rachel Carson published *Silent Spring* and I was reminded of her earlier warning of the damage we were doing to the earth in *The Sea Around Us*, which had been among the books Mr Brouard had read to us at school.

He had made all of us interested in words. When he heard one of us swearing, he discussed with us the origin of as many swear words as we could think of, until the fun went out of them. I remember Charlie Rogers saying "blimey's all right, isn't it, sir?" But when we realised it meant God Blind Me, we didn't think it was. He made literature come alive. We read Homer, Shakespeare, Milton, T. S. Eliot. He made us learn whole chunks of poetry. With his large feet on his desk, sitting back in the special chair he always said he needed for his back, he read us everything from Chaucer to *The Wind In the Willows* and encouraged us to paint pictures inspired by them. He used words to connect us to the world beyond the carefree confines of childhood: he told us about Suez and the Hungarian revolution and what was happening in Red China.

My parents remembered him, too. When one day I mentioned him, my father said he recalled Bill Brouard's interest in the Tanka people, following that capsize of the sampan. "He became fascinated by them. I don't know if you remember, but he used to do some part-time lecturing at the technical college in Hong Kong. Technical drawing. One of his students came from a family of junk people. He was particularly brilliant and Bill helped him get some sort of scholarship to MIT in America. They used to argue about the western view of evolution. This young student – can't recall his name - didn't believe that Man walked out of Africa and across the entire globe to end up on the estuary of the Yellow River. He reckoned his ancestors had always lived on the sea. Each man used to regard his craft as the fixed centre of his world, to which, by magic, he could draw islands and continents to him, hooking them like a fish when close enough, so that they remained still while he went ashore."

My mother said she had heard that Mr Brouard's wife had left him a year or so after our departure from Hong Kong. I had known that he was married, and had a vague memory of once meeting Mrs Brouard and their small daughter, who must have been about three years old at the time.

"I don't know all the circumstances," my mother said. "I think Margaret wanted to go back to England, and perhaps he didn't; anyway, she went, and took the little girl with her. Molly, I think her name was. As far as I know they're living with her parents in Devon."

Sometimes I thought it was Mr Brouard who had implanted in me the desire to be a writer. I had no desire to go to university, or art school. I could not wait to leave school to write and I was naïve enough to say so. I had already published several short stories, even sharing space with Graham Greene in a magazine called Argosy, but my teachers were unimpressed. "Journalism might suit you," said my headmistress, as though suggesting prostitution. We shook hands when I left and as I smiled and thanked her I wondered why she always had a damp lace handkerchief concealed in her palm.

I took a secretarial course and then got a job on *The Times Educational Supplement* in London and a bedsit in Barnes. At that time, when *The Times* was owned by the Astor family, it carried no bylines, which gave scope for people like me to write articles and book reviews, after which we could flog the review copies at a secondhand bookshop in Fleet Street. Not long after I had arrived I was asked to write a review of a biography of the Jesuit philosopher and palaeontologist Pierre Teilhard de Chardin. Being a conscientious person I began by reading de Chardin's *Phenomenon of Man.* It was elegantly written and poignant because it had been published after his death, the Jesuits having forbidden him to publish, but I wondered whether he was right to assume that humanity was progressing to spiritual perfection.

I had been brought up to believe in Darwin. Natural selection was the key to Man's upward ascent of the evolutionary ladder. Yet when I had read *The Voyage of the Beagle,* I was disturbed by his account of the three native Canoe Indians from Tierra del Fuego who shared part of the voyage with him. Two men, a boy and a little girl had originally been taken back to England three years earlier by the captain of the *Beagle*, Robert Fitzroy. Now they were being returned to their home. One of the men had died of smallpox, but the other, named – rather obscurely – York Minster – survived, together with the boy, Jeremy Button (a pearl button being the price paid for him) and the girl, who was given the name Fuegia Basket. They had been objects of curiosity in England and had learned to speak English. Fuegia had a remarkable talent for languages, and all had extraordinarily acute eyesight. Darwin wrote that he did not notice them until the Beagle arrived at their homeland.

Tierra del Fuego was a forbidding place of high rainswept mountains, peat bogs and bronze evergreen beech forests. Darwin was not impressed with the natives, particularly when he encountered six naked Fuegians in a canoe: "even one full-grown woman was absolutely so. It was raining heavily, and the fresh water, together with the spray, trickled down her body. In another harbour not far distant, a woman, who was suckling a recently-born child, came one day alongside the vessel, and remained there out of mere curiosity, whilst the sleet fell and thawed on her naked bosom, and on the skin of her naked baby!"

He described how they would sleep on the wet ground coiled up like animals, rising to pick shellfish from the rocks; "and the women either dive to collect sea-eggs, or sit patiently in their canoes, and with a baited hair-line without any hook, jerk out little fish. If a seal is killed, or the floating carcass of a putrid whale is discovered, it is a feast; and such miserable food is assisted by a few tasteless berries and fungi".

There were stories of old women being killed for food, and of fathers killing their babies. Darwin could find nothing to respect in their ability to survive – "their country is a broken mass of wild rocks, lofty hills, and useless forests...in search of food they are compelled unceasingly to wander from spot to spot, and so steep is the coast, that they can only move about in their wretched canoes. They cannot know the feeling of having a home, and still less that of domestic affection."   To knock a limpet from the rock "does not require even cunning, that lowest power of the mind". He did wonder where they came from:

> "Whilst beholding these savages, one asks, whence have they come? What could have tempted, or what change compelled a tribe of men, to leave the fine regions of the north, to travel down the Cordillera or backbone of America, to invent and build canoes...then to enter on one of the most inhospitable countries within the limits of the globe?"

Darwin also thought their culture, such as it was, deficient:

> "The perfect equality among the individuals composing the Fuegian tribes must for a long time retard their civilisation. As we see those animals, whose instinct compels them to live in society and obey a chief, are most capable of improvement, so it is with the races of mankind.   Whether we look at it as a cause or a consequence, the more civilised always have the most artificial governments...until some chief shall arise with power sufficient to secure any acquired advantage, such as the domesticated animals, it seems scarcely possible that the political state of the country can be improved. At present, even a piece of cloth given to one is torn into shreds and distributed; and no one individual becomes richer than another."

He was curious, therefore, about the desire of the three Fuegian Indians on the *Beagle* to return to this bleak place. Quite taken by the cheerful disposition of Jemmy Button, he observed: "it seems yet wonderful to me, when I think over all his many good qualities, that he should have been of the same race, and doubtless partaken of the same character, with the miserable, degraded savages whom we first met here".

Nevertheless York Minster, Jemmy Button and Fuegia Basket did want to go home, and so they were left behind when the Beagle departed.

It did not surprise me that Karl Marx was a great admirer of Darwin. He wrote: "Darwin recognises among beasts and plants his English society with its division of labour, competition, opening up of new markets, invention, and the Malthusian struggle for existence".

I kept thinking about Jemmy Button: why did he want to go home, if home was so wretched, and he had tasted the joys of civilisation in Victorian London?

Sometimes I wished I had gone to university, where I imagined everybody sat around talking about such philosophical things. I wished I could ask Mr Brouard what he thought.

One night when I was alone in my bedsit I wrote a letter to him. I told him about my curiosity on the subject of Darwin and Jeremy Button. I posted the letter to Gun Club Hill School in Hong Kong.

It was extremely cold in London at the time. My brother had kindly sent me an electric blanket, so I spent most of my time, when bereft of cash or an invitation, in bed. I was not a very adventurous young woman. I was often lonely and missed the tennis club at home. One night, having visited a girlfriend's flat in Knightsbridge, I was waiting for a No. 9 bus when a young man with an Italian accent asked if I knew which bus he should take to Richmond. I pointed out that he would need to get the No. 73 but that if he got the No. 9 then he might be able to change, on the other hand he could wait for the late bus – at which point he smiled, touched my cheek, said "I was going to ask you to come in my car, but you are too innocent", and departed to a BMW parked round the corner.

*

I did not receive a reply to my letter for several months, which meant that I had to write the review of the book on Teilhard de Chardin without his advice. There were no objections to my review – indeed there was no reaction at all. Then I received a small package in the post. It bore a French postmark. My original letter to Mr Brouard had been forwarded from Hong Kong. A short letter explained that he was staying with his sister, Frederika, who was married to a French doctor and lived near Rouen. With the letter was a shabby cloth-bound book called *Uttermost Part of the Earth,* by E. Lucas Bridges, published in America in 1949. "You may find this of interest," Mr Brouard wrote. "Let me know. It is yours to keep."

E. Lucas Bridges had been born on Tierra del Fuego in 1874. His parents were missionaries, inspired to settle on the island by Captain Fitzroy of Darwin's *Beagle.* Bridges had therefore observed the inhabitants at first hand, and *Uttermost Part of the Earth* was his account of their way of life. By then it was summer, and I read much of the book while lying on the warm grass of Hyde Park, London's surrounding murmur translated into the rhythm of the South Atlantic.

It seemed that there were two tribes living in Tierra del Fuego, collectively known as the Canoe Indians, but the most distinctive were the Alacaloof Inidans. They were anatomically and physiologically adapted to the climate of long, cold winters and short, hot summers, almost entirely dependent on the sea. They ate chiefly birds, seal, fish and shellfish. Curiously, it seemed that the men tended to remain on land, hunting otters and seals, gathering plants and lichens and wood for fires – and, perhaps most importantly, building dug-out canoes up to ten metres long. But it was not they who went to sea. The seafaring fishermen were the women.

Bridges described how the women were strong swimmers, mooring their canoes offshore, lashed to the seaweed-mantled rocks and coming ashore in the icy water. They would swim out not only with babies on their backs, clinging to their hair, but also carrying wood and the embers of a fire. So cold and bitter was the weather that they built fires on the boats, on a bed of stones and turf. And the women had charge of the canoes, travelling great distances. Sometimes fleets of the boats would hunt whales, although more often they relied on beached whales for fat.

Their language, which Darwin had described as "meaningless clicks", suggested they spoke an extinct language similar to those surviving in southern Africa. It appeared to have a vocabulary of over 30,000 words – which was perhaps why Fuegia Basket found it so easy to learn English and Spanish.

There was a note at the back of the book.

"Bridges died a year after this was published. The tribes he saw eventually merged, later to be superseded by the Ona Indians from Patagonia, who were quite different. They are all now extinct, any survivors having long since interbred with other mainland peoples. Where they once lived there is now a luxury hotel. But among its architects might well be one of the descendants of those formidable canoe women, for essentially they were no different from ourselves. They simply gave us a glimpse of how we once were."

I wrote to thank him for the book, and told him of my interest. And he replied a month or so later. This time he expanded a little. He said he was pursuing his ideas on the evolution of human beings, their origins and technology, and their links with the sea. He was therefore travelling a good deal. I think he had been surprised and perhaps pleased with my questions: he wrote at some length about his views on Darwinian theory.

"The success of the Industrial Revolution established the concept of evolutionary improvement in England – that is, if you think of it as success. Philosophers became interested in the way in which plant and animal breeders were able to improve their stock by selecting those which best suited their purpose, and killing the rest. The Reverend Malthus took the rather un-Christian view that Nature herself improved the population by allowing middle-class children to thrive, while killing off the larger families of the lazy and immoral poor...

"When Darwin and Wallace discovered that the simple processes by which individual animals adapted to changing circumstances, and how the 'survival of the fittest' could radically transform groups of them, the idea arose of an evolutionary ladder up which selected species climbed from tiny worm contemporaries of the horseshoe crab to become, successively, fish, amphibians, reptiles, mammals, primates, apes, ape-men, savages and finally Modern European. I suppose you might easily appreciate how a contemporary of the horseshoe crab could evolve into a lobster or a spider, given sufficiently extraordinary circumstances, but it's hard to quite see how a it could become a man. But then, of course, there was Mendel.

"Gregor Mendel, the saintly abbot of a Moravian monastery and a contemporary of Darwin's, wrote down details of his experiments on peas to show how heredity was controlled by what he called 'discrete factors' – what we call genes. He sent off forty copies of his paper to all the learned societies of Europe. None could understand such scientific precision, or troubled to acknowledge it. All but four copies were lost. Then, at the beginning of this century, one copy was found. Mendel then became 'the Father of Genetics'.

At this point he wrote a single line: "Am I boring you?" And then continued.

"Genetics has become an interesting new field of science. I've been in correspondence with Sir Fred Hoyle at Cambridge. He has this idea that viral particles from outer space may have been continually bombarding the earth in the heads of small comets, made up of ice, silicate smoke and organic molecules, forming all the essential building blocks of life. It sounds a little off the wall but I think there's something in it. A mature virus is a complex compound of protein and nucleic acid, and it doesn't do anything unless – and until - it alights on a specific host cell, when it penetrates the protective wall and comes to life like a genie out of a bottle. Its nucleic acid replaces that of its host cell, so the cellular factory switches to the reproduction of viruses. These usually kill the host cell, releasing a horde of viruses. That's what happens when you get a cold and start spreading it to everyone around you.

"But sometimes the nucleic acid of the virus allies itself with that of the living cell, its host, in a process technically called transformation. It gives it a new genetic pattern. Most species of plants and animals are subject to this sort of viral attack, and although most viruses have very specific hosts, some have more catholic tastes. And when a virus infects creatures of different families, it can alter their DNA.

"If you look at the long history of life on earth, the pathways of viral transformation represent a unique creative agency between otherwise separate classes of living things. And each time a new prototype was created, so it evolved defensive machinery, often of the most ingenious complexity, which then went on the offensive to occupy some vacant niche in nature, and colonised it. So evolution doesn't seem to me so much a matter of progress, but a complicated way of conserving whatever a virus, God, or what you will – has created.

"I think the science of genetics, touching as it does biochemistry, microbiology, even animal behaviour and engineering, will look increasingly at the creation and modification of living things. And it will give us the opportunity to look not just at the future, but the past. The remote past. The only clues we have now to prehistory are a few flint tools, some teeth and fragments of bone, from which the finders can weave their stories, just as no doubt Darwin's Fuegian Indians wove their folk tales. Our knowledge of DNA might change our ideas. Reason says that every living creature must have a mother, and always had, so that there must be a continuous line of ancestral mothers going back to the beginning of time: we are, as it were, part of a family which includes not only the living anthropoid apes but all the long-extinct ones which might have been more like us than any of our living cousins. But for the mother of this hugely diversified family we would have to go back a very long way. About, I think, sixty-five million years..."

Somewhat baffled by all this, I began to read rather more on the subject of evolution and prehistory, and to occupy something of a niche of my own on the *Educational Supplement* – books on anything about the origins of man or ancient history were directed at me. If the book was by a rather eminent author I was asked if I knew of a suitable reviewer. The deputy editor handled the book pages: he was an ex Latin teacher who famously lectured with a pet jackdaw.

"Thought you'd know who could do this," he said, presenting me with a copy of *The Living Stream* by Sir Alister Hardy, Professor of Zoology at Oxford. It was the published text of a lecture given at Aberdeen University, and the Professor described it as a "restatement of evolution theory and its relation to the spirit of man."

"I expect most of us will remember the feeling of awe that we experienced when we first realised that we were actually one with an organism that had existed some two thousand million years ago – that we were formed from part of the flesh of our parents and they from theirs, and so on back in one long chain into the past. We are part of a vast living stream flowing through time".

I sent the volume off to Mr Brouard in France.

He wrote an excellent review, including the paragraph:
"Yet I think Professor Hardy has another book to write. For years he has been fascinated by the possibility that Man has evolved from an ape adapted to a marine environment. As long ago as 1929, on an Antarctic expedition, he observed how the seals, whales and penguins all possessed layers of subcutaneous fat to help them survive in icy seas, and wondered if Man, the only primate to share this characteristic, might once have shared their ocean home. Did some primitive ape, perhaps driven to the shores of its continent, begin to adapt to the sea?"

"You can cut that bit," said the deputy editor. "Don't want to look as if we endorse the fellow's eccentricities."

With the review was a note from Mr Brouard telling me that he would be in London for a few days and as it happened would be seeing Sir Alister Hardy in Oxford, as the Professor had just written an article for *The New Scientist* called Was Man More Aquatic in the Past? He would be staying at the Strand Palace Hotel; perhaps I could suggest somewhere to meet for lunch?

When I look back at the 1960s I wonder how I could have missed so much that my contemporaries found so exciting, and to which they now look back with such nostalgia. I think many sins passed me by because I did not know they were there. I had been deeply affected by Rachel Carson's *Silent Spring*, and in London I joined Friends of the Earth and wore a lot of brown. Sex became very interesting but at the same I was deeply conventional and yearned for the chance to cook and iron shirts for someone. I fell in love several times with worldly and sophisticated young men. A number of older men said they had fallen in love with me, partly because I was so fresh and unsophisticated. It struck me that Mr Brouard was now among the latter, and I approached our meeting with increasing apprehension. I had suggested lunch at the Mermaid Theatre, which was just across from *The Times,* then in Printing House Square at Blackfriars. It was a sunny September morning when I left the office, accompanied by a tall, thin young man called Trepidation, whom I had always imagined wearing a dusty waistcoat and a gold watch chain.

3

My Big Toe

The Mermaid foyer was crowded with lunchtime people. I could see the theatre's founding genius, Bernard Miles, holding court over the quiche and salad. He had once told me I should go on the stage. I had never been sure quite why but had tucked the words away for occasional indulgence, along with the memory of someone overheard saying "you mean the girl with the beautiful eyes?", like a cache of chocolates.

He had said he would carry a copy of *The Times* but I recognised him anyway, although he had shaved off his moustache. He looked a little smaller than I remembered, a little slimmer – he had made a wonderful Ugly Sister with hardly any padding – but his face was still round, his eyes bright blue, although now behind gold-rimmed glasses. He was wearing a very old tweed jacket and a rather grubby tie. He did not recognise me at first, but rose as I approached, guessing it was me, and held out his hand. I realised that he looked smaller because I was taller than when I was ten.

"So. It is you," he said.

We ordered salads. He was drinking lager and I had orange juice. We made some very small talk about his journey and London and giggled over mutual memories: "Do you remember when you wrote 'Manners Makyth Man' on the blackboard after Jimmy Ross pinched Cheryl's bottom?"

"As I recall, I never rubbed that phrase off."

"And that time we did the gym display and you stood there and made the tiniest signals with your little finger, so Charlie Thomas could spot them and take us into the next routine?"

"Clever, wasn't it?"

"And the time we wanted to make balsawood ships like the boys instead of doing needlework, and you went to see the headmaster and got him to allow us to?"

"Only balsawood houses for the girls, I remember."

"Yes, and I wanted to paint mine grey, and you were two hours late for school because you'd searched everywhere to find a pot of grey paint?"

He smiled at the recollection. "Well, you were worth it. I couldn't say it then but you were special."

I glanced at him in faint alarm, but there was nothing at all suggestive in his manner, and he was not looking at me at all, but rather into the distance.

Then he said, "you remember when I tried to get you all to recite Macaulay – How Horatio Kept The Bridge and all that – and you were the only one who could really cope with it?"

"Yes, I remember. That was a pity."

"I did sometimes overestimate what you were all capable of."

"Sometimes."

Then I said: "Mum told me about your wife leaving you."

"Ah. Well. Yes. Foolish of me. I should have noticed she was unhappy, although I doubt whether that would have made any difference, in the end. We have come to a reasonable agreement over Molly."

"Oh. Good."

"It's all pretty amicable. I can see Molly as often as I want to – and she wants to."

Then he turned to look at me and added: "that is, so long as I can see."

I stared back at him, startled.

"I have a problem with my vision. That is, the likelihood is that I will have a problem some time in the future. I think I've noticed something already – I suppose one tends to look for signs, being aware of the possibility. I can't see so well in the evening, when it's nearly dark, and I've been walking into things. It's a curious genetic disease called retinitis pigmentosa. I don't know how fast it'll progress, but it will get worse. Curiously enough it actually results from a mutation in a gene, possibly in more than one. The light-reflecting cells in the retina gradually die off. My father had it. He was never completely blind; he said it was like looking through a pinhole, or walking in a dark tunnel."

"Isn't there anything they can do?"

"Apparently not. It's a degenerative process, and the progression is unstoppable. Most people are registered blind by middle age, even if they're still able to see something. If you look at the eye under a microscope you can see black pigment growing in the retina, blotting out the cells – and one's sight. But in my father's case he didn't become aware of it until he was in his forties, so I may have a while yet. Well, comparatively. Jean-Claude arranged for Freddie and I to have some tests with an opthalmologist in Paris, and it seems she's clear of it, but I have early signs of the disease in my visual field."

After a pause I said: "but you don't know how soon – I mean, you don't know when – "

"It's very variable. I could have years of reasonably good sight. It depends on the individual. And I can still hear. I can still listen to music. But the point is that I want to get things organised. There's a great deal I want to do before it gets too difficult. Travelling, particularly. I saw Professor Hardy yesterday in Oxford, and told him about my ideas. He said I ought to try and publish them. I said I couldn't see much chance of that: I'm not a scientist, I've only got a couple of external degrees and neither qualifies me as an anthropologist. But he was a nice man and extraordinarily encouraging, perhaps because he himself is something of a maverick in the world of orthodox scientific ideology. He did make me consider trying to get something down on paper, if only for myself, so that I can make some sense out of what is essentially a pretty heretical hypothesis. Some would say absurd."

"What, that Man has some sort of aquatic origin?"

"Well, there is undoubtedly evidence for some kind of link. But it's more than that. There are great conundrums about how and why Homo sapiens developed in the way he has. Perhaps we should start talking about She, for that matter. One thing in all this is certain: it happened through the maternal line. You have a mother. Your mother had a mother. Every creature that ever lived must have had a mother."

"Well – "

"Look at it this way. The sexual role of the male is technically simply to insure against the accumulation of genetic faults. In engineering terms, an electronic document can be safeguarded against damage by random agents like cosmic rays by 'marrying' it to a 'redundant male', so reducing the probability of any flaws appearing on identical sites. You don't *have* to do that, of course; you can take the chance. Likewise, in nature, females of some sexual species can be cloned without male intervention – and the progeny are identical daughters. You wouldn't be here if one mother in your ancestral line over the past millions of years had ever failed to give birth to a fertile daughter. It is a mathematical certainty that you can be traced back to a single individual."

"How far back?"

"Well, about sixty-five million years. To a female who survived the KT cataclysm."

"The KT cataclysm?"

"Sixty-five million years ago something happened to the earth. Some vast object, probably more than fifteen million tons, collided with it. It might have been a large comet, or an asteroid, and its impact energy would have been equivalent to the simultaneous explosion of all the hydrogen bombs in the world. As we know, it resulted in the extinction of the dinosaurs, together with many other reptiles and plants. The K is for Kreida, the German word for the Cretaceous age – the age before the catastrophe – and T is for Tertiary, the period of modern life that came after it. Geologists have defined it by a layer of clay about one centimetre thick, containing very high levels of a rare metal called iridium, which indicates the impact of something from outer space. The interesting thing is that some things did survive this impact: small things, the upland flowering plants, the insects, some mammals, certain reptiles, particularly marine reptiles – and the earliest primates."

"What – like apes?"

"Absolutely. And among these survivors was our ancestor. The common assumption seems to be that it was some tiny, shrew-like creature sensible enough to duck under a handy rock. But why? What if it was already an animal like us - walking upright, and on two legs?"

I glanced round at the bustling foyer, as if someone might have heard him, but no one was taking any notice of us at all.

"On two legs?" I replied cautiously. "But only human beings walk on two legs – "

"Well, yes: but it wasn't always so. It's true that only *Homo sapiens* walks and runs upright on two legs now, but for millions of years in the past the extinct southern apes of Africa also walked upright on two legs – and just as well, if not better, than we do. Which means, of course, that they must therefore have possessed all the incredibly intricate mechanisms for doing so. Including our unique big toe."

"Our big toe?"

"It's a key component. It has been said that human walking is an activity during which the body, step by step, teeters on the edge of catastrophe. Your big toe saves you from falling over. No other living anthropoid possesses such a toe. It's forward-pointing. It's both rigid and elastic. Each time you take a stride, your whole weight balances on it. It's like a tiny springboard. And the funny thing is that it's formed in the seventh week of pregnancy, when the foetus is only about fifteen millimetres long, which suggests that it is a particularly ancient hallmark of human beings. In fact the foot itself is highly specialised for walking. The whole human skeleton is uniquely designed. The spine is curved, transmitting the weight of the upper body to the pelvis - which is itself distinctive, with the hip joints at the extreme outsides. The thigh bones are angled inwards and the knees and ankles are very robust so they can support the entire body weight on one leg. That kind of design isn't something that happens overnight: if an orang-utan decided to jump down from the trees and walk – let alone run – upright, he couldn't do it."

"But our hands – you said they were anatomically primitive. Surely they're a mark of our sophistication as animals? I mean – look what we do with them. They're highly evolved. No other animal can do the sort of things we do with our hands."

"By primitive, I think you mean inferior. Yet I agree with you that they're remarkable things: the blind can see with the touch of their fingers. Hands can be calloused by work yet do fine needlework. Hands built the Great Wall of China – and inscribed the sayings of Confucius on a grain of rice. But they are, I'm afraid, primitive. Your hand has twenty-five joints and fifty-eight possible movements, but it is almost indistinguishable from the forepaws of fossil primates of fifty million years ago. A hand is simply a tool, and a tool needs to be adaptable. What it does need is a control mechanism that can use that adaptability. That control mechanism is our intelligence, our creativity. Our mind."

"Which, I suppose, is the main hallmark of the human being."

"Well, yes, *Homo sapiens* is certainly a creature with a large brain and the ability to think, to talk, to imagine, to create. The human mind led to the genesis of civilisation. But you see, I can't believe that we simply came down from the trees, grew big brains and an entirely different skeleton that enabled us to walk upright on two legs and become human. It isn't logical. To adapt and evolve such anatomical characteristics, and their physiology, takes time. A long time. Much, much longer than the timescale suggested by the current ideology of progress. Indeed, the scale of time, the chronology of human evolution, is somehow left out of the whole debate."

"You mean it would take longer to evolve than we think?"

"Yes," he said simply. "Let's look at the accepted facts of evolution. One is that a group of similar creatures possesses a genetic pool of sufficient variability to throw up individuals capable of adapting to any environmental change – possibly lethal change. Such individuals can reproduce their advantages, thus ensuring that the population adapts to the conditions. Second: if some members of the group are isolated from the others, and are thus unable to interbreed, then their descendants may ultimately discover that they are incapable of mating with those of their original ancestors. A new species has been created. But of course it takes time. Time measured in generations. For pathogenic bacteria, reproducing by division, generations take minutes, and thus they can redesign themselves very quickly to avoid extinction by man-made antibiotics. Humans, for whom generations take twenty years or so, need more time. And of course this apparently simple process has nothing to do with our idea of Progress, a false analogy with the growth of technology."

"Well – "

"The point is," he said abruptly, "I wondered if you might help me in getting my ideas down on paper, and into some sort of order."

"Me?"

"Yes, you. If you think you might be interested."

"Well, I am interested. I'm confused, but I'm interested."

He looked at me. We had reached coffee by now and I looked back at him over the rim of the cup. His blue eyes seemed quite normal. Then he said: "you didn't go to university."

"No."

"Why not?"

"Well – I suppose I just wanted to get out into the world."

"To write."

"Well, I hope so."

"Have you done much so far?"

"The occasional piece for *The Times*. And I've published a few short stories."

"What would you think about writing something for me? Let me explain. I'll be abroad a good deal over the next year or so – well, as long as I can still see enough to travel. I want to visit Africa, the Galapagos, Turkey – as many places as I can afford to get to. I'll have to travel pretty light, and if I use a tape-recorder rather than a notebook it won't matter if my sight starts to get worse. I'll still be able to talk. But I'll need someone to transcribe the stuff for me.

More than that, to put it into some kind of sense. Perhaps add your own ideas, your imagination to it. You could tell me when you don't understand something, or want to ask a question. It might turn into something with a life of its own."

"It might be rather fun."

"You're a writer. I'm not. But I do quite like the sound of my own voice, and I like reading other people's work – I can even write letters, but face me with a piece of blank paper and the prospect of producing something readable, and I'm paralysed. It took me a ridiculously long time to write that review, even though I knew what I wanted to say." He gave me a mulish grin. "And then you cut it."

"That was the deputy editor."

"I'm glad it wasn't you... So. What do you think?"

"I think I'd like to do it."

"You must be sure. It won't be that much work, because I won't put anything on tape until I've done enough research to be sure of what I want to say. There'll be times when I'm travelling or working in libraries or museums. I might even give up. But if I don't, if I keep on pursuing these thoughts of mine – well, you'll get some more tapes. But it has to be up to you to decide whether you want to transcribe them, whether you have the time, or the inclination. You might get tired of the whole thing. You'll probably be far too busy – although as far as I'm concerned there won't be any deadlines. You can do them when you can."

"Honestly, I'll do it."

"I just want you to be sure. You can stop at any time – this is not a contract. Although of course I will pay a retainer."

"I'll do it," I repeated.

Then he said: "I wouldn't want you to do it because of the business of my sight."

"I wouldn't."

He said he wanted to walk up to St Paul's. The sunshine was bright and a breeze was blowing gossamer seedheads off the rosebay willowherb in one of the old bomb sites along the way. He stopped at a tobacconist's to buy some tobacco for his pipe.

"Do you remember the old Somerset Maugham story about the verger of St Paul's? The cathedral authorities discovered that one of the vergers couldn't read or write, although he'd been there twenty years. So they dismissed him. He'd always wished there was a tobacconist on Ludgate Hill, so he rented a shop and started one. He ended up with a chain of tobacconists and a vast retail empire and gave a great deal of money to various charities. A journalist, interviewing him, was astonished to find that he couldn't read or write. 'What could you have achieved if you had been able to read and write?" the journalist asked. "I'd be a verger at St Paul's," he replied."

We stopped on the steps of the cathedral. "I don't know why," he said, "but I've always liked that story."

I smiled at him, in the bright sunlight, and he took my hand. "Thank you," he said. "I don't quite know what I'm going to do, or where I shall end up, but I'll be in touch. If you really are sure." "Quite sure," I said.

4

Footprints in Stone

Soon after that encounter I was promoted from dogsbody, covering news stories and writing more features. I moved to a shared flat in Shepherd's Bush and life became immediate and absorbing. I did not hear from Mr Brouard for some time, and he and the horseshoe crab slipped to the back of my mind. I was reminded of both, however, when two new books were published. One was *African Genesis* by Robert Ardrey, which seemed to put the origins of man very firmly in Africa. The other was *The Naked Ape* by Desmond Morris. I sent Mr Brouard a copy of each, and underlined two paragraphs in Desmond Morris's book which seemed to me rather convincing:

> "The ancestral ground-apes already had large and high quality brains. They had good eyes and efficient grasping hands. They inevitably, as primates, had some

degree of social organisation. With strong pressure on them to increase their prey-killing prowess, vital changes began to take place. They became more upright – fast, better runners. Their hands became freed from locomotion duties – strong, efficient weapon-holders. Their brains became more complex – brighter, quicker decision-makers."

And:

"So the hunting ape became a territorial ape. His whole sexual, parental and social pattern began to be affected. His old wandering, fruit plucking way of life was fading rapidly. He had now really left his forest of Eden. He was an ape with responsibilities. He began to worry about the prehistoric equivalent of washing machines and refrigerators. He began to develop the home comforts, fire, food storage, artificial shelters."

I received a short tape in reply. It said:
"So: from hunting ape to suburban householder? Curious. The creature who dwells in Beckenham and catches the 7.45 to Waterloo is, after all, no more or less human than the Bushman of the Kalahari Desert – and he is still out there gathering honey, killing small animals and plucking fruit. Wasn't it Mark Twain who said that what he liked about science was that one gets such enormous dividends of speculation from so small an investment of fact?"
"What I find more interesting is Morris's reference to Sir Alister Hardy's theory of the aquatic ape. He devotes some considerable thought to its plausibility. However he says that even if it does 'eventually turn out to be true', it will not clash seriously with the general picture of the hunting ape's evolution out of a ground ape. *I* think it clashes fundamentally."

Postcards arrived from various parts of the world: Turkey, Iraq, Argentina. One was from Cape Cod in Massachusetts: "I have been walking on the white sand of an inlet behind Nauset Beach, where the remains of a hurricane are battering the dunes. But in the bay behind them the water was calm, reflecting a clear blue sky, forests of reeds green and golden against the blue. And I found the shell of a horseshoe crab, quite perfect, complete with spiky tail. Of course they live off this Atlantic coast of America. It must have been shed by a young crab, for they moult many times as they grow to maturity. I gather the spawning is quite a sight to see, when hundreds of thousands come ashore to lay their eggs. I had the strangest sense of communion with an ancient past - the sea, the golden reeds, the horseshoe crab on the white sand."

About a year later a package arrived from Mr Brouard's sister's home in the village of Boury-en-Vexin. It contained another tape, and a photocopy of a page from American Natural History by Dr Roland T. Bird, published in 1939. The tape explained:

"This is intriguing. This chap Bird discovered some footprints in rocks in the Paluxy River bed at Glen Rose in Texas. It's well known for dinosaur fossils. The limestone rocks were once the mudflats of an estuary, and about a hundred million years ago, in the Cretaceous period, a few dinosaurs walked across it and left their footprints to solidify into stone – presumably the tide never reached as high as that again, so they didn't get washed away. Bird and his colleague took photographs, but the limestone slabs were put on show outside a hamburger stall until someone decided they were no longer a draw, and disposed of them."

Dr Bird had described them thus:
"On the surface of each was splayed the near-likeness of a human foot, perfect in every detail. But each imprint was fifteen inches long. When I heard that there were dinosaur tracks in exactly the same level of stone, from an apparently identical stratigraphical level,

my thoroughly revived curiosity could scarcely be contained. Even the possibility of such an association seemed incredible."

Mr Brouard added: "the photographs are almost unmistakably the footprints of a bipedal hominid. It must have been of giant size, judging from the length of the prints (thirty-eight centimetres) and the toe to toe stride, two hundred and ten centimetres. Just imagine for a moment: forget your preconceptions, and think of a large hominid, perfectly designed as a predator of the abundance of reptile eggs, and which in some ways resembled us more than any of our living primate cousins."

I sent him a note: "What was it you once said about Mark Twain and enormous dividends of speculation from so small an investment of fact? All you've got is one fossilised footprint that doesn't even exist any more. It sounds like one of those old films showing cave men battling against the dinosaurs. I know you think our ancient ancestor was some sort of two-legged egg-collector, but the general consensus seems to be that we were once a kind of tree-dwelling shrew. Somehow I don't quite see where your egg-collecting person fits in to the picture."

He replied immediately:

"*Purgatorious* was the name given to that small tree-dwelling shrew. I have to say Mark Twain was pretty unfair to science generally, but quite right about theology, cosmology and palaeo-anthropology...Look, all we've got of your shrew is a few isolated teeth with some primate characteristics. The fact that we tend to think of the last sixty-five million years since the KT cataclysm as the 'Age of Mammals' and the time before – the Cretaceous – as the 'Age of the Dinosaurs', rather obscures the fact that mammal-like reptiles may have preceded the dinosaurs. Mammals, as it happens, have been around for about two hundred million years – just as long as the dinosaurs. Curiously, when I was chatting to the curator of fossil vertebrates at the Canadian Museum of Nature in Ottawa, a chap whose specialism is dinosaurs, he mentioned that among them he had found the cap of a skull and sufficient parts of a skeleton to reconstruct a creature with a remarkably large brain, large eyes facing ahead, and the capacity to walk on two legs. It's extraordinarily like the fossil skeletons of hominids that Richard Leakey's found in Africa. He said he'd like Leakey to see it some time. I'd like to be there when he does.

"This isn't just speculation. It's based on logic. You can examine the way the living world has been created by looking at the development of modern industry. Think of it: every time a new invention is made, often by building on existing parts of often quite unrelated crafts or discoveries, it leads to a multitude of new industries. They in turn grow and develop through mass reproduction, competition, and constant modification to adjust to the needs of the shifting marketplace. And on the way a whole lot of pre-existing crafts and old industries disappear. Take the steam engine. It replaced the power of human and animal muscle with the power of fossil fuels and led to a vast number of new industries, notably by replacing human craft skills with machines.

"Darwin made a similar analogy between the improvement involved in selective breeding and the way living creatures can be transformed by adaptation to changes in their environment. That, combined with the startling improvement in living standards resulting from the invention of the steam engine, created a new humanist theology. And it suggested an extremely short timescale for the evolution of the human race."

I have always hated analogies. They seem to me to be a very male way of arguing a point. But Mr Brouard had one more to throw at me:

"Consider genetics. It gives us a new way of looking at the nature of living things. Do you recall I once explained a kind of natural genetic engineering – the result of an alliance between viruses and living cells? Such random unions, such transformations, would cause revolutionary changes in the living world, just as the steam engine changed the man-made industrial one."

There had been a good deal in the press just then about Fred Hoyle's theory that we were all constantly being bombarded with new viruses from outer space. Like most people I was inclined to be sceptical. Mr Brouard must have suspected it.

"The point is, analogies like these only serve to illustrate how successfully living creatures seem able to exploit every niche in the world market, as it were. If we go back to the Cretaceous age, before the KT cataclysm, it doesn't make sense to find that no predator existed to exploit the opportunity provided by the wealth of reptile eggs available. There simply must have been one – as perfectly designed as the horseshoe crab. It would be warm-blooded and therefore active when land reptiles were dormant. It would have forelimbs specialised for egg-collecting, and hind legs designed for high speed locomotion. Teeth could be simple for a diet of eggs and tender vegetation, a diet that would make the metabolic synthesis of essential vitamins unnecessary. In several ways our anatomy is less 'evolved' than that of the apes, although the evolution of our brains has now separated us from the rest of creation.

"So there we have her – our imaginary ancestor, destined to survive the KT cataclysm and radiate out into the entire hominoid superfamily. She's probably the result of some kind of breakthrough in natural genetic engineering, thereafter having evolved to occupy a particular niche. Her transformation – for we are talking of a female – into *Homo sapiens* must have followed all the normal rules of natural selection. Among them are those which require that isolated groups, in exceptional environments, shall diverge into new species.

"Let's go back to the Cretaceous and the time of Dr Bird's footprints. Remember the horseshoe crab? The one you brought to school in Hong Kong? We said that the twelve hours of the classroom clock could represent the six hundred million years of the horseshoe crab's existence. I recall Charlie Thomas asking how long people like us have been around, compared to that: the answer was three seconds. Well, on the timescale of the horseshoe crab clock, the Cretaceous was about two hours before noon."

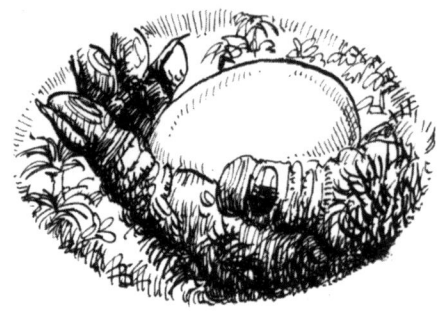

5

Poached Eggs

The sun was warm on her languorous body. The sun was warm everywhere across the earth, for it was a gentler place then, its climate almost uniform across the strange continents and shifting seas. And Rhea liked to lie on her mountain ledge and catch the last level rays of the sun, watching the remote mountains darken against the luminous twilight sky. The twilight was long, for this part of south east Africa was then fifteen hundred miles nearer to the South Pole. Rhea had eaten her fill of fruit and her mate had brought her tender shoots of the little upland flowers, although the aim of his courtship had been fulfilled. She was already pregnant. She had begun to build her nest here on the sunlit ledge.

"I have called her Rhea," Mr Brouard said, "because Rhea was the Great Goddess of the Aegean Sea, the Universal Mother of the Cretans, centuries before Homer began to write the Odyssey. Later still, Hesiod was to classify her in his Theogony as the mother of Zeus. Imagine her as one of the white-furred sifaki lemurs of Madagascar, although much larger. The Madagascans call them sun-worshippers, because they love to bask in the treetops, just as Rhea does on her rocky ledge above the dark world below."

A glossy green lizard shared Rhea's place in the sun, although he, unlike her, required its warmth for his very existence. So did the herds of dinosaurs that trampled through the ferns and cycads of the boggy forests, where the mosses dripped with moisture and the humid air was heavy with the humming of insects. So, too, did the alligators and crocodiles in the rivers and the turtles on the shores. While the air was warm, around 37 degrees Centigrade, they could hunt, forage, swim, run – and reproduce. They needed heat. It was more difficult for the larger reptiles. Some carried solar panels on their backs, and by orienting themselves towards the sun they could rapidly charge their metabolic batteries. Others gorged themselves on vegetation which could ferment within their vast stomachs to provide literally central heating. As darkness began to suck the light from the turquoise sky, Rhea could hear the great diplodocuses crashing under the canopy of conifers and gingko trees, far down in the gorge. It was their last chance before nightfall, when they would lose their vigour and slumber sluggishly in the sudden chill.

Yet for Rhea the night held no such torpor. The reptiles might be thermodynamically efficient compared to mammals, whose lives were dominated by the quest for food, but one thing they could not control: their eggs. The developing embryos were vulnerable to any sudden reduction in temperature. So they buried them, found warm places to lay them, nudged them under piles of fermenting leaves. They laid them all over the place. For Rhea and her kind they were a perfect and available food. No wonder, then, that over the preceding millions of years she had adapted to such abundance. Her forepaws were by now designed for the discovery and collection of reptile eggs. Her digestive system had been tailored to a diet not only of eggs but of fruit and tender upland plants, providing her with all the trace elements and compounds she needed. Unlike most other animals she had ceased to be able to synthesise certain vitamins. And not only could she walk upright, but she could run, climb over rocks and leap over obstacles, escaping with nimble ease the fury of some protective iguanodon.

Even as the sun briefly blazed and then slipped behind the distant peaks, extinguishing the warmth of the day, Rhea's mate emerged from the forest with his paws full of eggs. She made her characteristic singing sound in acknowledgement. He stood upon the boulders below and hurled the eggs, one by one, to her safe grasp, and then climbed up the cliff to join her. The night held no terrors for them.

But this night was like no other, for there was no dawn.

They had moved only a few yards from the ledge, making for the lichened lip of the clifftop above them by way of a deep crevice in the rock, when there was a sudden, blinding light. Instinctively they crouched together, under the overhang, as the illumination seemed to penetrate their very fur. They had no perception of catastrophe, no experience nor imagination to comprehend what was happening. They simply clung to the rock and to each other.

When the light went out, the blackness was absolute. The moon, the stars, were obliterated. Then the sound came, and the wind. The very rock beneath them trembled. The sound was like a scream, a scream not of any living creature but as if the air itself, the very sky, was rending apart. And the wind was no gentle current to shiver the great tree ferns, but something elemental, as if it was the scream made tangible, tearing at the very earth with its claws, uprooting the trees, ripping through the huge club mosses, adding to the noise the thunder of tumbling boulders as the land was split apart.

Rhea had no conception of time. All she knew was that the scream ended almost as suddenly as it had begun, and at last the tremor of the earth began to subside. Her vision was nocturnal, so the darkness seemed to ebb a little, and she moved on the rock. Her mate was still with her. The eggs, too, were safe under their bodies. They ate. And as their hunger and their thirst began to crowd out fear, so they began to forage further for food and water. The blackness was not quite complete, for there was the faintest loom of light in the eastern sky. A thousand miles away, the movement of tectonic plates that carried the continent of India towards Asia had opened a fissure in the crust of the earth. The outpouring of molten volcanic basalt had defied the cataclysm, and the light was the reflected glow of its vast fiery square miles on the radioactive dust that was to mask the sky for many months to come.

"No one knows exactly what happened on that night," Mr Brouard said. "It's thought that possibly an asteroid hit the earth in the area of the Gulf of Mexico – well, it created the Gulf of Mexico. There seems to have been virtual extinction of most living things, perhaps because of extraordinary volcanic activity, or contamination by radioactive dust. The nearest we can get to it is the possible collision of an asteroid with the earth in 1908, when a report came from the village of Nizhne-Karelinsk in northern Siberia of a blinding bluish-white light followed by smoke. That year was marked by an exceptional display of the Northern Lights and other atmospheric phenomena. It wasn't until 1921 that scientists investigated it. They found an area of about two thousand square kilometres had been devastated by something, but there was no sign of a crater. Years later further study found evidence of curious genetic effects on insects and plants."

I could hear him pause, put a record on the turntable: a Beethoven cello sonata.

"Life, you know, is extraordinarily resistant to sudden shocks. In geological time recovery can be surprisingly swift. It always puzzled me that although *before* the KT cataclysm every environment had been dominated by cold-blooded animals, *after* it they were supplanted by warm-blooded birds and mammals. It was puzzling because cold-blooded animals are – and always had been - much more thermodynamically efficient. After a good meal a python can endure starvation for a year or two, and a goldfish in a garden pool can last quite happily under thick ice throughout a long winter, but a mouse has to eat almost its own body weight of food every day just to keep alive. How could life on earth have undergone so dramatic a reverse through a single accident – however catastrophic?

"Then I thought of something. Do you remember a book that made a bit of a stir back in the 1950s – *The Death of Grass*? By someone called John Christopher. He imagined a virus exterminating all kinds of grasses, including, of course, wheat, rice, barley and the rest. Millions starved, civilised society imploded into chaos. Grazing animals and their predators died out as savannahs turned to forests. Only a few remnants of humanity managed to survive. In reality, of course, no single virus could exterminate around eight thousand different species of monocotyledons: but it is true that an ordinary garden weedkiller can selectively kill most of the larger class of dicotyledons, which includes most living plants. You could imagine an atmosphere contaminated by a selective herbicide...But this is fantasy. Just as the idea that the dinosaurs were too unintelligent to climb up the old 'ladder of life' is fantasy.

"Nevertheless something like it must have caused such a reversal. And a friend of mine came up with a clue. He was working at the Brookhaven National Laboratory in America on experiments leading up to the Nuclear Test Ban Treaty. One of the projects involved estimating the consequences of increasing background levels of ionising radiation – which was one of the results of nuclear testing – by putting a strong gamma ray source in a tract of typical woodland. The results were unexpected. The most vulnerable plants turned out to be the gymnosperms and spore-bearers – conifers, horsetails, tree ferns, the kind of ancient vegetation that had been dominant before the KT cataclysm, and on which most dinosaurs relied for food. Even a tiny level of radiation, about as much as you'd get from a dental X-ray, could, over time, cause serious damage to conifers: a whole forest could be wiped out quite quickly by exposure equivalent to a whole body X-ray. But deciduous trees were much less vulnerable, and small wild flowers were unaffected by an amount sufficient to kill a human being.

"Do you see what it means? Increased background ionising radiation, a consequence of the cataclysm, could have had a highly selective herbicidal effect – enough to transform the ecology of the entire planet. Creatures locked in to the food chain provided by the ancient vegetation of the valleys would have had no time to adapt to the upland plants on which mammals like Rhea could survive. And then, of course, there was the cold."

When at last a pale dawn came, and Rhea could see clearly again, the world had changed for ever. Dead plants rotted in the old marshy valleys. The bodies of the great herbivorous dinosaurs lay in the tumbled forests, victims of starvation. Some smaller reptiles had endured, and those that lived in the protecting lakes and seas. Creatures furthest from the terrible impact had had some chance of survival. As the months passed, so the light softened. One morning a hazy brilliance seemed concentrated in one corner of the grey sky: it was the sun.

As the sun returned, so did the upland flora, the tiny plants, the few wiry grasses, beginning to colonise not only their familiar rocky screes but the old world below, where the light and air now penetrated and the soil was rich with the humus. Their flowers began to bloom in the valleys. The air was warmer. For those creatures that had survived the cataclysm, there was a brief Indian Summer after the long chill. The rotting forests and the ignited fires of peat, lignite and coal in the ravaged earth gradually increased the proportions of carbon dioxide and methane in the atmosphere – the first greenhouse effect.

The mammals found new pickings in the lowland valleys, where the remains of the reptile population found their eggs vulnerable not only to Rhea and her kind but to the small shrew-like creatures who were to become the rats and mongooses of the future. Rhea and her mate foraged further and further for food and their agility gave them advantage. They found the eggs of lizards on land and along the lake and sea shores the offspring of the marine reptiles, the crocodiles and turtles for whom the oceans were safer haven. Less at risk were the eggs of the flying ptserosaurs and the warm-blooded creatures whose mastery of active flight allowed them to find sanctuary along the ocean cliffs – the birds.

On one of the warm dark nights of that brief time they came upon the horseshoe crabs, like a cobbled river on the sand, gleaming in the starlight. They dined well before dawn. And in that early light, in the opalescent air of the milky sun, Rhea gave birth to a single female infant.

6

Bird Life

"Imagine," said Mr Brouard, "a world which, once crowded with life, rich with different species, had become suddenly empty: a world in which Europe was a shallow sea, the Highlands of Scotland even then ancient islands. Most of North America had been inundated. The small separate continent of India was moving northward towards ultimate collision with Asia, and the crumpled uprising of the Himalaya. Perhaps least affected was Africa, gradually moving north towards Europe – it would take fifty million more years to make contact. In this strange new world those who had survived the cataclysm were given the chance to expand, to develop into new species. Any of them might have founded new dynasties, new species, genera, even orders of life, but only a single female could begin each line. One of them was Rhea. And one was a bird."

I had a friend at the time who took me birdwatching. He was a doctor who did not like people very much, but he loved birds. On the windy saltings around Chichester we watched the ducks flight in at sunset. We spent a weekend in Norfolk crunching along the shingle and heard the music of a flock of pink-footed geese, the variety of pitch in their individual calls making them sound like a cathedral choir. One golden summer afternoon we visited Peter Scott's Wildfowl Trust at Slimbridge on the Severn. Thousands of birds decorated the mudflats and the marshes along the wide brown river. We watched week old flamingos leaving their muddy mounds for a crèche, where they were cared for by a rota of adults. It seemed to me then that these were ancient birds. They fed through filters in their curious bent bills: "rather as whales do, pushing the algae and small invertebrates through the filters with their tongue, pumping out the mud and water," explained Brian. And we stretched out our hands to the Hawaiian Geese, and they came to us, reaching out with their golden necks, and took the grains of corn from our palms.

"They're so tame," I said in wonder, as I felt the bold tickle of their greedy bills. "It's always seemed so sad that most birds are afraid of man."

"They evolved on an island where they were no natural predators," said Brian. "They were never afraid. They were friendly to everyone – if you wanted a meal you could just reach out and wring their necks. Which is why, of course, they are now the rarest geese in the world. By 1950 there were only thirty birds left. Peter Scott took three of them and began to breed from them. It has been a very successful breeding programme, because they're now being re-established in the wild."

I described this to Mr Brouard in my next letter. My letters were infrequent but long, and I did as I had promised, transcribing his tapes freely and turning them into something that I hoped was a little less dry. If he felt I had not understood some point of detail he would telephone me, and I became accustomed to his rich voice, which never wasted time on pleasantries, although he was sensitive to my occasional hesitancy and would always ring off quickly if he thought he had chosen an inconvenient time. He was still living at Boury, and did not mention his sight. He was teaching English to professional and business people in Paris, travelling in twice a week with Jean-

Claude, his brother-in-law. He replied promptly to my questions about birds – for I did not understand how they could have co-existed with the pterosaurs. Surely, I said, they must have evolved from them?

"Why? There is no fossil record to indicate it. Bird bones are incredibly light and structurally delicate, so they simply disappear. The only fossil evidence we have is Archaeopteryx lithographica, which does seem to be a creature of transition between reptile and bird. It has both the bony tail and claws of a reptile and the wings and feathers of a bird, and it was found at the end of the nineteenth century in limestone that dates it at about 150 million years ago. It can't have been much good at flying. There is still a lot of debate about it, but it probably just managed to glide between perches. The feathers could, of course, have been for insulation: and in that may lie the clue.

"Feathers are made of hundreds of filaments of keratin, the stuff which your hair and skin and toenails are made of. And reptile scales. The filaments are made into a continuous membrane by millions of overlapping tiny barbules that hook them together, a bit like a zip. As an insulating material there is nothing like downy feathers – hence eiderdowns, the down from eider duck nests being the finest of all. And they are almost weightless. The trouble is that if you fixed a wing to a lizard it just wouldn't work. The wing may be light but the effort of flapping it against the pressure of the air requires quite a powerful force – and that needs strong muscles anchored to a breastbone with deep keel, as it were. Reptile bones are far too heavy to get the thing off the ground. Birds have bones like paper, reinforced with internal struts like an aeroplane wing. And, of course, they're warm-blooded – so they could have survived lengthy cold periods. They would have been able to reproduce. Because they couldn't cope with the weight of developing eggs inside them, they laid them in nests which must have been pretty inaccessible to most predators."

I had remembered something else that Brian had said, as we watched a dark spiral of starlings come in to roost in hawthorn trees at dusk.

"They are extraordinary successful as a zoological class. I mean, despite the way we carry on making them extinct, there are an awful lot of birds. Well over nine thousand different species. More than twice as many as mammals. In terms of evolution, they must go back a long way."

I said, "when you say species – you mean a blue tit and a long-tailed tit are different species?"

"Yes."

"So they don't interbreed, even when they're sharing the same bird table?"

"No."

"Why not? Wouldn't you think they might get together one day, and sort of fancy each other?"

"Well, perhaps, once, millions of years ago. But not now. Although birds may live quite close together, they form separate populations – sympatric populations."

"Sympatric – what does that mean?"

"A sympatric population is one that is separated from others by its behaviour. Although in theory it may be capable of interbreeding with them, it doesn't. An allopatric population, on the other hands, is separated by geography. In that case they simply haven't the opportunity to get together. The individuals from both these populations tend to adapt and evolve into a great diversity of sub-species. If the isolation is prolonged and complete enough, they evolve into different species. And different species cannot interbreed."

"But blue tits and long-tailed tits are about the same size. Not that different."

"Well, they're a different colour, and design. But more than that, they behave differently. Long-tailed tits are clubbable sort of birds and like being together. They have a different call, a different song. And long-tailed tits have – well, long tails. Also they have completely different nests. Have you ever seen a long-tailed tit's nest? It's a fascinating piece of construction: oval-shaped, made of moss and cobwebs and hair and lined with feathers, and it's so small they have to fold their long tails over their heads inside – the entrance is always very small, too, high on one side. A blue tit, on the other hand, finds a hole in a tree, or uses a nest box, although the hole has to be a pretty specific size – big enough for a blue tit but not for a sparrow or a great tit. Now, I don't know which came first, the long tail or the nest-building, but it makes it impossible for a blue tit to fancy a long-tailed tit. Nests seem to be pretty crucial in the bird world. Think of the bower bird, spending hours making a nest to attract a female, or a cuckoo, simply taking over another bird's nest and chucking out its eggs."

"And yet," I said, "we are just one species. We are all over the world, black and white and tall and short and different in lots of ways – but we're still one species. We can all breed with each other."

"Exactly so," said Mr Brouard, when I relayed this conversation to him. "Yet all birds are related to each other, just as we are related to other primates. They too are survivors of the KT cataclysm."
"Like us."
"Like us."
I had telephoned him: he was in expansive mood.

"After the Indian summer of that strangely empty world, the climate began to change again, governed as it was by the heat circulating in the main currents of the oceans – themselves determined by the distribution of sea and land. The gradual shift of the continents was to lead to a drastic drop in global temperature. The reptiles that had survived that long could not function if they had no warmth. They could not charge their internal batteries, so they could not reproduce. Only the most heavily armoured, like the turtles and crocodiles in the seas, lived on. And there were parts of the earth that were warmer than others. Rhea had seen the light in the sky, the reflected light of the molten volcanic magma.

" As it cooled, it formed a triangular plateau of basalt covering most of southern India – the Deccan. It was like a giant hotplate. Convection currents heated both the sea and the upper **atmosphere**, and the warm westerly winds carried its benison to the south-east coast of Africa. Perhaps the last of the pterosaurs flew there, gliding on the rising air currents by means of the leathery membranes on their forelimbs. But they too were to die out, to be replaced by a competitor who was fortunate enough to have warm blood and feathers. For Rhea and her descendants the birds were to form a vital part of their diminishing food. As they filled the air, the sea and, flightless, even the land, so those distant hominids followed them."

"Not much hard evidence, though."

"True. There are very few fossils from those millions of years, and particularly few early hominid fossils. Some human-looking teeth found in Africa have been dated about eight to fourteen million years ago – give or take, I suppose, the odd million. Anthropologists called their owner Ramapithecus, but there is doubt as to just what one means by human: it may be that her descendants are among the great apes. Then there's Australopithecines, the Southern Apes. Their fossil remains date from about five million years ago. There are quite a lot of them, each being given a different name: Australopithecus robustus, africanus, bosei, etc. It seems to be generally accepted that they were bipedal: they walked and ran on two legs just like us. Some of them seem to suggest a transitional phase between ground walking and living in trees."

"Which would support the idea that we came down from the trees and walked on two legs."

"Why?"

"Well – "

"I suggest the opposite. Australopithecine fossils are all older than those of tree-dwelling apes. So, logically, if you can ignore the Darwinian ideology that says we must be progressing up some metaphysical ladder from lower to higher animals, the transitional fossils might suggest some ground apes actually went up into the trees."

"It is very depressing, your belief that we aren't progressing at all, that we're all actually descending that metaphysical ladder."

"It shouldn't be. I wish we could free ourselves from the quasi-religious notion that we must be going either up or down, to perfection or perdition. The French zoologist, Baron Cuvier, once said: 'the true method is to view each being linked to all the radiations of organised nature; only this can give the idea of nature which is truly worthy of her Author.'

" In other words, we should take things as they are, identifying logical connections. For example, some of those early hominids, in an increasingly harsh environment, may have followed the radiating patterns of bird populations along the milder coasts of Africa. There was less danger from predators and a better chance of finding food from marine animals. Some may have moved inland, where their ability to walk and run gave them some advantage in the face of predation by other animals; they could also use their instinctive dexterity with their forepaws, their hands, as a weapon, hurling a round pebble with extraordinary accuracy at an attacker. Perhaps, later, they discovered other uses for pebbles and broken stones. They were also very obliging in that they died in a part of Africa where the geology meant that their fossil bones were easily revealed. But they were not our ancestors. We may share a common ancestor with them – but we are different."

"Yes, but we are very close to them. Chimpanzees, for instance. And gorillas. Genetically, aren't they our closest relatives?"

"Yes; and, genetically, we're very close to cockroaches. And fish."

"That's just silly."

"Well, let's look at the gorillas. They are very well adapted for life in the trees, but as they are very heavy animals they tend to spend more time on the ground. It's a compromise. Whereas we have spines specifically curved to transmit the weight of our upper body to the pelvis – itself of a distinct shape, with hip joints at the sides and inwardly angled thigh bones to bring the knees together – gorillas have spines curved in a permanent stoop. We have our unique springboard of a big toe: a gorilla's big toe is designed for walking on tree branches. Now, you could say this is the result of genetic selection in response to our environments. But if you accept that the bipedal locomotion of the hominid goes back such a very long way, then somehow it makes more sense to me to think in terms of selective atrophy of the multitude of special features in our own complex design, rather than the reverse."

"Well, you mean our big toe, and the spine – "

"There are other features, too. Look at the human face. It's essentially flat. All other mammals have a protruding muzzle, which is essentially what you see of a bone called the premaxilla. Sometimes this bone provides for side-mounted eyes, like horses, or front-facing, like cats – and apes. You might think the human face would simply be a sort of continuation of this arrangement. But it's not. The side bones of the face extend forward and inwards over the premaxilla bone to produce the framework of the nose and force the upper jaw, and consequently the teeth and shape of the lower jaw, into a parabolic shape. And this occurs in the human foetus at about the same time as the equally unique formation of the big toe."

"But Rhea wasn't human, was she?"

"No, but it is possible that we have inherited some of her particular features. And because of some special circumstance, some logical connection in the story of humankind, we have retained them and adapted in a particular way to our environment, just as the chimpanzees and gorillas have lost the requirement for them and adapted in a different way to their environment. For the next chapter in the story of *Homo sapiens sapiens* I think we must follow the horseshoe crab to a point in time about ten million years ago, and to a place beyond the south-eastern shores of Africa."

He sent a new tape soon after that. It was summer. By that time I had gone freelance and was doing features on a fairly regular basis for several national newspapers. I was also writing a novel, of course. I had been lent a caravan by friends who owned a smallholding in Cornwall. John and Yolande had very little cash, growing potatoes and keeping hens while John did shifts as an odd job man at the local naval air station and Yolande looked after their three small children. She was already pregnant with their fourth. In those days they had no electricity, only calor gas, and the cottage was so small that they had bought the old caravan for guests. They seemed idyllically happy to me and I think they were. I tapped at my Adler Gabriele in the caravan under the shade of an oak tree and yearned for a family of my own. Through the open door I could hear children's voices, barking dogs, and Yolande's laugh. I was very envious. The novel continually eluded me and it was a relief to have to listen to Mr Brouard's mellifluous voice.

A few hundred million years ago all the continents of the earth were one, which we now call Pangaea. By the time of the KT cataclysm, Pangaea had broken up into great tectonic plates, crusts of the sea bed, floating on a viscous magma that forced the plates apart then and still does today. They were to become the new continents. And among these vast shifting masses of land was a smaller fragment, a micro-continent.

Sail a ship six hundred miles east from Madagascar into the vastness of the Indian Ocean. Go in November, when the trade winds moderate and the doldrums move south with the sun, so that the sea is treacle calm and clear. It will suddenly begin to undergo subtle changes in colour and mood: from indigo to turquoise, from deep ocean swell to lazy ripple. White sand will appear beneath your keel. You are sailing over a part of the forty-five thousand square miles of the sunken Mascarene Plateau: the cradle of mankind.

The northern mountains of what was once this micro-continent now form the islands of the Seychelles, and these give a good idea of what it must have been like originally. The southern part of it was battered by the south-east trade winds, and lay within the notorious cyclone belt of the Indian Ocean. It's now completely eroded away, forming the Saya del Malha and Nazareth Banks.

On the eastern coast, battered by the wind and waves that swept across five thousand miles of ocean, mountainous cliffs gradually crumbled into the breaking surf below. The monsoon rains fed a great river that formed a vast delta on the western plains, where marsh and salting nourished shimmering forests of papyrus reed. Inland, out of the winds, it was luxuriant with indigenous flowers and shrubs, which in turn fed and sheltered the creatures that inhabited it. Among them were animals whose skin was bare and who could swim as well as they could run upon the white sand of the sea shores. They flourished here, although they were found nowhere else on earth. The island provided the single most important requirement for the origin of a species: isolation.

7

Women Divers

"How's the novel going?" John asked that dread question one evening as we sat over a bottle of wine in their cottage kitchen. Yolande was saying goodnight to the children: we could hear her high Roedean voice admonishing one of them.

"Oh, all right," I said.

"I could hear you at the typewriter this afternoon," he said genially. He was a very gentle, quiet man and I knew he wasn't just pretending to be interested. He wanted to know.

So I told him that actually the novel wasn't going at all, and that I had been transcribing Mr Brouard's tapes.

"Isn't that rather tedious?"

"No, not really. I mean, I'm interested in his research. And I rather enjoy putting his words down on paper in my own way. I suppose it's also quite useful as a way of avoiding doing my own writing."

"And you said his sight is going?"

"Well, very gradually. Although he doesn't say much about it. That's why he's trying to pack a lot in before he loses it, travelling, getting all the latest published work – and unpublished, some of it, I think – talking to people, visiting museums, that kind of thing. I can talk to him on tape when I send his back with the transcripts, or telephone him if I need to ask something directly. It's quite fun, actually."

"It must be a grim prospect, knowing he will lose his sight."

"I think he may keep a tiny bit in the middle of his field of vision for quite a long time. But yes, I think it is hard for him. Yet he seems to do a lot inside his head – he always had a way of painting pictures with words. He could always see clearly in his imagination."

"And he's imagined an island."

"Well, yes, I suppose it is imagined. But he believes it did exist. That it still exists, under the sea."

"Where?"

"East of Madagascar in the Indian Ocean. He says that sixty years ago, if you had sailed to that point, you would have seen a tiny islet called St Brandon, with a few palm trees and maybe a fishing boat – that was all that was left of it. And that disappeared in 1947."

"And these – these hominid creatures were isolated there?"

"Well, that's what he says."

He reached for his glass of red wine. "I remember an island," he said thoughtfully. "Before we were married Yolande came out to join me in New Zealand, where I was working my way around the world. After that we travelled on together. One of the places we visited was an island called Cheju, off the coast of South Korea.. It was one of the most beautiful places I have ever seen. When we were there it was winter, and the mountains were covered in snow, although in the lowlands it was green and lush with extraordinary volcanic rocks. There were white sand beaches and water like clear glass. We had some days of battering wind and rain when it didn't seem so different from Cornwall, and although they weren't in flower then there were acres of azaleas. It is so isolated that its language is quite different from the mainland. There were extraordinary women there who dived for pearls and shellfish to depths of around twenty metres. They wore only thin cotton bathing costumes, without aids of any kind, although the water was very cold. They could stay down for several minutes. They were called the Haenyo, and most of them were the breadwinners of their families. Women seemed to outnumber men anyway, but these women were particularly strong, independent characters – charming and quite delightful in their way, friendly and smiling, but with great pride in what they did."

"I remember," said Yolande, taking the chair next to him. "There were all ages, too, some just children, some quite old women."

"They used a kind of diving reflex," John said. "I knew a bit about it, having done biology at university, and it was remarkable to see actually in action. In a deep dive like that the heartbeat slows right down and somehow rations the supply of blood to give the brain and heart muscles priority. It happens in other aquatic creatures – whales, sea lions and so on – but not in any other terrestrial mammal."

"They were quite fat, too," said Yolande. "Well, not exactly fat – but they were very smooth and rounded."

"Women do have a higher percentage of subcutaneous fat," John observed.

"I'm only too well aware of it," said Yolande. She rose, then, and found, among the clutter of objects that crowded all the surfaces in their cottage, a shell. It was curved like a trumpet, heavy to hold.

"We bought this from them. It's a conch shell."

It was the emblem of Triton, son of Poseidon, who was half man, half fish, and who could summon the waves to him at will.

8

Sex in the Sea

The last of the rain was scudding through the tasselled shiver of the papyrus forest that lined the white shore.   Sunlight suddenly glittered on the skein of the waves and a shoal of tiny blue fish darted away from her shadow in the clear water. She stopped running. Her skin glittered too: she touched her arm with a finger, watching the drops of moisture disappear.   When she lifted her small face to the sun she was intrigued by the red glow that penetrated her closed eyelids.   She was intrigued by many things, although she could not have put them into words, for she knew no words, nor even thoughts, if thoughts were more than simply unfilled spaces in her mind, unformed, questions unanswered because they could not be asked.

"We might call her Thetis," said Mr Brouard, "the divine silver-footed Thetis, daughter of Nereus, the Old Man of the Sea, most beautiful of the Nereids, who could change herself into a fish or a fluid wave.   You may remember, she was married to a mortal."

She could see the rocks ahead, where the wind was always strong, out of the shelter of this part of the southern shore, and where the mussels would be thick in the pools. What mattered to Thetis were not the strange sensations in her head, but those that she could feel on her tongue and in her belly: the fat mussel in its sharp shell, the roundness of a turtle egg in her palm, the slippery squirm of a fish speared by a reed point. Sometimes, too, there was smell: the smell of fruit when she followed a chattering gang of monkeys beyond the papyrus forests and shared with them sweet bananas and paw-paw, the musk smell of some big cat that made her run back to the sea again. Then there was the feel of the cool sea in the morning after a night when the fleas had been biting within the nest of reeds where she rocked with her siblings, or the warm-egg caress of a dolphin's greeting.

And yet – and yet, sometimes she was aware of more than these immediate physical sensations. She would watch the red sun's descent into the sea with a kind of hunger that food could not satisfy. When she frayed the papyrus fibres with a mussel shell and twisted them together, and then wove them into the beginning of a new nest, and saw that she did it well, she felt a kind of satisfaction, which was curiously enhanced by the way others saw it too.

One day, as she was watching one of the males carefully balancing his nest on piles of the discarded shells that strewed the shore above high tide, she found herself feeling much the same sensation as when she did something well. When something worked – well, that was a pleasure. And, watching him, she saw that he could crouch beneath the nest and shelter from the rain. Inland there were trees to provide such protection, but here on their own shore, where the sea was their sanctuary from marauding animals, there was only the white sand and the shimmering reeds.

He looked up, aware of her long before that moment, but not conceding it until now. She had not been with a male before, but now he came towards her and led her into the waves. This was a different smell, a different feeling: a new pleasure. Or was it pain? She did not know. But as his arms tightened around her and she felt him pressing against her buttocks, she wriggled round and looked into his eyes, and clasped him to her belly.

"Peleus," I suppose we could call him," said Mr Brouard. "The mortal man married to Thetis by jealous Zeus...But it is a fact that mammals which copulate in the sea have female sexual organs modified for ventro-ventral approach – not just dolphins and whales but less completely aquatic creatures like beavers and sea otters. Our usual method of sexual intercourse is just one of the characteristics we acquired over the millions of years that we flourished on the island. We would have adapted to a semi-aquatic environment, discovering certain things, learning from them, perhaps as certain macaque monkeys do. There was a study of macaques on a Japanese island in the 1950s, in which they found that a particular female would take freshly dug yams to a pool to wash them clean of soil. When they scattered rice on to the gravelly ground she would take handfuls to the pool and wait until the gravel sank, and the rice floated on the surface. Other macaques imitated her, and these improvements, skills, whatever you might call them, were part of instinctive behaviour – even when clean yams were substituted for dirty ones. They called her Imo." I could hear him grin as he added: "Reminds me of Ino of the Slim Ankles, who saved Odysseus from drowning..."

He continued: "The point is that we are talking about a very long time. Long enough for these early creatures to become a single species. Long enough for them to develop the kind of learned behaviour that the macaques do. It is very likely that nest-building became a part of such behaviour, as it is not only for birds but many mammals, including primates today. Over the millennia, as the eastern mountains eroded and silt expanded the estuarine delta of the river and its tributaries, such nests could be engulfed in shallow water. A study of the Swamp Hornbill of the Danube basin showed how they provide practical protection against land-based predators and pests – and against equally dangerous ones in the sea. There was abundant material for them – the reed forests of the delta, like those of the Marsh Arabs in southern Iraq. Handling the fibres, dry or wet, parting them, pulling or cutting them with the edge of a shell, would stimulate new techniques, twisting, tying, weaving – all based on the nest-building instincts. Have you read Thesiger yet? Then you should. Before the Marshes of Sumer are lost for ever. They are one of the last fragments of the Ancient World. According to the legends of Sumer, transcribed on to stone tablets by the Babylonians in about 2000 BC, the god Enlil – whom the Babylonians called Marduk - built a reed platform on the waters, and thus created the world."

I read Wilfrid Thesiger's *The Marsh Arabs* and Gavin Maxwell's *A Reed Shaken By the Wind*. Mr Brouard's words seem prophetic now. That beautiful place, six thousand square miles of golden reeds and water, has now been almost completely destroyed, although the other day I read that since 2003 fresh water has been returning to flood the land.

In the early 1970s a writer called Elaine Morgan published a book called *The Descent of Woman*. It was in the style of earlier books on human behaviour by a writer rather than a scientist – *African Genesis* and *The Territorial Imperative* by Robert Ardrey, who was a Hollywood screenwriter. His idea was that man was innately a killer, which was why we had evolved from aggressive predatory apes to the not much less unpleasant creatures we are now.
Elaine Morgan had a different theory, drawing on Sir Alister Hardy's ideas about the aquatic features of human beings. She added a feminist twist to the debate with a lot about male as opposed to female aggression, and the female orgasm, and tears, but she did seem to me to pre-empt much of Mr Brouard's ideas. She wrote about the diving reflex that John had described; about subcutaneous fat, learning to use tools by cracking open shellfish – even the fact that the vestigial hairs on the human body follow exactly the lines that would be followed by the flow of water over a swimming body. It was all rather fascinating and well written and it was to begin a continuing argument between the proponents and opponents of the theory of the aquatic ape. I wasn't quite sure how Mr Brouard would take it. It was a very popular book, although not with most anthropologists. I sent him a copy.

Anxious to know how he felt, I telephoned him. I could hear a Bach fugue in the background.

"What do you think of the book?" I asked him.

"Well, her theory does have a provenance going back several years – she acknowledges her debt to Alister Hardy, of course. But she's moved it forward a good deal. There are a number of minor errors, which she'll no doubt iron out in due course – although I suspect the anthropological establishment will use them to demolish her, especially as she isn't a scientist. On the other hand she, like Hardy, clings to the traditional concept of progressive evolution of *Homo sapiens* in Africa."

"Nothing about islands," I observed.

"No, nothing about islands."

"She seems to think the aquatic bit was a turning point in the progress of evolution."

He said crisply, "I thought we'd dispensed with that word progress."

"Well, I know, I just think – "

"Can you remember what I said about the time factor? The six hundred million years for the horseshoe crab – and yet you think *Homo sapiens sapiens* evolved in a few hundred thousand?"

"No, I can see what you mean, but surely it does seem that Africa is the cradle of human evolution. I've been reading about the discoveries in Kenya and Tanzania. Jonathan Leakey has found this fossil which is about two and a half million years old, and seems to have human characteristics – a bigger brain, smaller teeth, that sort of thing. Couldn't it be a sort of missing link? Between the Southern Apes and us, I mean? He's called it *Homo habilis.*"

"Yes," he said. "Man the Toolmaker, I think. Jonathan Leakey's father, Louis, and his colleagues have decided to call it *Homo. Habilis,* I imagine, because the fossils were found with some stone implements – pebbles flaked to produce a scraping or cutting tool. Mary Leakey, Louis's wife, discovered such tools in the Olduvai Gorge in Tanzania and although they've since been found elsewhere they are now known as 'Oldowan'. They vary in date and sophistication. But it is perhaps worth remembering that none of the finds in the Great Rift Valley, of which the Olduvai Gorge is a part, would have been made had not the area undergone massive upheaval less than half a million years ago. The movement of geological faults resulted in exposure of layers of deposits, revealing all this archaeological material. It is an extraordinary stroke of luck: but it means that a great deal rests on this particular part of Africa."

"Well, yes, but surely that is what makes it so valuable – from what's been found here we can interpret so much more – "

"And of course that is the fun of it. Imagine the excitement as you come across a fragment of cranium – then another – then the painstaking tension of reconstruction of a cranium, a jaw; the estimation of the brain size by water displacement. Then the naming: should it be a sub-genera of the genus *Australopithecus* within the family *Hominidae*, i.e. *Paranthropus* (the name the enthusiastic paleontologists gave to some South African fossils, meaning 'beside or equal to man') or *Zinjanthropus* – 'East African Man'? No: look at the size of the skull, the tools – let's call it Man and be done with it: *Homo* it is, and *habilis* because it was obviously clever enough to be making tools (well, not cleverer than a lot of apes, but then this must be different...) It's all fascinating stuff and I only wish I could be there too," he added, for a moment sounding quite serious.

"Well," I said. "You sound a bit sceptical."

"Well, a little, perhaps. These finds are exciting. But it is easy to extrapolate whole worlds from them. Now, I have no doubt that there were populations of hominids in Africa who occupied various ecological niches and adapted to their particular environments. As individuals, subject to physical disease, injury and congenital variation, they were probably as different from each other as we are. But what I don't believe is that we evolved from them – not even from our friend *Homo habilis*. He, or she, happened to be a hominid which – like us – retained more primitive features than others. She had a slightly larger brain than most of her family. But she was not human. Because the African niche which she occupied, the environment to which she had adapted, were not the unique and extraordinary circumstances which led to the creation of the human animal, and its marvellous conscious mind."

"Yes, but how – "

"I know, it is confusing," he said. "But let's go back to first principles. We belong to a kind of 'super family', all evolved from a very distant ancestor. Because of our destructive domination it now consists only of our own species, and a few surviving species of anthropoid apes. Two million years ago there were probably hundreds of different species in Africa, far more like us than any of our existing cousins. From their distant ancestor, over tens of millions of years, they had occupied various ecological niches, becoming allopatric or sympatric populations, isolated from another by geography and behaviour – "

"I remember," I interrupted eagerly. "A sympatric population is separated from others by behaviour, and allopatric by geography – by simply being in another country or something. Blue tits and long-tailed tits. Because of their behaviour, the way they nest, that sort of thing, they have become different species, so they can't mate with each other."

"Exactly so. Individuals from such populations adapt and evolve into a great diversity of sub-species, and if the isolation is prolonged and complete enough, into different species, which cannot interbreed."

"But we can."

"Indeed. We can. Our differences from humans of other races or cultures are truly little more than skin deep - because they result from comparatively recent colonisation by early *Homo sapiens*. It has been a period of adaptation over tens of thousands, not millions, of years."

"All right, then: but if *Homo habilis* isn't human, then what about *Homo Erectus?* Richard Leakey has found an almost complete skeleton of a twelve year old boy in Kenya – and that's supposed to have a brain almost as big as ours – "

"Well, it had once. Yes, I think *Homo Erectus* is human. Like the fossils found in Java and China as far back as the end of the last century: like the little boy, they date from about 1.6 million years ago. I would suggest calling them *Homo sapiens erectus*, for I believe they may have been a sub-species of *Homo sapiens* – an extinct human race. Just like the later neanderthals, who were taxonomically *Homo sapiens* neanderthalis."

"Taxonomically?"

"Taxonomy – the theory of classifying living organisms."

"Look, I may have read up some of this, but I'd rather not

be blinded by science." I realised what I had said and added, "sorry."

"No, I'm sorry. Look – this is complicated. But imagine the island. Millions of years pass. In that time, the island hominids adapt to their environment, establishing themselves as raft or nest-building creatures, semi-aquatic, capable of increasingly complex tasks in circumstances which required them to use particular skills – not to run fast or swing from trees. They were essentially still the animals which had crossed that KT boundary, not humans, although their adaptation had meant an increase in sensory and motor mechanisms. It is likely that the areas of the brain to do with visual association had expanded."

"So how come they turned up in Africa and Asia?"

"You're forgetting timescales. At this stage, any such aquatic apes that found themselves on the coast of Africa would almost certainly have been unable to survive, let alone reproduce, in such a hostile environment. By the time we get to the fossil remains of *Homo sapiens erectus*, we're talking about a creature which had already evolved into a recognisable human being. We're talking about millions of years of evolution in isolation on the island. Only at this stage could they leave their imprint on Africa – and indeed, on Asia."

"Why only then?"

"Well, first of all, look at the geographical position of the island. It was vulnerable to cyclones, winds, ocean currents. Over the timespan we're talking about – millions of years – it's inevitable that eventually millions of these early human beings would have been marooned on the coasts of Africa by the south-east trade winds, and on Asian shores by the south west monsoon drift. Think of the Galapagos, and the way they were populated by unique creatures carried on the Peru Current. So it happened in Africa."

"And by then they would have been able to survive?"

"Well, the sea passage would have been the easiest part, and the sudden change of environment would have eliminated all save those who by chance had already become partly adapted to changed circumstances. They would have suffered every kind of attack from bacteria and insects to mammals. But some would have survived, and a few females would have managed to reproduce – to have daughters. Natural selection can act very rapidly to eliminate characteristics which are more of a liability than an asset, and the flimsier skull and extravagant demands of cardiac output required by the larger brain developed on the island would have been just such liabilities. In some respects the successful survivors would tend to revert towards their distant land-dwelling ancestors."

"What – get more like the apes?"

"In a way, yes. The point is that what on the Island were advantages were disadvantages in this very different environment. Take sweating, for example. It's a curious kind of cooling system. Essentially, you break down blood and exude salt water through glands in the skin. It works well for a semi-aquatic creature with a large amount of subcutaneous fat and a skin that needs to be able to screen against harmful ultraviolet light, while remaining pale enough to reflect other radiation, like infra-red. But it's not so good for a terrestrial creature in a hot dry environment. On the other hand, the human brain – and these were human – gave them massive advantage in terms of anticipating danger and dealing with all kinds of difficulties. It gave them the ability to learn the methods of survival from their distant cousins, the 'southern apes'. In time they would have competed all too successfully with them."

"So – the ones that coped better with the conditions, and survived, were to become *Homo sapiens erectus*?"

"Well, we aren't talking about a great many *erectus* fossils. None has been dated earlier than two millions years ago. But the discovery of any fossil at all means that there was once a population of reasonable size in that particular spot. It also requires a reasonable population of fossil hunters... And there is no doubt that such early human beings did successfully occupy a particular ecological niche in Africa. For example, if we look at the routes they might have taken – albeit at the mercy of wind and current – there are precise landfalls that provided them with environments very close to that of the island, like the Zambezi delta, or the shores of Djibouti and Ethiopia, which were then lands of great rivers and estuarine marsh. Nevertheless, as I said, there is a limit to how much we can interpret from fossil discoveries, though no limit to how much we might enjoy extrapolating."

I heard the doorbell: "Look, I'll have to go," I said quickly.

"Yes, of course. I seem to have talked far too long."

"No, of course you haven't – "

"Nevertheless, I forget you have other things to do."

"Well – "

"Perhaps one day we could meet again," he said suddenly. "In Boury, perhaps. It would be good to see you again, and talk face to face."

"Well, yes, it would – "

"The real story begins with the Pleistocene. The epoch of the ice ages. It began about two million years ago. That's about one minute four seconds on the horseshoe crab's clock. But it's our world: the one we still live in today."

9

Monet's Vision

The Pleistocene was to remain a mystery for some time. My first novel was published later that year and prompted a good deal of publicity. The plot concerned espionage and naval skulduggery and although my father was the chief source and the rest was from my imagination, I told a Sunday Mirror reporter on the telephone that I had picked most of it up at indiscreet naval cocktail parties. The Ministry of Defence demanded to see a copy before publication. I was photographed on a windblown warship and subsequently received some very strange letters and telephone calls from middle-aged men. My flatmates (I was then living in South Kensington) were highly amused and dealt effectively with the telephone calls, although I did accept a tip for the Derby and one invitation to lunch. Long afterwards I wished I had dismissed most of them less summarily, for they all appeared to be rich and lonely, but at the time I was besotted with someone and, as they say, had eyes for no one else. Which was the chief reason I only occasionally wondered why no tape appeared from Mr Brouard. I telephoned him once and was told he was away, but he did not call back.

Nevertheless I was aware of developments in the continuing quest for the origins of humanity. In Ethiopia a team of French and American anthropologists discovered a diminutive fossil skeleton identified as *Australopithecus afarensis*. It was female, about three million years old, and walked upright. They called it Lucy. And around this time, in Tanzania, Mary Leakey came upon a trail of what looked like human footprints made in a layer of volcanic ash over three and half million years ago.

In September I was asked by the *Daily Telegraph* Magazine to write a feature on Monet's garden at Giverny in Normandy. After the artist's death in 1926 it had been left in the care of his son's sister-in-law, Blanche Monet, but when she died after the war it had fallen into neglect. In 1966 it had been bequeathed to the Academie des Beaux-Arts, but only the most basic repairs had been done to the house and nature had reclaimed Monet's water lilies and irises. Now it had been entrusted to the man who had restored Versailles, Gerald Van der Kemp. With new funding he was now to begin the restoration of the house and garden that had been Monet's abiding passion.

Giverny was only some twenty miles from Boury-en-Vexin. I telephoned Mr Brouard and got Jean-Claude:

"Je regrette, he is out – he will return this afternoon. His daughter, she is visiting him here."

"His daughter?"

"Oui, Molly. You do not know her?"

"No," I said.

I took the ferry to Caen and drove westwards to Vernon, a sylvan little town on one of the coils of the Seine. It took longer to drive across France then and I stopped for a night at an auberge in a village near Bernay. My room had a high mahogany bed and a crimson damask bedspread. I ate blanquette de veau and drank red wine brought in a stone jug. As I departed in the morning Madame Huguet was milking a white cow in the orchard. The sun slivered through the poplar trees along the dust-edged tarmac.

Monet's house at Giverny was shuttered, pink paint peeling, rose trellises collapsed along overgrown paths and the lily pond full of silt. Yet there was a real excitement about the project. Old plate photographs – in colour - taken by an amateur photographer in about 1917, provided extraordinary evidence of how the garden had looked in Monet's lifetime. An elderly artist called Andre Devillers remembered visiting Monet, and discussing the palette of roses, delphiniums and dahlias. There was hope of more cash for the restoration, particularly from America, as Giverny had hosted a small colony of American Impressionist artists around the turn of the century.

"Annenberg, Rockefeller – even the *Reader's Digest*," Mr Van der Kemp said cheerfully. "I believe many such people will help with the work. I think Monet would be very pleased to see his garden returned to its beauty. It is, perhaps, an irony to think that he could not fully enjoy it towards the end."

"Why couldn't he?"

"He was going blind," said Mr Van der Kemp.

"But he was still painting?"

"Of course. Ten years before his death he wrote: 'if I have recovered my sense of colour it is because I have adapted my work methods to my vision'. To the end he was painting his Water Lilies."

I drove to Boury-en-Vexin three days later, through the gentle French countryside with its woods and open pastures. It seemed spacious, almost empty, with stands of trees instead of hedgerows, scattered hamlets and straight dusty lanes, compared to the crowded English countryside.   Boury itself was a small stone village with handsome houses, a farm and a small, silvery, seventeenth century chateau. The main street had cobbled pavements and from Jean-Claude's instructions it was easy to find the house: tall and gabled with a gravelled forecourt behind high wrought iron gates. I pulled the iron bell-pull with sudden apprehension.   Trepidation tapped me on the shoulder.

Jean-Claude Melchior was slightly built, with bright brown eyes and one of those floppy moustaches that might have given him a faintly comic look, were it not for the self-mocking amusement in his glance. His wife, Mr Brouard's sister, Frederika – always known as Freddie – was a graceful fair-haired woman, perhaps an inch taller than Jean-Claude.   They shared the house in Boury with Jean-Claude's parents – his father was a retired gynaecologist and ex mayor of the village – their two children, then in their early teens, and various visiting relations.   It was that kind of house, spacious, with lots of rooms, tiled floors, tall shuttered windows, open fires and a drawing room kept for best.   There was also a very small whiskery dog, several ducks, M Melchior senior's donkeys, and a golden retriever called Nuke, who ate peaches off the espaliered trees that lined one of the orchard walls.

"And this is Molly," said Jean-Claude.

She was taller than me, big-boned, with red hair (like her father's) drawn back in a ponytail.   Her eyes were hazel, not blue, like his.   She was wearing jeans and a Peanuts T-shirt and no make up at all – not that she needed to, having fine pale skin with freckles, and good cheekbones.   (I was never seen without eyeliner).

"Good to meet you," she said.   We shook hands and she smiled in a friendly way, but I was aware of the suspicion in her eyes. I felt uneasy: an intruder.

"Well – let us find William," said Jean-Claude.   I sensed that he, too, was not quite comfortable with the situation.   I glanced at Freddie and I could not read her expression.   I realised that I was the stranger here.

The back of the house looked out on to a lawn with a stream and woodland beyond.   A gate in a high stone wall led through to the orchard, with apple and cherry trees, and the espaliered fruit.   The outbuildings on one side, continuing from the house, had been converted into guest and games rooms.   It was here, Freddie explained to me, that Mr Brouard had made his home for more than a decade.

He heard us approach along the gravelled path and came to the open *porte-fenetre* to greet us.   He had grown a beard, neatly trimmed with scissors, peppery but still tinged with red.   His eyes were still bright blue.   I noticed that his gaze was very intent, very focused.   He held out his hands and I took them in mine, and he bent down to kiss me briefly, twice, then once more, on the cheek.

"Well – we'll leave you to talk, and see you for lunch," Freddie Melchior said.   I saw her touch Molly's arm.   "Don't let Nuke eat all the peaches."

We sat for a while in his study, with the sun outside and the big golden dog resting against his leg. The room was dark and small, lined with shelves of books and files. The two tables and the floor were stacked with books and papers, neatly arranged. There was a telephone and a tape-recorder. We talked as if it were only a few weeks, not over a year, since our last conversation, and for once we spoke about our lives as well as human evolution.

He asked about my writing, and why I had not yet married. He would have expected it by now, he said. I explained that I had had two near misses, one that got away and one that I got away from: that my mother was of the opinion that I was too particular, but I was actually perfectly happy on my own.

"Besides," I said, "I have a lot of friends, and I'm an aunt, too, now. My brother's got a little boy. But what about you? I was interested to meet your daughter – she must have been just a baby when I was at Gun Club Hill School."

"Yes, Molly has been a delight," he said. "We rather lost touch through her teens, when she was at school – she boarded at a convent in Surrey. Not my choice, but then I had no right...Then she went to Oxford. She did extremely well. French and politics: she got a first. I saw her several times while she was at Oxford. She had a year in Toulouse at a law firm there, and she's just got into the civil service. She's aiming for a job in Brussels."

"Clever girl," I said, feeling old and inadequate.

"Well, she is very bright."

For a moment I remembered those pale hazel eyes. Then I said: "Well. But why no tapes recently? I've been waiting for the Pleistocene for ages – "

"Ah," he said. "Yes. Our own epoch. Well, it's all there – " He gestured at the neatly labelled boxes on one of the shelves: labelled in braille.

"Oh," I said.

"My sight is worse," he said. "So I thought I should learn braille. To be prepared. I have some difficulty in reading. But I can see the brightness of the sun, the dog in the doorway there – you, if I concentrate on the central point."

Then I said again, "and the tapes?"

"I didn't want to impose," he said, with a sudden awkwardness.

"Impose? Why on earth should you think that? I like transcribing them. I've missed them."

"Have you?"

"Of course I have. Besides, I promised you. Have you given up your quest for the origins of mankind?"

He smiled at me, then. "No. It keeps me going..."

"Then why – "

"Oh, something you said, perhaps; you have been busy with your life, your writing, whatever men there have been...I am an old man – "

"Rubbish. You're not old. I'm a great one for sugar-daddies, anyway."

He laughed. "Well, I don't think I qualify for that – but seriously, I didn't want this silly obsession of mine to become a burden. It isn't fair. And sometimes I wonder what it is all for. Just to keep me occupied, learning braille, getting transcriptions, having someone to read for me – Freddie and Jean-Claude and the children are wonderful, but Chloe and Jack are growing up, and I can contribute very little to the household. I made some reasonable property investments in the sixties, which helps financially, but I don't find it easy to be so dependent on them."

"Well, I would like you to go on sending the tapes. And letting me argue with you on the telephone. I'm intrigued, for heaven's sake – I mean, there are new developments and discoveries in this field all the time. You can't just stop now."

"Do you really mean that?"

"Yes, I do. Can I take some tapes home with me now?"

"Well – if you really want to – "

I touched his hand. "I really want to."

He put his hand on mine, smiling at me. I swear there were tears in his eyes. "Molly said – " he began.

"Molly? What did she say?"

"Well – she didn't spell it out, but the implication was that I am an old fool, and unfair to you."

"She had no right."

"She was thinking of me – and you."

"Well, she had no right to think of me. She doesn't even know me. And just because you can't see so well doesn't mean you've lost your marbles, does it?"

"No," he said, and we both laughed, then.

"Come for a walk," he said. "Let's go out in the sunshine."

We walked in the orchard, and the dog Nuke stole the peaches, and we did, too, and we listed the number of things that a warm, ripe peach reminded us of, which made us both giggle.

Lunch was laid on a long table in the garden, so that everyone could be seated. Orange and roast pepper soup was followed by beef niçoise, fruit and apple tart, and there were jugs of red wine. "For Zeus!" cried Mr Brouard at one point, pouring a libation on to the grass. it was a very happy occasion and I felt privileged to be there. I did not say much because my French was not very good – certainly not as good as Molly's – but Jean-Claude's father and I took rather a fancy to each other and I managed to follow the gist of his conversation, which was on the subject of how Normandy had always been English while the Ile de France was most definitely French. The fortress of Boury, it seemed, was a crucial factor, Richard the Lionheart having laid seige to it on this very spot (unsuccessfully) in 1198.

"You should visit the chateau," said Molly, from the other side of the table. "It was rebuilt in the seventeenth century, although I believe the current owners are descended from the original family. It's quite charming. You might find it interesting to write about. I could put in a word. Is it the sort of thing you do?"

I had thought of it, so lovely was the little chateau I had glimpsed from the street, but somehow I suddenly went right off the idea.

Before I left, on that bright sunlit afternoon, I went with Mr Brouard to collect the box of tapes from his study.

"Odysseus sprang to mind for this bit," he said. "See what you think."

The sun had gone round, shining through the open glass doors. Molly's face was in shadow. "What are you doing?" she said.

He said he was giving me some tapes to take back with me.

"But I thought – "

"She is happy to transcribe them for me," he said quietly. "For which I am most grateful."

The hazel eyes were hard.

"Well. It's very kind of you," she said.

"Not at all. I enjoy it. I think your father's work is fascinating."

They all followed me into the forecourt as I carried the box to the car. There were many kisses of farewell and Jean-Claude said into my ear: "I am very glad you came today. Please continue to think of him."

Mr Brouard took my hands and said he had asked the bright-eyed goddess to be with me. "Athene," he added. "I know," I said. "Remember, I did the Odyssey at school."

10

Building the Boat

Our planet does not revolve with perfect precision around the sun. Its orbit varies by perhaps one tenth of one per cent over about 100,000 years. The tilt of its axis, relative to its orbit, varies by as much as four degrees in a 41,000 year cycle, and the timing of its approach to the sun is affected by the gravitational pulls of other planets. Such alterations may have little effect on us – in particular, on our climate. But when continents move, when patterns on earth change, then the consequences can be dramatic.

For millions of years the sun and oceans had been in harmony. The world had been a place of calm, of warmth, despite the imperfections of its spin upon its axis. Then, about two million years ago, something happened. The continents had moved. It was their instability that affected the earth – specifically, now, the polar regions. In high latitudes the summers could not melt all the snow that had accumulated during the previous winter, and it turned to ice. Glaciers expanded. The polar ice caps extended across vast areas. It was the first of many ice ages to come. Each was to last hundreds of thousands of years.

When the grip of the ice age was harshest over the earth, sea levels were reduced by some ninety metres, and the whole planet cooled, for much of the sun's heat was reflected back from the shining mirrors of the ice fields. Then, as the earth's alignment shifted again, its orbit changing, the heat of the sun increased. Sea levels rose again in the long warm spell that followed, before the next ice age began. Such intervening periods are known as interglacials, although one might last as long as an ice age itself. Sometimes it seems there are shorter warm intervals, perhaps ten to twenty thousand years, called interstadials. We may be living in such an interval today. If so, and this interstadial reached its warmest point about five thousand years ago, our climate could be getting colder again. On the other hand the last ice age may be over, in which case the world can look forward to a hundred thousand years of increasingly warm climate, perhaps exacerbated by the activities of *Homo sapiens,* if still in existence... The polar ice caps will recede, and the sea levels will rise much higher than today.

No one really knows the exact sequence of events, said Mr Brouard on the tape. We know a good deal by analysing oxygen isotopes from ancient marine deposits, but to go beyond the last ten glaciations and interglacials is more difficult. All we do know is that about two million years ago the climate of the earth began to change, and its inhabitants had to adapt to new environments. The people of the island in the Indian Ocean endured cooler, wetter weather. But more than that, the very foundation of their world was changing: the island itself.

From what remains of the Mascarene Plateau, albeit under the sea, it is probable that the southern half was once a single island. A river, rising in the east, flowed down to the western sea. Then, about a million years ago, there was another rise in the sea level. The ocean broke through the eastern cliffs and turned the river into a stormy strait, cutting the island into two. Who knows how it might have happened? Was it an infinitesimal process, a gradual nibbling of the waves on the granite rocks, a seepage of salt, a trickle that chiselled its way through some deep ravine? Perhaps there was a sudden deluge, a breaking apart, a final triumph of the ever-rising ocean. Great boulders, trees, fish and animals were caught up in the turbulence of an ancient Charybdis. The northern part of the island, now beneath the ocean, was in recent times called Saya de Malha: the southern, Nazareth. On the twelve hour clock of the horseshoe crab, this divide took place only about a minute before noon.

I heard him pause on the tape, heard the clink of a mug, the sound of him relighting his pipe. Once again he ceased to speak from his notes, but as if talking to me from that room in Boury, with the dog lying in the sunny doorway.

It may have been the catalyst for the island people. Their reliance on a settled environment had long been undermined. Unlike their ancient forebears who had been carried to the coast of Africa, and over previous millions of years had learned from their *Austrolapithecine* cousins how to survive, they had had to acquire different talents. They were not threatened by predators, at least not such powerful predators as in Africa, but by the very thing on which they depended: the sea. Their old floating nests were no longer safe. Some improvement was a necessity. Some rare inventive genius came up with a clever way of lashing bundles of reeds: another saw how it was possible to tie a knot, to weave, to cut the fibres with a sharp-edged shell. Others would copy them, as happens even among tribes of Macaque monkeys. And then, perhaps on some calm morning, someone looked across the sea to the northern part of the island, and in his mind, in that extraordinary forebrain possessed only by *Homo sapiens*, as yet undeveloped, thought of a way of reaching it. A way of moving on the surface of the waters. A boat.

He said then, as if recalling a memory: In the legend of Sumer that the Babylonians call Enuma Elish there is a description of a time when there was nothing. 'No reed-hut had been matted, no marsh land had appeared...Only Apsu, of the sweet waters, Tiamat of the salt waters, and Mimmu of the clouds 'co-mingled their waters as a single body'. I remember once standing on a still morning at the mouth of the Shatt al Arab – the shore of Iraq. It was misty, with low cloud. Pools of water, rising out of the mud, or from a recent river flood, mingled with the salt sea water of the Gulf, glistening over the flats. It was as if sky, sea and earth were one.

I wanted to talk to him then, to challenge him. He picked up the telephone almost immediately, as if waiting for it to ring.

"But you're not saying these were human beings, like us, nearly a million years ago?"

"Essentially, yes, I am. But they didn't have our overgrown brains, and everything that goes with them. And whether the moment of creativity came and went, simply passing through the mind of that individual creature, to return to one of his or her descendants – well, who could know. But what had been instinct, the instinct to build nests, to survive, had been honed and extended by the life they had led in their semi-marine environment, all the time adapting to conditions through awareness of techniques of survival rather than escape from predators. Their enemies were wind and sea, storm, cold, probably some predation by insects and marine creatures – shark, jellyfish, squid. All the time they were pushing at the boundaries of sensory perception, or inventiveness – but like the macaque monkeys, they were adapting by instinct, not by deliberate creativity. Until, perhaps, that instant of realisation that it was possible to turn something into something better."

"A nest into a boat."

I could hear him chuckle. "You sound a little sceptical."

"Well – "

"Keep listening," he said. And rang off.

What began then was an integration of mental evolution and developing technology unique in the natural world. Intelligence began to matter. Each improvement in intelligent perception enhanced the chances of improving the ability of the island people to move across the waters, to fish, to carry cargo, to integrate land and sea. For tools they had an infinite variety of shells. They could cut, carve, dig, shovel.   Canals could be excavated as we know they have been for thousands of years, for irrigation, for draining marshland, for transport on reed boats similar to those which are used today on Lake Titicaca. And at some point between the splitting of the island caused by one great rise in sea level and the moment of final destruction, they built a reed boat. It was the beginning of conceptual thinking.   It was the concept of a boat.   And a boat that was probably at least as effective as Thor Heyerdahl's Ra I and II in which he and his crew crossed the Atlantic. It was unwieldy, unable to sail other than with a following wind, subject to all manner of catastrophe, but Eratosthenes and Pliny both described boats like these trading between Sri Lanka and the mouth of the Ganges.

But there is more to it than just the intelligence of an individual. Those who had the best boats would best survive climatic disaster, and on that infinitely slow basis those with such intelligence would pass it on: thus does natural selection work. Skills in handling reeds, in weaving or tying knots, expand the area of the brain controlling hands and fingers.   Similarly, the part connected with visual perception and translation of visual signals into manual activities would have to expand. And building a boat is not a solitary occupation. The individual creativity requires some social organisation, often complex co-operation – someone needs to hold the bundle of reeds while someone else lashes it to another.   An inventive macaque monkey might work out a way of washing sand to sieve out rice grains, but because such an improvement isn't part of a tangible object, a permanently inherited thing – like a nest, then a boat – they aren't part of a permanent culture.

But if several islanders became involved, then more, as time went on, so there was a new need for some mechanism which would make it possible to transmit information.   Not only would these elements of technology require to be passed on to others, but to each new generation. Just as the natural organisation of heredity provides a kind of immortality to the patterns of all living creatures, so the artificial organisation of master and apprentice, craftsman and labourer, gives immortality to the creations of human ingenuity. And that particular organisation of individuals requires communication. Language.

Human beings are unique among land mammals in being able to control their breathing, specifically in blocking off their breathing passage, both consciously and unconsciously, to prevent water entering the lungs. Adult humans cannot breathe and drink at the same time, like baboons or other animals. But babies can. And during its first year of life a baby makes the same sort of sounds as a young chimpanzee. Then, during its second year, something happens which doesn't happen in chimpanzees. Its larynx descends to a lower position, taking the base of the tongue with it. From that moment the baby can no longer eat, drink and breathe at the same time – but it can begin to talk. There does seem to be a physiological link between the capacity for speech and the ability to survive underwater.

He broke off the tape at this point and added: "Birds use language – no doubt Rhea used sounds in the same way, although of course when it comes to birds it's usually the male of the species that sings to define its territory or attract a mate. And then there are whales and dolphins, the only other animals with systems of communication comparable with ours. But by human language I mean communication with words, symbolic sounds."

The development of language and hearing required phenomenal expansion of those parts of the brain directly associated with them. New circuits had to control the muscles of the tongue and larynx, combined with association areas for interpreting messages. Temporal areas dealing with memorised storage, neural transmitters dealing with hearing, eyesight, motor control of hands - all had to be enlarged to manage all the new information. The evolutionary pressure on the brain to provide sufficient capacity to memorise and process a huge quantity of ideas meant that the cross-connecting circuitry expanded the frontal lobes of the brain by as much as thirty times.

Once again he stopped for a moment, drawing on his pipe, and digressed a little: "You know, the curious thing about this part of the brain, the frontal lobes, is that it seems to be a kind of blank screen on which the brain can compose imaginary pictures from collected data – yet it's more than that: this is the area of creativity, of a sense of beauty – madness. I've always been rather intrigued by the story of a young railroad construction worker called I Phineas Gage. It was 1848 and he was using explosives on a railroad in Vermont. He inadvertently tamped a steel rod into a blasting hole and the result was that the rod, over a metre long and about two and half centimetres in diameter, went through his left cheek, destroying his left eye, through the front part of his brain and out the other side. But he wasn't dead. He could actually talk to the surgeon who removed the rod. I believe Phineas Gage's skull – and the steel rod – is still somewhere in Harvard University. The extraordinary thing was that Gage not only survived, but was able to function normally – except that his personality seemed to have changed. His motor functions like speech and movement were unaffected, but he could no longer handle his emotions. Or so it seems. He later suffered epileptic fits and died quite young."

I paused, reaching for my coffee mug, glancing out of the window. A woman was pushing a baby in a buggy along the pavement below. She was talking to the baby with all the gooey intimacy of a mother who thinks she is unobserved, and the baby was looking back at her, fascinated by this strange language. I had a sudden recollection of myself in a pram. It was the only memory I had from such an early age, but it was always vivid. My mother had been pulling me up a hill in Bath, the city where we lived at that time. She had her back turned to me as she pulled the pram like a horse in the shafts. And I, imprisoned, unable to move, was also unable to express my fury at this impersonal back in its camel coat. I could not speak. I do not know whether I cried. All I can remember is the angry frustration of not being able to speak, to tell her to turn round so that I could see her face.

As the island people became fully sapient human beings, so their range of technological skills became ever wider and more complex: processing reeds for containers, protecting the growth of selected plants, planning fishing and hunting. Social patterns of behaviour would emerge, the beginnings of ritual, of tribal loyalties. The territorial instincts of the animal kingdom would play their part in creating new tribal loyalties. Animals often display altruistic, benevolent actions, chiefly because they exercise a genetic protective mechanism, but these too would result in the creation of ritual and taboo.

But this expansion of the frontal lobes of the brain created a problem. Giving birth to a baby with a big head was constrained by the size of the female pelvis, and bipedal locomotion placed limits on the enlargement of the pelvis. What made things easier was for babies to be born increasingly prematurely, so their heads were smaller and more malleable. Such a modification did not require any great evolutionary step, but rather the judicious selection from the existing range of hereditary variations in the endocrine glands, which control the rate of growth and maturity. And they are themselves controlled by a part of the forebrain called the hypothalamus. Tiny amounts of hormones secreted by glands and specialised nerve cells may have far-reaching effects.

One consequence of babies being born more prematurely was that they required more, and longer, parental care. On the other hand, human babies can be born easily under water. Immersed in amniotic fluid in the womb, a baby cannot use its lungs, so the transition to breathing air via warm salt water of similar temperature is not a problem. Babies of normal weight have enough fat to give them buoyancy, and will swim instinctively until they are a few months old.

These, then, were the people of the island about half a million years ago. They were people who had been formed by some hundreds of thousands of years of adaptation and evolutionary pressure to become human: to think, to talk, to imagine, to create. In terms of race, identifiable by the colour and type of skin and hair, they were a Mongoloid people. Their hair was black and straight, their bodies smooth, ranging from pale amber to brown, their eyes dark and narrow. But, essentially, they were people like us.

I turned off the tape recorder and looked at my watch. It was a quarter past three. Were they really like us? Hard to believe, looking out at London. A winter afternoon in London. Did a young female agonise over some male three hundred thousand years ago? Did she sometimes sit alone under a pandanus tree, thinking about him, wishing she could be like the rest of the world, which sometimes seemed to exist entirely of pairs, within a charmed circle she could not enter? Perhaps such melancholy was a twentieth century phenomenon. I made myself a mug of tea and leafed through *The Times*. Mrs Thatcher had remarked that many people feared being swamped by people with a different culture, Ted Heath had denounced her. Fourteen people had been killed by a bomb in Belfast. I wondered if it would have been better for the world if those remote ancestors of ours had never made it to land. And then I saw another small paragraph. In Washington, Mary Leakey had announced the discovery of what appeared to be human footprints, four million years old. I calculated how long that would be on the horseshoe crab's clock: it worked out at almost five minutes.

11

Farewell to the Island

The reeds were dying. Old men said they could remember old men telling them about a time when the lagoons had been shallow enough for the water lilies and the white ibis to flourish, but now the black frigate birds came to steal and scavenge over the waters. The golden plumes of the reeds that once rippled along the white shores were sparse and dry. Where once you could paddle through the green shade of their forests for a day and more, and never see the brilliance of the sun, the salt waves now scoured the tall stems and took back into the ocean great brown fans of silt. Although it was the spring month of calm, when the wet winds from the north-west wearied at last, and those from the south-east had not yet begun to blow, vast skeins of marsh and salting were covered by the waves. They lapped against the granite rocks that once guarded this rim of sand. On the other side of the island, where the dry gales ate into the rocks, what had once been a great lake guarded by cliffs was now part of the ocean itself.

He had walked a long way from the place where they were building the new boat. It was as if he knew that he was looking upon the island for the last time. Perhaps they all knew it, now. In the songs the old men sang at nightfall were pictures of how it had been, when great cliffs guarded the western coasts from monsoon wind and rain and cargoes of coconut and pandanus fruit were carried along the canals from the heart of the forests. There were even tales of times before the channel had opened between the north and the south parts of the island, when it had still been a great river, its source high in the mountains beyond the place where the fruit bats sang to the coco-de-mer. But of course these were only imaginings. All they knew now was that the sea had begun to encroach on the great western lakes and and its spume on the winds was killing the orchids and the sea hibiscus. The canals were full of mud and the air was always moist. Sometime he thought the dolphins and the flying fish were calling to him, that the ocean itself was home, and not here, on this sick land.

When he reached the great ocean strait that lay between the two parts of the island, he saw a boat making the crossing – something only possible, at least with any cargo, during the two quiet months of the year. Even in his lifetime the rain and wind had increased. He watched as it rode the swell of the transparent turquoise water far below, catching the currents, then finding the breeze in its golden sail. Shoals of fish scurried over the white sand, keeping just beyond its seeking shadow. He sat down on a rock to watch. A lizard darted, stopped, looked up at him with tiny alert head cocked. A sound made him look round to see two tortoises pulling at the coral pink flowers of a creeper, and he could not but smile at them as their eyes regarded him, their long necks extended, watchful, but not afraid. He thought then, for the first time, if all was to be lost then they too must die; perhaps not for a long time, but if the old men were right, and the sea must claim the island back, then everything would disappear into the waves. Perhaps it would be possible to take some of these creatures with them: the tortoises that outlived even the oldest of the islanders, the turtles, the flying fruit bats that squabbled in their roosts in the forests, the darting geckos, the tiny lemurs, and the birds whose eggs they shared.

It was late. The sun was beginning its descent. He rose to his feet. The tortoises watched him, flowers trailing from their mouths. He wondered if they might one day have some sense of foreboding, as he had: perhaps they, too, might become alert to a menace in the air, in the shifting seas, the power of the cyclones. But of course they would not. For a moment he envied them their innocence, the emptiness of their minds. Would it not be so much easier not to think at all?

From here on the hill he could see the old patterns of the canals and the reeds still cut and coppiced for harvest. Across the marshes of the distant bay, where his people were building the new boats, the shadows of their islet homes were woven like the mesh of a great net. Longest of all the dark shadows was that of the great reed house built upon the old long mound in the centre. The sea beyond was like a blue rim to a flat pearl shell. For a moment he drank in the beauty and significance of that view. Then he began to run down the bouldered slope. There was a pleasure in running when the air was calm. He crossed the pools, the mangrove swamps, the white sand, towards his people, among whom was the woman he had long since chosen as his own.

She looked up as he approached. The low sun glistened on her long dark hair. Her amber skin was white-crusted with salt from the sea. With the other women she was lashing together bundles of golden soaked reed, twisting the lengths of corded fibre rope made from the bark of the sea hibiscus. Her baby hung upon her hair and cried and she sat back to put it to her breast. Beside her was a green turtle shell containing three ripe mangoes, and she offered him one as he squatted on his haunches beside her.

At the sea's edge, across the white sand and the dark skein of saltings, men were beaching the boats after a day's fishing, unloading the baskets of fish and crabs. Soon, before the swift darkness came, they would gather to share the food at the great mound, where the geckos and black robins nested in the high reed roof. Then they would return to their own small island homes. These days the reeds were in so short supply that other vegetation, pandanus and palm and paw-paw, was used to build them up out of the water. Children were still playing, searching for shellfish on the rocks. As the sun sank into the dark sea, so the light began to be absorbed into the turquoise and violet sky. A skein of fruit bats rose from the forest and a flight of white terns circled, roosted in the tall screwpine trees.

As he rose to help unload the boats, he saw another craft appear beyond the headland, and recognised it as the one he had seen crossing the great channel. So fitful now was the evening air that it hardly moved, only coming in with the currents, until it grounded on the sand and three men leapt from it to haul it up the shore. There was something about it that intrigued him. As he walked closer he could see it was the way they had set an oar on the curve of the stern, and the shape of the oar was different. He welcomed these people from the north part of the island, and asked them to join them for food, for he was the leader of his people along this south-western shore.

So they sat long into the star-bright night, while the fire smouldered and the women and children slept on their nest-islands on the soft mats of reed and pandanus leaves. They talked of what must come, and when and how they should gather together all their own people, and he spoke of his desire to take what creatures they might put upon the boats. Some thought him foolish, but others said it would mean food – the turtles and the birds would provide eggs. Water could be carried in dried gourds, food in baskets and sealed bags made from tortoise and turtle shell, caulked with the fibres of the sea hibiscus bark. All knew which fish could yield sufficient fresh water to survive on the ocean.

"And yet we know not where we go, what landfall we might make," said one of the north people.

He answered: "No. Perhaps the ocean will become our home. For many days, at least. But I believe there is some other land beyond the sun's rising and setting, for you know how many strange creatures come here from some distant place, the tiny birds that find some crevice on the eastern cliffs, the seeds that grow into plants we have never seen before."

One of the old men said: "it is not the destination I fear, but the departure, for I am old. I shall have no joy in leaving all the things I have cared for, the gardens I have made, the canals I have dug, the reeds I have harvested, the fruit and wild plants I have cultivated. It has been my life. I have always believed I would die here, and that my spirit would leave across the sea in the boat my son will build for me."

"Yet if we do not leave, the time will come when it will be too late: there will be no reeds left to build our boats, no food to take, no fresh water. It is better to go now."

"For you, perhaps," said the old man. "I shall stay, and await what may come, for I will die before it." His black hair was still thick but his beardless face was seamed like an old turtle. His brown skin hung on his bones like the wings of a fruit bat. There were tears in his eyes. And the others felt his sadness, and were silent, hearing only the sound of the waves, the rustlings of the forest, the strange eternal music of the constant stars.

12

Calypso and the Dentist

They were not the first to leave. For hundreds of thousands of years before, others had gone before them. But those departures had been random, involuntary, sometimes on their fragile nests, carried by wind and current. Most had drowned. Those who remained had endured change. Each generation had heard tales of the time when the sea had broken over the western cliffs, when the island had been one, not two. Even when the Pleistocene was young, more than two million years ago, the mountains had been eroded into the silt that filled the estuaries on the western coasts and turned them into swamp and salting. Such was the power of the south-east trade winds that had gathered their force over five thousand miles of open ocean.

Of those who were last to leave the Island, many more must have drowned. The winds took them, the waves overwhelmed them, the fish fed on them. Yet the climate of the world was mild, and the ocean swell covered great parts of the continents. Tides and currents carried the island people to distant shores. Most were blown westwards in their reed ships to the coast of Africa. Wherever they found landfall in an estuary, where sheltered shores, reed forests and lagoons allowed them to recreate their lost world of the island, they could hope to continue their way of life. The vast marshes of the Zambezi delta, relatively safe from predators from land or sea, provided such a haven. And as their numbers increased, so some were carried northwards in the south west coastal drift, continuing to occupy any suitable shore. One such landfall would have been the Gulf of Djibouti, immediately to port as they entered the Gulf of Aden.

It is worth looking at Djibouti, although it is a comparatively small country now, about the size of Massachusetts. Once it was called French Somaliland. It only gained its independence last year, the last French territory in Africa to do so. Like all African countries its borders are artificial, created by Europeans. Essentially it is part of East Africa, bordering Ethiopia, Eritrea and Somalia. The French originally acquired it in about 1860, chiefly because the British had by then taken Aden across the Gulf of Aden at the mouth of the Red Sea. Djibouti had nothing else to offer, save its strategic position. It is one of the cruellest, hottest, saltiest countries on earth. The Afar Region, which it shares with Ethiopia, is the site of a triple junction of three tectonic plates of the earth's crust. Each is moving away from the other – hence past and present volcanic activity. Some of its mountains are still active volcanoes. Yet parts of Djibouti are hundreds of feet below sea level, forming great salt depressions. In the 1930s Wilfred Thesiger followed its only river, the Awash River which rises in the Great Rift Valley in Ethiopia, and found that it never reached the sea. It flowed north for some five hundred miles and ended in a series of salt lakes and shimmering salt pans in the desert. He writes about it in his *Journeys Through Abyssinia*. It is a place where nothing, you think, could exist: and yet it does, and it has.

It is perhaps no surprise that *Australopithecus afarensis*, otherwise known as Lucy, was found in this part of Africa. The chance of finding any fossils depends on the size of two populations: on the original one, and the current one of palaeontologists looking for them.

The original population was probably considerable, and we know there are plenty of the latter. I don't think it will be long before new fossil examples of 'modern man' are found here, and I could bet they will date back almost two hundred thousand years. But will anyone wonder if they originally arrived not across the land, but by sea?

You can get a glimpse of what East Africa was like, about two hundred thousand years ago, by following the Awash River today. Although its rich wild life has diminished, even since Thesiger described it, it provides a riverine forest of shady acacia woodland and grassy savannah. Oryx, gazelle, leopard and baboons are among its many native mammals: in its waters are crocodiles and hippopotami. You can see hornbills and bee-eaters, coucals, turacos and hawks. The sea off the coast is full of abundant fish, turtles, dolphins and shellfish.

When the island people made landfall here the sea level was about a hundred feet higher than it is today. The Awash River must then have reached the sea. The lakes that now replicate themselves in a hundred mirages across remains of the salt sea bed were part of a vast area of shallow seas and marshes. Its reed forests provided the familiar raw materials for building boats and settlements, for exploiting wild life and recreating their traditional society. Where now a few nomadic people follow their goats to the next pool of shade, hoping that a grove of dessicated thorn trees may mark a water hole, there was once a great estuarine wilderness. Here, as in other similar parts of Africa, the Mongoloid human islanders could flourish. Their numbers were small at first, their venturing sporadic. It would be a very gradual diaspora, but by the end they would reach almost every part of the world. From the beginning they were moving to all points of the compass.

Many were carried further north on the back of the south-east trade winds and the north-east monsoon, finding landfall, though not always sanctuary, in the great deltas of the Tigris and Euphrates, the Indus, and the Nile delta beyond the Red Sea, with its immense forests of papyrus. Sea levels were still high and much of Russia and the Ukraine was covered with ocean. The vast estuaries of the Volga and the Don linked the Black Sea and the Caspian in the north.

The Mediterranean was open to the Red Sea and the Aegean, and westward was the Atlantic.

For the islanders who made their final landfall on the shores of the eastern Mediterranean, it must have been a kind of paradise. It was not then scarred by thousands of years of man's agriculture, by over-grazing and deforestation. The Nile delta was one huge whispering forest of papyrus reeds, a watery world of lakes and woodlands, rich with bird and animal life. Along the coasts of the Aegean virgin forests of oak, fir and cypress stepped down to welcoming shores. Game flourished: fruit, nuts, wild gourds and honey were there for the taking. Fish filled the seas. From the Caspian Sea to the Black Sea, the Mediterranean and the Atlantic Ocean, across the thousands of square miles of sea that covered Russia and the Ukraine, the seafarers could move on the waters that recreated for them the abundance and beauty of their legendary home.

I stopped typing and sat with my fingers still upon the keys of my old Adler Gabriele, remembering a passage from *The Odyssey* that I had always loved.

A large fire was blazing on the hearth and the scent from burning logs of juniper and cedar was wafted far across the island. Inside, Calypso was singing with her beautiful voice as she went to and fro at her loom, weaving with a golden shuttle. The cave was sheltered by a copse of alders and fragrant cypresses, which was the roosting-place of wide-winged birds, horned owls and falcons and cormorants with long tongues, birds of the coast, whose business takes them down to the sea. Trailing round the mouth of the cavern was a thriving garden vine, with great bunches of grapes; from four separate but neighbouring springs four crystal rivulets were channelled to run this way and that; and in soft meadows on either side iris and wild celery flourished. It was indeed a spot where even an immortal visitor must pause to gaze in wonder and delight.

Yet by their very nature the people of this watery and fruitful world left almost no trace of their existence. Their ships, when discarded, rotted. They used virtually no stone tools. One of the few remaining clues to their existence was left by those islanders who went further north, reaching the windy shores of north west Europe: to be precise, a pebbly beach in what would one day be England.

In 1935 a retired dentist and amateur archeologist called Alvan Marston was exploring a gravel pit near Swanscombe when he noticed a fragment of fossilised bone. He sent it off for identification. It turned out to be part of a human skull.

"Incidentally," Mr Brouard remarked at this point, "Marston was completely obsessed. I worry that I may be a little like him. He found a matching piece of the left-hand side of the skull the following year, but he spent another twenty years, at times enlisting his family to help, before he found the right-hand side."

During the interglacial when the some of the islanders reached Europe, some three hundred thousand years ago, the south bank of what is now the Thames was a beach. Behind it were tall cliffs, now eroded, part of the North Downs. For more than a century this ancient shore has been excavated to provide gravel for the building of London. Marston's discovery was a hundred feet down. There were other finds: bones of mammals, and a great quantity of tools – or, rather, many tools of a single design, the oldest and most universal stone tool ever found. Stone hand axes have been discovered around the coasts of Europe, Asian, India, African and Indonesia, and their design varies very little, although whenever slight changes have been made they appear to have been universally adopted. No one knows their precise use, except that such tools have been used for making dug-out wooden canoes from the trunks of trees.

Measurement of the amount of fluorine accumulated in the bones put the date of both the skull and associated animal bones at about 300,000 years ago, during that interglacial period. Of a similar period were the hand axes, given the name Acheulian after the site of their first discovery at St Acheul in France. And Mr Marston's occipital and parietal skull bones, with a cranial capacity of about 1,300 cc, were reliably judged to be those of a young woman of the species *Homo sapiens*, with almost as large a brain as any young woman today.

"Incidentally," said Mr Brouard, as if leafing through something on his desk, "at that time the human brain might well have been smaller and within a thicker skull, because hundreds of thousands of years of seafaring after that date would have caused an increase of intelligence, simply through natural selection... Ah, here it is. Yes. A curious little study... The survivors of shipwrecked castaways in open boats, or on desert islands, like Robinson Crusoe, tend to be particularly intelligent. Experiments on rats showed that the quickest way of breeding super-intelligent animals was to drop them in a lake on which had been scattered a considerable amount of jetsam, and then breed from the few that made it to shore. Remember, the floating populations of island people would have had to endure perhaps cataclysmic waves, tsunamis, as well as frequent capsizes and shipwrecks."

Was she one of the lucky ones, I thought, washed up on the shore of the Thames?

I mentioned her to the man with whom I was in love at that time. He was a Welsh hypochondriac artist who painted like an angel and whose greatest pleasure was to visit those few galleries that hung him to look at his own work. He bought his clothes in Moss Bros's Dead Men's Department, including a massive greatcoat that had kept its late owner warm on the Murmansk convoys. Whenever I eat cherries I think of him eating them out of a brown paper bag and spitting the stones into the gutters of Soho. He was one of those men who do not do a lot for one's self-esteem.

"You could put a cup and saucer on those hips," he observed when I once wore a bikini.

We had been to see a Laurel and Hardy film in a cinema in the Balls Pond Road and were in his favourite Chinese restaurant. It was lit by bare bulbs and the tables were covered in oilcloth. No one spoke English.

"But was she really like you?" he said. "I don't mean small and fierce, but with a brain like yours? Aren't we talking about the time when Neanderthals roamed Britain?"

"No, rather before then, I think."

"Well, surely that means she was a low-browed, shambling creature that ate raw meat?"

"Look, I haven't done all the tapes yet."

"Well, get on with it. I'm curious about this Neanderthal business. I once met a man who swore they were still living in the Urals. He claimed to have seen one once, a great hairy thing living in a cave. He said that a Bolshevik general called – well, it doesn't matter – no, Topilsky, I think – came across some strange footprints in the snow while pursuing White Russians in the Pamir Mountains. He traced them to a cave, too. Then he shot the thing. He had it examined by a doctor who thought it had all the typical Neanderthal features, particularly the fact that it was thickly covered in hair, like a bear."

"I expect it was a bear."

"Well, possibly. But what I don't understand is how your islanders sailed across the seas, having been living with the dolphins, all beautiful and intelligent, and then turned up here near the Dartford tunnel unable to do anything except presumably kill a mammoth with a lump of stone."

"Well, nor do I."

"Well, ask your Mr Brouard," Geraint said.

"All right, I will."

"Okay. Sea bass with ginger for you?"

13

The Ice Trap

First, I began listening to the next tape.

In 1856, three years before Darwin published *The Origin of Species*, a gang quarrying limestone in the Neander *thal* (*thal* being German for valley), seven miles east of Dusseldorf, unearthed a human skeleton. The skull fragments, pieces of collar bone, shoulder blade and bits of arm and leg bones were taken to Professor Schaffhausen at the University of Bonn. He pronounced them as belonging to "a savage and barbarous race derived from one of the wild races of north-western Europe, spoken of by Latin writers and traced to a period when the latest animals of the Flood still existed".

There was intense controversy. In 1863 Thomas Huxley, Darwin's great advocate, decided that this Neanderthal Man was some kind of reversion to a simian ancestor. Someone else thought the skull was that of an imbecile. Because the skeleton had been removed from the quarry without any other finds being recorded, it was difficult to date it precisely, but it appeared to have died about a hundred thousand years ago during the last period of glaciation. Various names were proposed for it: *Homo neanderthalensis* in 1864, and *Homo sapiens neanderthalensis* a hundred years later. The arguments went on for years.

Then, in 1908, an almost complete specimen of an adult male was found buried in the floor of a cave near a village called Chapelle-aux-Saintes in France. This time the spot was carefully recorded, together with finds of mammal bones including woolly rhinoceros, reindeer, hyena and wolf, and a lot of flint tools, all dating from the same time of intensifying cold some hundred thousand years ago.

"It made headlines," Mr Brouard commented. "Everyone was looking for evidence of progressive evolution, and here was a chinless, shambling caveman. The experts decided that despite a skull capacity of about 1620 cc, close to the highest limit of modern man, he couldn't walk upright and had a receding forehead, jutting head carriage and slouching, if bipedal, gait. It wasn't until 1955 that the skeleton was re-examined by several professors of anatomy. They discovered he was actually crippled with arthritis, and would otherwise have stood and walked as easily as any modern man.

"Only a year later they found a whole Neanderthal family at La Ferrassie in the Dordogne. This time the male skull was even larger than that of La Chapelle with a capacity of 1641 cc. What began to become clear from subsquent piecemeal finds all over southern Europe was that the anatomy of these people was remarkably uniform. They were all generally of medium height, with strong muscles and greater breadth in the body; the men probably weighed about seventy-five kilos. They had large, broad feet – like the Alakuf Indians who go barefoot in snow and ice – and the adults' heads tended to be longer, broader and flatter, although those of young children tended to be more like ours. They had a brow ridge with exceptionally large nasal passages and big facial bones which suggested large beaked noses. Certainly over the past few years Neanderthals have been considered almost civilised.

"All right, so I can hear you thinking, how come? Who were these people? What happened to the islanders? Let's go back a couple of hundred thousand years or so. Those who had made their home in the north of Eurasia, that northern part of Europe, perhaps began to be aware that their world was getting colder. The long, warmer interglacial was ending. Year by year, century by century, they adapted to lower temperatures, to sunless skies."

"Well, why didn't they move south, then?" I said silently, but he was already replying on the tape.

But remember by then they had lived there for generations. For them it had always been home. There was perhaps some folk memory of their voyages across the seas, but that was all, handed down in some ritual form. But look - if we can't tell whether the world is getting warmer, going through a brief cold spell or heading for another ice age – well, we can hardly blame them for remaining in the part of the world that had become familiar to them. But there's another reason. During each ice age northern Europe became colder more swiftly than other parts of the northern hemisphere. It was walled in to the south by an almost continuous mountain chain, stretching from the Caucasus to the Pyrenees, with the Mediterranean beyond. Normally, the southward march of the ice at the onset of each glaciation was gradual, measurable in living generations but leaving time for plants and animals to migrate south and stay within their accustomed climatic environment. But in the north of Europe the extension of the polar ice was accompanied by simultaneous glaciation of the mountain barrier. It was a freezing vice. As its grip tightened, escape routes to the south were cut off by frozen rivers and encroaching glaciers. Those who did not sense the change, who did not follow the migrating birds at the end of another cold summer, were trapped. And for them, it was forever.

Those who survived did so because they managed to adapt to snow, ice and bitter cold. Lakes and rivers froze. Only the hardiest plants and creatures could endure the winters until the brief summer came again. People had to adapt to an impoverished diet, replacing birds' eggs, shellfish and fruit, with an almost entirely protein-rich diet of meat and fish. Fittest to deal with these new conditions were those with strong teeth and skulls engineered to provide anchorage for larger jaws, just as the earlier *Homo erecti* who had learned to live with the great apes of Africa had thus adapted by the ruthless laws of natural selection. But the characteristics which enabled individual *Erecti* to survive had been to do with agility, good night vision, fast reaction to danger, immunity to insect-borne disease. It did not matter if redundant parts of the frontal lobes of the brain were sacrificed to improve the strength of skull and jaws. The superior imagination of an over-sized brain was outweighed by its vulnerability and the strain it put on the heart and vascular system. It was quite different for the people of this icy northern world. They were free from disease-carrying pathogens and concealed predators. Like the Inuit today, they were the hunters. But they had to keep warm, to find shelter, to take advantage of short summers: they had to anticipate trouble. So they needed fire. They needed ways of hunting large animals like wild cattle, mammoth and reindeer, methods of trapping and snaring smaller sources of food – and they had to build protection against snow and wind. They needed to *think*.

"The Inuit," commented Mr Brouard, "have brains about ten per cent larger than the average European, because they have always needed intelligence and creativity to survive."

Nevertheless the brain is always vulnerable, particularly to a drop in its internal temperature, and that can happen because of something as simple as a small nose – experiments in military survival show that chilled air in the nasal passages can cause damage to the brain. So a large, preferably beaked nose with narrow nostrils would help to pre-heat and humidify inhaled cold air. Pronounced brow ridges helped to protect the eyes.

Subcutaneous fat would be useful at very low temperatures, although it is primarily designed – so it seems – to insulate against cold water rather than air temperature. Women probably needed more fat for insulation and a reserve of food when suckling children.

A fur coat – now, that was certainly a good idea. Sightings of so-called 'wild people' like those observed in the fifteenth century by a German traveller called Hans Schiltberger, have always been described as being covered in a pelt of hair. In 1917 a Bolshevik general called Topilsky found one in the Pamir mountains of southern

Russia. Unfortunately for the creature it was shot as it emerged from a cave. Topilsky had it examined by a doctor, who said that although it was thickly covered with hair it was definitely human.

So Geraint was right, I thought.

The island people, adapted to their semi-marine environment and to the warmth of an almost perpetual world climate, would have had no need for abundant body hair, and indeed it was probably regarded – as it is in many parts of the Far East – as rather repulsive. But like any mammal forced to live in a cold climate the northerners would tend to grow more hair, and those who did were much better able to survive. Under that severe pressure they would begin to acquire a complete coat of guard hairs and underfur on both body and face. Unfortunately that would exacerbate another problem: lack of Vitamin D.

Human beings need Vitamin D. Without it their bones lose calcium. Children get rickets and adults' bones become weak and deformed. The main source in the human diet is eggs and fish oils – both increasingly less available to the people of ice age Eurasia. A substitute is the action of ultra-violet light in sunshine on the skin, but in a world where the skies were invariably grey and the skin covered in ever-thicker hair, it was effectively screened. Those best able to counter the deficiency were those with reduced levels of melanin, the protective polymers in skin, hair and eyes, and there would have been rigorous natural selection in their favour. Inherited albino tendencies were suddenly advantageous. Such a reduction in melanin meant that not only skin but eyes would change – from dark brown to blue – and hair would increasingly be fair, almost white. Which also provided camouflage in the snow.

Something bothered me. When I sent back the transcriptions I added a query: "OK, so they were getting Vitamin D – but what about Vitamin C? I thought that was essential? How were they getting that if there wasn't any fruit or veg? Didn't Shackleton's men suffer from scurvy?"

The reply came by return.

Once again, look at the Inuit peoples of Canada and Greenland. We know they have a highly adapted physiology, but it's true that they still need Vitamin C. And we know they don't get scurvy. People have argued about why they don't for years – some say they manage to get some from berries during the summer, but the amounts would be very small. But then in the 1920s an explorer and anthropologist called Stefansson made a study of Inuit diet. What he reckoned was that they got their Vitamin C because they didn't cook their fish or meat - or, if they did, cooked it very lightly. Cooking destroys Vitamin C. Shackleton's men weren't keen on eating raw fish or meat, even if they could cope with it. And the Inuit ate other things like the skin of beluga whales, which the Inuit called muktuk, which is said to contain as much Vitamin C as oranges. So, it seems, do the stomach contents of caribou – another Inuit dish.

Stefansson actually tried the Inuit diet for years, and then finally tested it under clinical conditions in 1928. For a year, he and a colleague lived on a meat-only diet, more or less entirely protein and fat. They didn't get scurvy, they were perfectly healthy. As it happens Stefansson always enjoyed a good steak, together with an occasional grapefuit, and coffee.

"Mind you," he added, "I wouldn't suggest you try eating raw meat – you might not suffer Vitamin C deficiency, but other than in the frozen north you might have trouble with E.coli."

"But what you're saying is that the Inuit people are like Neanderthals?"

"Only in aspects of their diet. The Inuit are a Mongoloid people, like the original islanders. A different race."

I doodled on a scrap pad: a large man with a lot of pale red hair, blue eyes and a beaky nose appeared, eating a large raw steak. He looked just like Geraint.

"The fact is," said Mr Brouard, "we don't have that much evidence of what Neanderthal people looked like. There aren't that many fossils. And of course we don't know what kind of hair they had or what colour their skin was. But it is almost certain that they did have a covering of hair – a hundred thousand years of adaptation would make that inevitable. We do know that they used tools for all sorts of purposes, because all the fossil evidence is associated with distinctive flint tools first found in a village called Le Moustier in France.

"Mousterian sites, with or without Neanderthal bones, are found all over Europe, North Africa and the Near East. Archaeologists have managed to deduce a surprising amount about Neanderthal culture as it existed between a hundred thousand and, say, thirty-five thousand years ago. We know that they were skilled hunters: blades of spears and hand axes, with flaked-flint knives for skinning and butchering game, have been found concentrated in what seem to be hunting outposts. There were tool kits for dealing with wood, bone, ivory and leather. Curiously enough burial sites have been found that suggest they looked after each other – in Croatia a man appeared to have been nursed back to health after a skull fracture, and in another an old man was found with flowers (now just pollen grains) in his grave. Apparently they even cleaned their teeth...

"But there's something even more interesting – well, to me, anyway. We do know they were hunters. Over thousands of years, possibly a hundred thousand, they probably hunted such animals as the mammoth, woolly rhinoceros and great aurochs – the wild cattle – almost to extinction. And why? Not just for food, but for the same reason that in more recent times the Inuit have hunted the walrus almost to extinction: for their hides. As the ice age intensified the landscape was a bleak one, the tundra of the sub Arctic with few sparse and twisted trees. Reeds, once so much part of their life, had long since withered in that glacial trap. Across the northern plains, the steppes, the endless winds turned the earth to dust. Like the Inuit peoples of today, these hunters needed to exploit the rivers and lakes in the short summer. They needed boats. Boats were a part of their inheritance. And only the hunted animals could supply the materials they needed.

"Perhaps someone found a drowned mammoth floating down river, and had the idea of using the skin to cover a bone rib cage. I don't know: but the technique of building such skin boats, using bones and pliable timber like birch saplings, has lasted into this century. The basic design is still used for boats like coracles and kayaks. Fossilised firesticks have been found in Yugoslavia – it's very likely that they could make wood tar, a kind of pitch, with fire, perhaps for caulking the seams of the hulls. With such boats, light enough for perhaps a single man to carry, they could explore the summer rivers and find new territories, new sources of game. And in winter the same essential design, upturned, provided shelter."

Geraint, reading my transcription of this conversation, observed: "So how long did it last, this cold spell?"

"About a hundred thousand years."

"Long enough. What happened to the ones that got out before it started? Or never went that far north in the first place?"

"Well, they settled around the coasts of western Europe, the Mediterranean, Asia Minor – maybe beyond. Anywhere it was warmer, I suppose."

"And they didn't get pale and hairy and hunt mammoths?"

"No, of course they didn't."

"And they didn't die out, like the Neanderthals."

"No."

14

Following the Sun

The world had always been open to the islanders, for wherever they found haven, they still remained a people of the sea, almost a part of it, mobile, skilled, in tune with wind, wave and current. For over two hundred thousand years, as the cold tightened its grip on the north, like the birds, they followed the sun. In the northern hemisphere they colonised the western coasts of Europe, the Eastern Mediterranean, Asia Minor and beyond, settling along the estuaries, the marshlands, exploring the rivers. As generation followed generation, so they diversified: some to find shelter and resist the cold, some to continue their migration; some to hunt, some to avoid the menace of wild animals on land but retaining their links with the creatures of the oceans.

Unlike their kinsfolk trapped beyond the mountains they had no need for radical adaptation, for they were free to escape the ice and sail south. Their diet of fish, molluscs, the eggs of reptiles and birds, the plants of the salt shore and the fruit of the forests that stepped down to the edge of the sea, was entirely suited to their lithe brown bodies and their way of life. They were like the birds, or the dolphins with whom they played.

They had no need to hunt the great cattle and mammoths of the northern interiors to build their boats, no need for shelter or permanent home on land. Their skills lay with reed and rush, in the dexterity of the needle in sewing, weaving, knotting, the handling of fibres, timbers and cordage. They could employ their imagination to design, to improve, even to appreciate the aesthetic of a curve, the satisfaction in a detail. They had the inherited experience to know the winds and the waves. In the brilliant skies of nights without light, save for such elements as the glow-worms, the aurora borealis or the phosphorescence in the curl of wave, the patterns of the stars were as familiar to them as the spoor of game to their cousins in the north. They moved as freely as the dolphins. And like them, they left no trace of their passing.

"What happened to the poor old Neanderthals, then?" said Geraint. "Seems to me they weren't too bright. After all, they could have noticed it was getting colder."

"It took thousands of years to get colder."

"Well, I know, but you'd think that after a few chilly summers you'd have reckoned you could find a warmer spot. It wasn't as though they'd got mortgages, the children in school, that sort of thing."

I explained about the time, and the icy barrier of the mountains, but I wondered if there was something in what he said. It must have been a bleak prospect, enduring such apparently eternal cold. Even the Inuit these days could go south. At least they knew that where the ice ended there was a world of sunshine and warmth. I went back to the next tape.

For people of the ice age there were only a few weeks of summer. Then for a time the earth softened, the thorny shrubs that hugged the ground were starred with flowers, and veils of insects rose above the boggy pools. Green leaves unfurled, translucent, on the stunted birch and willow trees. The rivers flowed, the lake ice melted. There were fish and sharp berries again to eat, sun to help the curing of the boat skins, lichens and mosses to fatten the herds of wild horses, the cattle and the deer. It must have been a time of sensuous pleasure, even of spiritual renewal. Perhaps, as they looked up at a benevolent sun or the brilliant stars in a clear night sky, saw the rushing water and the shimmering grasses, they knew the sense of something lost, something beyond their world, which is one of the hallmarks of the human.

About forty thousand years ago, a subtle shift began to become evident in the world of the ice age. The winters were milder. The summers warmer, each year just a little longer. The ice began to melt. It was the beginning of the first warm interstadial of the last ice age. Climate and sea levels were close to those that existed only ten thousand years ago, at the beginning of our own time, be it interglacial or interstadial.

The Neanderthal people were not dependent on the sea: as the land masses seemed to rise again out of the oceans, so they carried their light skin boats further up rivers and into the mountains in search of game. They began to foray further south. For over a hundred thousand years they had exploited the wild game of the tundra, learning to live on the wind-riven plains, but as the climate subtly changed, so did the vegetation on which the massive musk ox, the mammoth, the auroch, were accustomed to feed. Their reproductive cycle was slow, their offspring born singly. There were more Neanderthal people, but their prey was less abundant. So the northern people took their light hide boats down the great rivers to the Black Sea, to the Caspian, foraging further south like the gyrfalcon and the white foxes to find new hunting grounds. They began to filter down as far as the Sea of Marmara and the Aegean.

Some of the Neanderthal people, perhaps by finding their way along its coasts, under cliffs and along sandy shores, crossed the Black Sea. From the marshy deltas of the Kizilirmak and Kilkit rivers they ventured into green forests of oak and beech. It was a new world of mist and rain. They followed the rivers up into the wooded hills, then higher still, where the winds sang in pine and cedar trees. They came upon high alpine meadows mantled in shining grasses and decorated with daisies and wild crocuses. Game was abundant, sometimes dangerous: lions and leopards shared their prey. When they reached the source of the river in the mountains they came upon lakes, and new rivers springing from the rocks, but flowing south, and some followed them down into the limestone foothills and tawny plains that descended to the sea.

"This was Anatolia," Mr Brouard commented at this point. "A unique cradle of living creatures, surrounded by four seas. It was like an island, isolated from land and beyond the sea. Even during the ice ages it must have had an extraordinary wealth of plant and animal life, encompassing so many different climates and topographies. Then with the coming of the ice it became sanctuary for hundreds, perhaps thousands of new species. Even today it has almost as many species of wild flowers as the rest of Europe combined. More than three thousand are native to Anatolia, found nowhere else on earth. This is the home of over thirty species of wild wheat. Barley, chickpeas, apricots, cherries – all originated here. And the country has over eighty thousand species of animals, including monk seals and turtles along its coasts. It is as if Anatolia was the greenhouse of the world."

A bit uncomfortable for the Neanderthals, I reflected, thinking of all that hair...

But other people were moving north, away from the ever more encroaching sea, towards those golden plains and the blue foothills of the Anatolian mountains. In the time of the ice, when sea levels had fallen, the sea people had settled in a place that perhaps held ancient memory for them: then an area of islands and marsh – the Persian Gulf. It too was somewhat isolated from the rest of the world by surrounding mountains, but to the north was the great open delta of the Tigris and Euphrates across which they could move inland while never quite leaving the sea. But as the climate changed and sea levels rose again, they were destined once more to endure the flooding of their island home. This time the enforced diaspora was less daunting, for they could sail north and know that there would be sanctuary. The rivers were generous, wide and navigable for hundreds of miles. Thus, as the Neanderthal peoples ventured south, so the sea people moved north from the marshes to the plains, travelling along those great rivers towards the distant hills.

We know that at this time something began to happen to the Neanderthal people. Something that made them disappear for ever. Something which would transform humanity.

15

Blue-eyed Baby

The mountains were behind them now. The great river they had followed from its source now wound through lion-coloured limestone foothills. It was wide and blue under the sky, bordered with rushes, and green oak. Above it the sun bleached high stony bluffs in the diamond air, but the river was cool and deep. Over the past years the northern hunters had travelled almost three hundred miles from the Black Sea coasts, often carrying their hide coracles, like the leather boats Herodotus would observe thousands of years later when the Euphrates river became one of the great trade routes of the Near East. They had found new game, snowy peaks, red ochre plateaux, waterfalls. They had come upon lakes whose waters were too bitter to drink, and others like inland seas that stretched blue to the horizon. Snow fell in the winters. Vultures circled above. But the people survived, foraging ever more widely, seeking the haven of the south.

Then, one day in summer, a hunting party set up camp on the shore of the great river. Their boats were drawn up under the alder trees. The men had gone to search for game and the women and children were left to work and wait.

While their children slept or played their mothers occupied themselves with the preparation of food, curing and drying the meat. Animal skins were spread and pegged for curing. Some worked on the boats, patching hides, piercing eyelets for new lashings, replacing bone and horn. Perhaps they did not notice that one of the youngest children, less than a year old, had crawled out of their sight behind a thicket of thorn and wild cherry trees. Like its mother, it was covered in a pale furry pelt. It looked a little like a baby monkey.

No one saw the strangers approach. They had landed downriver on an opposing curve, pulling their light boats on to the shore, then moving inland to forage for small mammals, the hares in their burrows, the eggs of ground-nesting birds, the first of the summer fruits. They carried sling-shots and light axes and they were watchful, for they had little protection against the larger predators. They wore animal skins to protect against injury and cold but their bodies were smooth-skinned, their eyes as dark as their hair. Before they saw the Neanderthal people they heard the infant, now so far from its mother that fear had touched it. It sat in a little meadow, almost hidden by the shimmer of ripe wild barley, for it was of a similar golden colour, and cried.

Its mother heard the cry, and rose to find her baby, but already one of the strangers had picked it up – gingerly, in case it might bite or scratch, but it showed no inclination to do so, indeed was as warm and soft as any small animal. It ceased to cry, looking up with blue eyes. The man who had found it, astonished, called to his companions to see this phenomenon, but they were alarmed, aware that an apparently abandoned infant might have a mother nearby, and moved away, back to the safety of the boats on the shore. Even as they turned, so the mother appeared, followed by others. They walked upright, some of them had babies clinging to them, but they were heavy, covered in hair of varying shades from white to reddish brown. Their faces were low-browed, their teeth bared in anger as they cried in fear and fury. For a moment each group hesitated, transfixed by the other, caught between curiosity and alarm. Then one of the strangers took his sling-shot, put a smooth pebble in its soft leather pouch, and raised his brown arm. The distance between them was some thirty metres, but his aim was true, and the foremost Neanderthal woman dropped and died almost instantly as the pebble entered her brain.

It was the child's mother.   Her companions moved back, touched by terror: the strangers turned and ran, carrying the baby with them.   When they reached their boats they put the child in a rush-lined basket and lashed it to the mast, moving out on the current of the Euphrates, catching the wind in the wide sail.   They were many days on the journey south to more familiar lands, the beginning of their marshes, the lagoons, and the reed forests.   They managed to coax the Neanderthal child into drinking wild honey and water and eating a little raw egg until, reaching their home settlement, it was presented as a trophy, a pet, to the community.

One of the women had more than enough of her own milk to feed it as well as her own baby, and was charmed with it, as indeed were they all, for not only was it a curiosity but delightful to feel and hold.   And as it grew, it became apparent that it was intelligent and strong. From a charming household pet it became a valuable servant who could work tirelessly, and indeed do more than most of its captors.   Everyone, as they say, wanted one.   Neanderthal infants become one of the most sought-after quarries of hunting parties along the rivers, especially females. To have several became a sign of wealth.

Over thousands of years this society of the old sea people flourished in that charmed area of the Persian Gulf, southern Iraq and the edge of Anatolia. They were secluded from the world outside by its surrounding mountain ranges, but in any case they had no need to go outside its boundaries, for everything they needed was there.   As the ten thousand years of that interstadial passed into another period of glaciation in the north, so they enjoyed the benefits of climate, lower sea levels and reliable rainfall.   There was abundant produce from sea, land and air.   It was an enclosed society, perhaps a time that passed into legend as one of the earliest of golden ages. Its people were confident of their world, which now stretched as far as the eastern Mediterranean.   A new permanence pervaded it. People began to design and erect buildings on shore.   Into their lives came new concepts of wealth, of accepted hierarchies – and of slavery.

At this point the tape stopped, then started again, and I heard the sound of Mr Brouard knocking out his pipe. A bird somewhere called, a sharp blackbird alarm.

"Slaves do not write history," he said, and I could hear the laborious and rather disgusting process of relighting his pipe. "At least, not until they are freed," he added, before the tape continued.

Slaves they have underpinned our own world for millennia. Curiously enough it is because of the very fact that they are a tradeable commodity, to be bought and sold for money, that they are generally well looked after, at least in terms of being fed and housed. When Africans were brought to America to work on the plantations they were regarded as valuable possessions. They probably fared rather better than the so-called free apprentices who had come out from Britain, or transported prisoners, many of whom were brutally treated in New England states. And of course at home in England children were being sent up chimneys and into the fields. When the plantation owners had to face the possibility of losing their slaves, they were pretty upset.

About twenty thousand years ago, in the by now settled and comfortable lands of the old sea peoples, they were getting very worried about the possibility of losing their Neanderthal slaves. They had begun to kill the goose that laid the golden eggs – through taking infant females they had simply reduced the supply. You could say they had introduced another new concept – exploitation. There was only one answer. It had probably already begun. There must have been Neanderthal females perhaps less hairy than others, more to the taste of those who in any case must have been curious about what it was like to have sex with them. The Mongoloid sea people and the Neanderthal had to be encouraged to interbreed.

Remember the story of Jacob and Esau in the Old Testament?"

I always wished I'd read the Bible properly.

Their father, Isaac, the son of Abraham, married Rebecca,

and she had a somewhat troublesome pregnancy – so much so that she appealed to God, who said:

> *Two nations are in your womb,*
> *and two peoples, born of you, shall be divided;*
> *the one shall be stronger than the other,*
> *and the elder shall serve the younger.*

> *When her days to be delivered were fulfilled, behold,*
> *there were twins in her womb. The first came forth*
> *red, all his body like a hairy mantle; so they called his*
> *name Esau. Afterwards his brother came forth, and*
> *his hand had taken hold of Esau's heel; so his name*
> *was called Jacob. Isaac was sixty years old when she*
> *bore them.*

> *When the boys grew up, Esau was a skilful hunter, a*
> *man of the field, while Jacob was a quiet man, dwelling*
> *in tents.*

When Isaac was close to death – by my reckoning over a hundred – he wanted to give Esau his blessing, for Esau was his favourite, although not Rebecca's. It was she who warned Jacob of Isaac's intention, so that he might pre-empt his brother, but Jacob pointed out that Esau was 'a hairy man, and I am a smooth man'. So Rebecca brought Esau's clothes and put them on Jacob, and then put the goatskins on h is hands and the smooth part of his neck.

> *So Jacob went near to Isaac his father, who felt him and*
> *said, 'the voice is Jacob's voice, but the hands are the*
> *hands of Esau'. And he did not recognise him, because*
> *his hands were hairy like his brother Esau's hands; so*
> *he blessed him.*

It seems to me quite probable that the ancient distinction between those with body hair, and those without, has its origins in the conjunction of Neanderthal and sea people. As the part played by a servile Neanderthal population in the society of the Gulf area became increasingly important, and the need to maintain that population more urgent, the only answer was to allow some kind of captive breeding between the two - despite what must have been a strong taboo against it. They were, after all, the same species, although by then separate races.

There is evidence of both the interbreeding and the taboo in ancient legends. The Sumerian Epic of Gilgamesh tells of Enkidu, created by a goddess to become the equal and competitor of Gilgamesh, king of Uruk. Enkidu lived among the wild animals of the plains, 'his body all hairy, his locks like a woman's'. Gilgamesh sent a prostitute to seduce him and lure him to the city. And in Genesis in the Old Testament there is a kind of retelling of the story in reverse:

> When men began to multiply on the face of the ground, and daughters were born to them, the sons of God saw that the daughters of men were fair; and they took to wife such of them as they chose. The giants were on the earth in those days, and also afterward, when the sons of God came into the daughters of men, and they bore children to them. These were the mighty men that were of old, the men of renown.

Were the sons of God the sea people? And the 'daughters of men' Neanderthals? Is this ancient passage another link with that distant interbreeding?

I had a sudden recollection of Mr Brouard telling us about the discovery of the Turin Shroud. He had known a great deal about Jesus, and the Bible, but he had said he was an apostate. "And you can only be that when you take the trouble to find out as much as you can about something you want to believe in."

"What is an apostate, sir?" Jimmy Reed asked.

"Someone who has decided they don't believe in something after all."

I switched the tape back on, faintly disturbed.

What is certain is that the result of such interbreeding would have been a hybrid between Neanderthal and the Mongoloid sea people. And what is also certain is that when such racial taboos break down, different races mix rapidly. In this case the result was a hybrid people that we call Caucasoid. And if you look at the geographical area occupied by this hybrid people, before their vast expansion in historic, as opposed to prehistoric time, then you can see it was almost exactly that of the Neanderthal heartland. You can trace it simply by 'joining the dots' of outlying Mousterian sites where their stone tools were found. What is certain is that these new people combined the hunting skills and technology of the Neanderthals with the maritime culture of the Mongoloid sea peoples. We use the phrase 'hybrid vigour': well, they possessed it.

And because they were strong, intelligent people with particular qualities of stamina and endurance, thousands would have escaped from that enclosing society. It is inconceivable that they could be controlled. They would have left the golden land to move into the Mediterranean, into Europe, or south and east into the Gulf of Oman and the Indian Ocean. Inevitably, as they met both Mongoloid sea people and Neanderthals, interbreeding would have occurred.

The Neanderthals were continuing to move south in other parts of Europe, but we know that they disappeared remarkably suddenly, considering they had successfully colonised northern areas for over a hundred thousand years. Within a few thousand years, say a hundred generations, the population of Europe and beyond became a new hybrid Caucasoid race. It had all the variability of any hybrid. Heights, body shapes, the colour of skin and eyes, all were different. Noses might be anything from a Neanderthal beak to a flattened Mongoloid snub. Thin lips and beetling eyebrows were evidence of Neanderthal inheritance. Body hair covered the spectrum from smooth to hairy. Some Caucasoid people have almost as much body hair as a gorilla but are not regarded as anything but normal, although the least hairy Neanderthal females would probably have been more attractive to the sea peoples. Scalp hair could have been anything from blonde to black. A genetic side effect of hybridisation may make premature baldness quite common among adult males and many dark-haired Caucasoids prematurely grey.

About sixty years ago, they found some human skulls in two caves on the slopes of Mount Carmel in Israel. They were around forty thousand years old and they showed precisely the mix of Neanderthal and modern Homo sapiens characteristics which suggest continued hybridisation. Over hundreds of generations a breakdown in sexual segregation would have widespread consequences. The population ceased to be either purely Neanderthal or purely Mongoloid, but a mixture. Modern man.

Geraint said: "I always thought it was odd that we shave every day. I mean, why do we feel we have to scrape hair off our faces? Maybe it has something to do with our Neanderthal inheritance."

"You don't shave every day."

"No, well." And he smiled his sweet smile, and I looked back at him, reflecting on his blue eyes and pale freckled skin and the sandy hair that grew down his back, until he threw something at me.

16

The Ubiquitous Flint

Some time after this, Mr Brouard visited the United States. I received a rare letter, and a strange little drawing. He was staying with a friend at Rutgers University in New Jersey and had been invited to see horseshoe crabs spawning on the shores of Delaware Bay. The sight had moved him.

"I had no idea how complex they are. They not only have two compound eyes, but others which can detect the ultraviolet light of the moon, and the cycles of light and dark. No one seems to know how many there are, or indeed the precise details of their lifecycle, but to see them emerging here from the moonlit ocean is an extraordinary sight. The females are much bigger than the males, who wait for them at the water's edge. I discovered that horseshoe crabs are being used for drug testing, because their blood – which, by the way, is blue – reacts to bacterial contamination. Inevitably a percentage do not survive being captured and bled for this purpose, although most do, but the worst is the way they are increasingly being

119

used as bait by the fishing industry.   Thousands, at least.   I find it difficult to understand how we can so carelessly discard such an ancient and fascinating creature, especially one that has survived so long."

He had drawn the horseshoe crab's clock, the one he had described all those years ago.   The hours were marked from 1 to 12, but the face of the clock was divided into different periods of time, from the Cambrian to our own, the Quaternary.   There was something rather chilling about this demonstration of just how long the horseshoe crab had been around, compared to us: it had lived since the beginning of time, but the whole of our recorded history occupied less than the last half second.

Following the letter and the little drawing I had a card from Washington, followed by another tape.   He had returned to his preoccupation with the mysterious disappearance of the Neanderthal population, and he had found that some of his discussions in America had caused one or two raised eyebrows.

It isn't a simple matter of black and white.   The real position is much more complex.   Caucasoid populations have recently – that is to say, in historic, as opposed to prehistoric times – expanded phenomenally worldwide. Negroid populations in Africa and America have had considerable mixture with Caucasoid genes.   The gene for black skin tends to be more dominant, which means that many black men and women in America are otherwise almost entirely Caucasoid.

I could see why he had received a few old-fashioned glances.

In the Old World, around three or four thousand years ago, Caucasoids extended into India, where they became a majority.   They also reached Africa, as coastal Arab people.   Nowadays, partly through admixture and natural selection to climate, they range from fair-haired Scandinavians and red-haired Scots to black Arabs and Indians.

The one thing that is nicely exemplified in the United States today is how quickly black and white interbreed, as soon as artificial segregation barriers break down.   Once there is free mobility between races, it is pretty well instant.   In the prehistoric days of the last Ice

Age there would have been much the same swift change – although, given the different circumstances of longevity and opportunity, it might have taken many generations instead of a couple.

During the 'classic Neanderthal' period, from about a hundred thousand to thirty-five thousand BC, there would probably have been some riverside trading contact between the Neanderthal hunters of the northern tundra and the itinerant sea peoples, both travelling along European rivers like the Danube and the Rhone. A whole range of useful basic commodities would have been traded – maybe, too, a work of art: the occasional decorative figurine or piece of jewellery, unlikely to have been made by the very utilitarian Neanderthal people, has been found in Mousterian sites. But there would have been complete sexual segregation until something else happened – something gradual, but which – as now in America - resulted in swift breakdown of such segregation. As a result of miscegenation – interbreeding between races – in that part of the Middle East where slavery had become endemic, the original Mongoloid population would increasingly include bearded pale-skinned individuals.

As they extended their range, by river and land, so they would encounter some Neanderthal individuals not that dissimilar from themselves. Sexual curiosity and attraction would overcome the old barriers. Once that happened, the emerging vigorous new race revolutionised life on the great northern plains. Probably less because of the racial change from pure-bred Neanderthal to hybrid Caucasoid than from the fruitful marriage of cultures. At this point, the 'Middle Palaeolithic' became the Upper Palaeolithic, with its record of beautifully flaked flint tools, occasionally associated with skeletons indentical with those of modern Europeans. Throughout the traditional Neanderthal world of tundra south of the ice, the new people increased in number until they ranged from western Europe to the remotest corner of north-east Asia – and sometimes even beyond.

For instance, let's look at the mysterious Ainu people of Hokkaido, an island in the northern Japanese archipelago. They are now at the edge of extinction after centuries of oppression, racism, forced assimilation and general intolerance, all of which the Japanese authorities tend to play down. They are, undoubtedly, a people very different from all other indigenous people of Far East Asia: heavily bearded, with thick wavy hair and a very distinct European appearance. They're pretty much indistinguishable, in fact, from your classic Highland Scot. No one has yet explained their origins. Their culture reached its height about eight centuries ago.

Now, we know that every ice age has peaks which occur at intervals of fifteen to thirty thousand years apart. Then the ice cap extends southward. But curiously enough, in the past, even then the plains of Alaska remained sufficiently free from ice to allow summer grazing for game. And during these peaks, the increased accumulation of ice lowered global sea levels by about ninety metres. The Sea of Japan dried out. An isthmus, some six hundred miles wide, joined Siberia to Alaska across the Bering Sea – although Canada itself was covered with ice about a mile thick. At any of these times grazing animals, mammoth, musk ox, woolly bison, could cross into North America. And it seems that during the last such time, fifteen thousand years ago, our Upper Palaeolithic hunters could have followed them there, and left their typical flint spearheads to mark their presence.

These flint tools are similar to those used by mammoth hunters throughout Eurasia. They are identical in design to others found in the French village of Solutre – which gave its name to the contemporary Solutrean period of the Upper Palaeolithic.

When the ice age came to an end, about ten thousand years ago, imagine what happened to those Caucasoid pioneers as the sea began to inundate their lands. In such a tectonically unstable area, the end might well have come with a catastrophic great wave – a tsunami. Those left separated in America would have become – well, American; those bordering the Asiatic mainland would rejoin other tribes around the mouth of the Amur River, which now forms the boundary between Russia and China. But what of those who, together with wild animals, sought refuge as the sea swirled across the low-lying bed of what was to become the Sea of Japan? They would have found some haven on the hills which now form the islands of Japan, there to remain until Japan was invaded by the Mongoloid sea people from the south, who drove them north from Honshu. So are the Ainu, then, some of the last remaining descendants of those hybrid Neanderthal hunters?

I looked at the postcards he had sent me. One of them bore a drawing of a fluted flint spearhead. The postmark said 'Clovis'.

The tape continued: this is perhaps the clue to some of the original inhabitants of the American continent. Spearheads like this were found in 1932 in the small town of Clovis in New Mexico, and thus the theory arose that because they are so similar to those of Asia, hunters must have walked south – from Asia via Alaska. Tricky, because they must have found some sort of corridor through the ice. I've been discussing with some people at the Smithsonian. Most support the traditional theory – which of course rests on the assumption that Palaeolithic people had no access to boats. The sea didn't mean anything. So they populated the world by walking – well, originally by walking from Africa. But others are beginning to think this assumption is no longer valid. Many coastal archaeological sites now give clear evidence of earlier Mongoloid immigrants, who could only have reached them by sea. (As, indeed, must have the native Australians, over four times longer ago than the Clovis people).

There is a real debate going on. There is anatomical evidence linking native Americans – Red Indians – with the present inhabitants of Mongolia, but that would only be valid if there had been no racial change since the last ice age. I have a feeling that genetics is going to answer some of these questions. I believe it will reveal a basically Mongoloid pattern, relevant to the once ubiquitous sea people, with a small trace of ancient Caucasoid genes.

Is it fantasy to suppose that when the ice cap had retreated, and the northern hemisphere began to enjoy centuries of warmer climate than we know today, the Mongoloid sea people migrated as far north as the great Amur River? That when that warm era was followed by exceptional cold, these same people appear to have adapted by taming the wild horses of the steppe? As if the mobile life of the seaborne nomad was thus translated? In war and defence few could then match these horsemen. Their heirs were Ghengis Khan and the Ottoman Turks. Under their ruthless pressure, the hunters of the Upper Palaeolothic retreated into western Europe, where they were to give expression to their own understanding of the natural world.

17

Painting Caves

I was keen to hear more about these new people of the Upper Palaeolithic, but no new tapes arrived for several months. Other things preoccupied me. I finished my second novel, and it was accepted. I was also doing a lot of features. One was about the free miners of the Forest of Dean for one of the colour magazines. Geraint accompanied me on my research trip, as he often did. We both found it intriguing, a part of England neither of us knew at all, an insular forest planted on a high saucer of coal. In the dripping woods we tripped over old rusting rails that had once been part of a concentrated industrial landscape. The Wye that curled in such sylvan serenity below the lofty peak of Symond's Yat had once been as busy with the sound and smoke of shipbuilding as the Tyne. We went down a coal mine owned by one of the privateering free miners, and discovered that iron too had been mined in the Forest. Six hundred acres of caverns and tunnels lay beneath our feet.

The vast complex of limestone caves, glowing with the reds, terracottas and siennas of the iron ochres, was first mined over four thousand years ago. The stone had to be chiselled away to reveal the iron, both oxides and ore, and there was much evidence of the miners – many of them children.

"You might have expected," Geraint said, "to see cave paintings in a place like this, like the ones at Lascaux and Altamira. They have the colours here. Perhaps they simply aren't old enough. Or are we too far north? I suppose this was Neanderthal territory, when it wasn't covered in ice, and they don't appear to have been artists."

"But then," I said, "the miners may have chiselled them away."

Nevertheless the shop sold jars of red and ochre oxide powder. Artists often bought them, they said. Geraint was seized with the idea of trying his hand at cave paintings and bought a boxful. He could remember visiting the caves at Lascaux before they closed in the early 1960s, and the vivid images of bulls, horses and deer now came back to him.

"I could never understand," he said, "how they painted them without light, other than some sort of lamps fuelled with animal fat. At the time I didn't really question what kind of people painted them, but now I'm curious..."

We spent a good deal of time after that visiting quarries so that he could coax lumps of stone out of the quarrymen, combining these trips with his usual quest for pubs that brewed their own beer, or small cider-makers, of whom there seemed to be many in those days. His first attempt at painting on a flat piece of slate was not altogether successful. He managed to make a palette of earth colours, mixing the powders into pastes with water, linseed oil and even Unibond. He was able to produce violet and black from manganese oxides and white from zinc but there was no source of blue and green. His studio on the Isle of Dogs, which was hardly immaculate, was covered not only in paint but very fine powder that stained everything it touched. He finally completed three paintings, one on a piece of granite and the others on flat sheets of pale limestone. He did a lot of preparatory drawing at London Zoo. He was enchanted with the scatalogical preoccupations of monkeys and apes. One of the paintings was of a rhesus monkey, the other of a baboon. The third one was of a Zebu bull, a large Indian ox. I had read that it was a descendant of the original wild cattle, the aurochs. Geraint was filled with enthuasiasm and suggested I ring Mr Brouard for more information.

"Isn't it a long time since you had one of his tapes?"

"Yes, it is."

"Well, ring him," said Geraint.

When I rang Boury I spoke to Jean-Claude's father, who spoke very little English, and said Mr Brouard was not there. He gave me the Melchiors' telephone number in Paris and I tried that, but there was no answer.

Geraint's stone paintings were exhibited at a gallery in Camden, and there was considerable interest in them. He did not, of course, like to prostitute his Art by pandering to such popular taste, but the money was surprisingly good.

It was, for me, a happy period of my life.

In the spring of 1980 a tape arrived.

It was very short. It was Mr Brouard, but he did not sound quite like himself: there was nothing about Neanderthals or indeed anything else to do with the evolution of man. He said his wife Margaret had died of cancer two months before. Molly had taken him to England for the funeral. He would have got in touch but it did not seem a good time. Afterwards he returned to Brussels with Molly, where she was working, and he felt he should stay on for a while, as she was very down. She had been very close to her mother and had nursed her through the final weeks of her illness. He did not say so but somehow I felt that he was blaming himself for his ex wife's death and his daughter's depression.

"I wish she had more friends," he said. "She works very hard and is making a great deal of money, but this is not the kindest of cities and she seems very lonely. I thought we'd hold fire on the tapes for a bit. It upsets her if I spend too much time on my work. And it's difficult to do research here. I'd got everything so well organised in Boury and Paris. Perhaps you could keep an eye on new discoveries, new thinking. Just send me a tape if you can."

He did not mention his sight.

I sat there by the window, having started the tape with such excited expectation, and looked out at the acid mauve of a lilac tree in the garden opposite.

My second book was published in June, not a good time for publishing second novels, I thought, reading only the second review I could find anywhere – and that only seven lines of the faintest praise. I sent a copy to Mr Brouard, together with a tape in which I told him about the success of Geraint's cave paintings.

But I had begun to believe Geraint was not in love with me. He did not say so but I knew.

I went down to see John and Yolande in Cornwall and helped with the newest baby. Its delicious skin and smell and chuckling laugh did me no good at all. I went for long walks along the beach and wondered what I had done with my life: I was nearly thirty-five years old, unmarried, and I had not written a great novel. I had had a lot of love affairs but I still had no idea how one consolidated a love affair into marriage and children. John and Yolande were no help at all.

"Well – she pursued me," said John. "I just gave in."

"Quite true," said Yolande. "I was sixteen and I knew he was the man for me. So I followed him to New Zealand."

He smiled at me, a little rueful.

Geraint said, "it's just that I don't think we've really got a future together. It isn't that I'm not very fond of you. I am. I just don't want to be married to you. Or anyone. I like coming across new people."

"Women."

"Yes," he said. "Yes, I do. I don't think that's a suitable basis for marriage."

"I suppose not."

So we parted, although we were always to remain friends.

During that long autumn I was busy with freelance work, and did some television presenting for Harlech Television in Bristol, although the producer said the two halves of my face didn't quite match, and the camera liked symmetry. On one visit home to my parents, who had retired to Bath, I found my father had drunk the bottle of champagne he had always kept in the fridge to celebrate the announcement that his only daughter was to be married.

"Well, he got a bit down one day," my mother said. "Your trouble is, you're always looking for a straight stick. And there's no such thing."

The following February, when Prince Charles and Lady Diana Spencer announced their engagement, I found a straight stick at a party in the Barbican.

He was a reader in physics at Imperial College. He was tall, dark, very thin, and wore glasses. I noticed him first because he was reading a book by James Thurber in the corner of the very crowded flat, oblivious to the very high decibel level. I had always felt an immediate affinity with people who liked Thurber. It probably got us off entirely on the wrong foot because long afterwards he said he had never heard of James Thurber, it was just that he was rather bored, and had taken the book off the shelf. His name was Alexander Kidd, but he was known as Al.

We were married in April, the same Saturday as the Boat Race and the Grand National, which was won by Aldaniti, on whom my father had placed a bet for us. I had written to Mr Brouard in Boury to ask him to the wedding, which was at my parents' church in Bath, but had not really expected him to attend. Nevertheless he did come, accompanied by Molly. I met them at Bath Spa Station on the Friday evening. I had booked them in to a hotel in Pulteney Street.

He looked a little older. He had put on weight and his trimmed beard was greyer, his red hair thinner, rather long around his ears. His eyes were as blue as ever. He carried a white stick, which I found disconcerting. Molly looked much the same, although bigger, her hair short, still no make up. She shook my hand unsmilingly and said "he said he had to come."

I smiled at her and took his hands. "I'm so glad. Thank you for coming. It can't have been an easy trip."

"I couldn't miss your marriage," he said.

I drove them to the hotel. Molly seemed determined not to

leave his side but I insisted we go for a walk. "I'll make sure he's all right," I said.

"I'll be fine," he said.

We walked along the sunlit elegance of Pulteney Street to a little park where I had played as a child. It had been given in remembrance of a subaltern killed in the First World War. Under the great mature trees, given space here to reach perfection of height and spread, there were, in summer beds of tulips, pansies and forget-me-nots. There was also a garden for the blind, with a lily pool and walks shaded by pergolas entwined with roses and clematis.

"I buried my hamster alive in this park," I recalled. "It was when we arrived back from Hong Kong, and were living in a hotel in Pulteney Street. I kept him in a garage at the back. Afterwards I read that hamsters go stiff when they're cold, so you might think they're dead, but they're not, if you warm them up they're perfectly all right. I couldn't sleep. I kept getting nightmares of him coming back, giant-size."

"Well, at least he didn't suffer any distress. Just went from a death-like sleep into death."

"I try to think so."

"A good way to go. But then I would like to be burned, not buried."

"And your ashes scattered on the sea."

"Yes," he said, smiling.

"Which sea?" I asked curiously.

"Somewhere in the Southern Ocean," he answered. "Off the coast of Antarctica."

"Why?"

"Just a fancy I have."

We strolled on past blowsy pink tulips. It was like Monet's garden at Giverny.

"I like parks," he observed. "Much neglected these days, but urban treasures...So are you happy?"

"Yes, of course,"

"Why 'of course'?"

"Well – it would sound a bit funny if I said I wasn't."

"True."

"Tell me," I said: "have you stopped your work on human origins?"

We reached a bench in the sun, and sat down. Golden fish rose in the dark water of the lily pond before us.

"No," he said. "Just – paused."

"But you're back in Boury?"

"For the moment. However Molly would like me to live with her, and that would mean moving to London. She's been appointed to the European Community department at the Foreign Office. Assistant head of department."

"Oh. Would you like that? I mean – living in London?"

"Well, perhaps. I don't like imposing on Jean-Claude and Freddie."

"I'm sure they don't think you do."

"Well. We shall see. But – France is good for research. I know my way around. I have an excellent new amanuensis in the village, a man who makes cider for a living but has an interest in my subject."

I thought of Geraint. "Good cider?"

"Excellent. Also very good brandy." Then he said – perhaps I had mentioned to him in one of the few tapes I had sent him that Geraint was a cider fanatic – "how is that friend of yours, the one who painted his version of the cave paintings of Lascaux?"

"Very well," I said. "At least, he was the last time I saw him."

"He's not coming to your wedding?"

"No. He said he would feel like a spectre at the feast."

"Ah."

"He's given me one of his paintings, though. One of his cave paintings, a prehistoric bison."

"I'd like to see that. The art of the Upper Paleolithic age is fascinating. There are examples of rock art all over the world, some of it very ancient – in Australia and Africa, for instance – and it seems to coincide with great strides in technology. And it also coincides with the time when the new hybrid peoples, the joining of cultures, took place about forty thousand years ago. The first part of the last ice age had melted into a warm interstadial that lasted about ten thousand years. After the ice was on the move again. The classic period of Neanderthal culture had ended. The new people began to occupy their lands."

"So they are the people of the Upper Paleolithic?"

"That's how it's described – easier, perhaps, to think of successive waves of new people and cultures. There are several, but you can roughly classify them as the Aurignacian, which began about thirty thousand years ago, followed by the Solutrean and finally the Magdalenian, which really takes us up to the end of the last ice age, and real changes in the world. But there is something else that distinguishes these cultures, something which I hesitate to classify because I think many people in the distant past were conscious of beauty in things, or had some drive to reproduce what hey saw. But the sculpture and paintings of the Upper Paleolithic are very distinctive. And, as your friend Geraint has demonstrated, they are undeniably what we call art."

"Well, then I assume I'll be hearing more about it? When am I going to get some more tapes?"

He smiled at me with his now very concentrated gaze, moving his head a little, as if he had to work hard to see anything. "I think perhaps we could wait a little while. There is a lot of research to do, and it takes me longer than I would like these days."

"Has your sight got worse?"

"You are always direct. Yes, I think probably it has. It's as if less light penetrates to what is left of my retina. I cling to the belief that there will always be something – that essential pinhole. I can only see a small part of any object at one time, although I can still detect it – even the page of a book is visible if I take a bit of time to scan it. I don't know if my vision will disappear completely. I must admit I am afraid of going into total darkness. As long as there is some light, I feel I am not totally alone."

"You won't be alone, even then. But if you can, then please send me some more tapes."

"You may be more distracted from now on. Your life will change."

"I'm still working. I'm still me. I miss hearing your voice."

"I miss yours. Your queries, your scepticism, your observations."

"Well, then – "

"It hasn't been easy, with Molly. I feel – responsible for her."

"But it was her mother that left you, wasn't it?"

"Yes, but even then I felt guilty. I simply hadn't been aware that she was so unhappy. I thought everything was fine. And part of that was that I was so preoccupied with these new ideas about the origin of our species – there was so much new research coming out, so many fascinating new discoveries and theories."

"And she wasn't interested?"

"To be honest I don't think I tried to interest her. And, you see, perhaps that was a way of rejecting her. Worse than if I had tried and she had been uninterested. She was not self-sufficient, like you. She needed someone all the time."

"We all do, don't we?"

"No, I don't think so. Not mentally, perhaps. That is to say – I do, physically, now, and I wish I didn't. Sometimes I can't bear knowing that I do need someone. I have felt very low recently."

His voice was quiet. I had never heard it anything but full of vigour and enthusiasm.

"Please send me the tapes again," I said.

"Your new husband might not be too happy about it."

"Al won't even notice. He's so wrapped up in his work. I'm not absolutely certain he'll remember the wedding, except that he's got a reliable best man."

He smiled, then, and said he would see, it would depend on how things went with Molly and the possibility of moving from Boury.

As we walked out of the park he said: "I wish I could have seen the caves of Altamira. Now I never will." Then he turned and took my hands and added: "Perhaps, one day, you will let me take you to see them – and I might see them through your eyes."

"All right," I said.

18

The Man of Honour

"Please, Papa, please may I come too?"

Don Marcelino Santiago Tomas Sanz de Sautuola looked fondly down at his young daughter, Maria. He had thought her still asleep, like the rest of the family, but she had run out of the manor at Puenta San Miguel to find him. It was a fine spring morning in this year of 1879, the sun already hot. He had already mounted: his horse was impatient, skittering on the dusty forecourt.

"You wouldn't enjoy it. I'll be working in a dark old cave. No fun at all."

' "Please, Papa. You said it was exciting – I just want to see the bones and fossils and things. I won't be in your way."

She was beguiling as always, although she would be a distraction. "All right," he said. "If you promise not to complain... How long will it take you to fetch your pony?"

He waited for her under the cypresses, watching the sun slant through the shade and catch a prism in the fountain. Then together they rode through the open gates of the manor and into the lane that led up into the rolling limestone hills of Cantabria, that sliver of land on the north coast of Spain. The land was his almost as far as they could see, its fields dry-stone walled, its farmhouses red-roofed among the olive groves. Not far away was the old town of Santillana del Mar. He loved this part of his estates, his passion intensified by the knowledge that beneath its thin turf and rocky outcrops was another, ancient world.

The entrance to the cave had been cleared, and it was not difficult to make their way out of the sunshine and into the cool dimness beyond.

"It's dark," Maria said.

"I told you. And it will be darker yet...Wait until I've lit the lamps."

As he lit the acetylene lamps she asked: "is this where you found all the bones?"

"Yes, and teeth, and many oyster and mussel shells. And flint tools, like the little knives, the bone awls and the needles. Look – here's a shell. See, inside it has this pigment – "

She scratched it with a finger: "it's red stuff."

"Sometimes it's black. Now, follow me. I'll show you where I found the giant bear."

It was four years since he had first investigated the entrance to the cave. It had been discovered by a hunter looking for his dog, eleven years ago now, in 1868, and subsequently reported to him. Everyone on the estate knew of Don Marcelino's enthusiasm for all things old. Indeed, he was an enthusiast for a great many things: he took a direct interest in the running of all his estates, even as a young man appointed to organise the Valladolid Agricultural Exhibition. He had introduced eucalyptus trees to Spain. He had a magnificent library, a fascination with geology and was vice-president of the Monuments Commission in Santander. He had found the giant bear on his first visit to the cave, and shown these and all the other fossil bones to his friend Don Juan Vilanova y Piera, professor of geology at Madrid University. Vilanova had identified them as those of bison, wild horse, and the extinct giant stag. "But what it most fascinating is that they have been split – and this splitting is the work of man, with the object of extracting the marrow."

Since then Don Marcelino had done a great deal of research into other known Spanish caves, and the year before had visited the Second Universal Exhibition in Paris. He had been impressed by the work other amateur archeologists were doing, particularly in France: there were several collections of objects from the Perigord, arrowheads, knives and flint implements which had been found in association with bones of the very same species he had found in his own cave. He could not wait to get home and start a real excavation.

"Look," he said to Maria now, lifting the lamp. "We are now in the great cavern. I don't know how high it is, but immense, I think...Now, if we duck down here, there's a smaller side cavern. Mind your head, it's very low. The floor slopes down. Just follow me very carefully."

"It's like a dragon's den," she whispered.

"There are no dragons," he said firmly. "Just all sorts of little things hidden in the dust of the floor...You see, here, black ash, as if fires had once been lit here in the darkness. And this is a piece of bone."

"Why would they want to come in here?" Maria asked.

"Well, perhaps to escape some predator: perhaps it was warmer in here. At least it was shelter."

"But it's dark."

"Well, then they must have had some kind of light. Perhaps animal fat, burned as we burn oil, with a wick; or tallow candles."

He was right: Maria did get bored. As he squatted on his heels, meticulously scraping the earth and picking out anything that looked at all interesting, flint and fossil fragments, putting them in his leather bags, she took one of the lamps and began to wander round the chamber. He kept an eye on her, in case she should stumble or go out of sight, but he was absorbed in his work.

Suddenly he heard her give a cry, and scrambled to his feet, cursing the low roof – he was a tall man and there was a protrusion of rock just at that point.

"Maria! What is it?"

"Papa, Papa! *Mira, toros pintados*!"

"What do you mean? Painted bulls? There's nothing here but us – " he said, clutching her to him.

"No, look up!" she commanded him, and lifted the lamp.

He must have hit his head on the damn roof a dozen times: he had stooped and cursed and never looked up. Now in that moment of revelation he saw that just above their heads the whole ceiling - which was perhaps sixty feet long and thirty feet wide - was covered in what seemed like a vast painted relief sculpture. A panoply of great animals glowed in vivid reds, browns and blacks above their heads. The very protrusion on which he had just banged his head had been turned into a three-dimensional bison.

"Bison," he whispered. "A whole herd of bison..."

They crouched down together and craned their necks to look up. Don Marcelino shaded the flickering cold flame of the light and in a strange way the colours seem brighter than before. It was like being in the midst of the great herd, with bison grazing, running, sleeping – and here a charging boar, a wild horse.

"We are the first to see these," said Don Marcelino, "since they were painted."

And they remained in awed silence, broken only when Maria said: "And I found them. Aren't you glad I came, Papa?"

"Very glad," said Don Marcelino.

When, at last, they emerged from the darkness of the cave into the spring sunlight, Maria said: "does it have a name, Papa?"

Don Marcelino looked up at the green hill behind them. The sun was low, the shadows of drystone walls and thorn trees patterning the turf. "This is Altamira," he said.

He left for Madrid the next morning to tell Don Juan de Vilanova of the discovery. Vilnaova was sceptical, but was persuaded to return with Don Marcelino. One glance convinced him that this was something marvellous.

They began a systematic investigation of the caves, and they were not disappointed. Earlier pictures appeared behind the herd of bison, outlines of charcoal on the white limestone; they found wild horses on the other side of the chamber, and on one wall were three imprints of human hands, one as if the hand had been coated with paint and then pressed on the rock, the others as if the hands had first been held in place and then painted round it.

"They're all left hands," said Maria, about to put her hand where the long ago painter had placed his.

"Don't touch – " said her father hastily.

"That must mean the painters were right-handed," observed Vilanova.

The roof of the main cavern was too high to reach, but the walls were covered with animals, some etched into the rock, some drawn in charcoal. There was a great head of a bison, drawn as if in wet cement by fingers.

"They are the work of a master – this man, these men, were true artists," said Don Marcelino. "Who could deny it? They are simply beautiful works of art, so sure of their form, so subtle in drawing and colour – "

"Yet they must be – perhaps fifteen thousand years old, or more," said Vilanova. "Everything else in here is typical of the Magdalenian culture of that time, and there is no evidence of anything later: we are looking at paintings made in the Upper Paleolithic, late in the period perhaps."

"You know they have found pictures carved on bone in the Dordogne, scratched on small fragments – I saw some in Paris last year. Those were found with objects from the Magdalenian culture. They were acknowledged as authentic – I myself heard them described not as the work of children, although they are nothing compared to this – but as 'the childhood of art'. I would say these paintings are by a true artist who might hold his own with any today."

They went ever deeper into the caves, through caverns and into narrow tunnels beyond: eighteen metres in all. They found paintings of aurochs, stags, ibex and boar, wild horses, chamois and mammoth. All possessed the same quality of vivid life, although at one point Vilanova said thoughtfully:

"You see the way the bison's hooves lie – it is as if the animal was painted not from life, in death, as it lay on the ground."

"But its eyes..." said Don Marcelino. "Its eyes are alive."

When they had completed their careful investigation and

recorded all the paintings, Don Marcelino began work for publication. He needed a way of illustrating all the evidence, and he thought he had just the right person for the job. Some time before he had been asked if he might help a destitute Frenchman who had been stranded in Santillana del Mar. The man was dumb, but intelligent and a gifted artist. Don Marcelino decided he was capable of drawing copies of the cave paintings, and together they worked on the treatise, with the advice of Vilanova. The following year, in 1880, *An Account of Certain Prehistoric Discoveries in the Province of Santander* was published. It was scholarly, even dry, and the details of artifacts, fossils and molluscs were as precise and scientific as the paintings. Don Marcelino was careful not to allow his enthusiasm to empurple his prose.

The pamphlet was greeted at first with incredulity: then with scorn, ridicule and anger.

One academic wrote: "Primitive man was little more than a gorilla, incapable of conceiving arts and sciences...Furthermore, how could it be credited that paintings in powdered ochre could be preserved for thousands of years in a deep, damp and pitch-dark underground cavern?"

Fiercest in his condemnation was Emile Cartailhac, professor of prehistory at Toulouse University who considered himself – and indeed was considered – to be one of the most eminent experts in the field. He refused to travel the two hundred and fifty miles from Toulouse to Santander to see the paintings but nevertheless declared them to be a fraud. When a respected paleontologist called Edouard Harle did call to see them, he found out about Don Marcelino's itinerant and conveniently dumb French painter, who by then had moved on in his travels and disappeared. That was sufficient to convince the establishment. The cave paintings of Altamira were a hoax.

Don Juan de Vilanova sought to defend his friend, but it was simply said that he had been duped and was too proud to admit it. People began to say that local youngsters had decorated the caves in the years between its first discovery and Don Marcelino's investigations. Some said the paintings were Roman.

Sitting alone in his study in that bleak year, Don Marcelino heard the door open, the rustle of skirts, the touch of his little daughter's hand.

"Papa – why don't you fight? Tell them we found the paintings – tell them they're not a trick, they're real!"

He smiled at her eager face. "Why should I? All Spain knows I am a man of honour. I do not care to argue the matter. If they cannot take the word of an honourable man, then that is up to them. I know the truth. It will make no difference, in any case. I have done all that I can. I have enough to do here on the estate."

"Uncle Juan says he will fight them."

"That I can understand. It is not his honour, but his judgement, his professional position, which they have questioned. If I can help him, I will; but I fear that if I take his part it will only bring him more ridicule."

Vilanova did fight them. Later that same year he delivered a speech at the International Congress of Archaeologists in Lisbon. The evidence for the authenticity of the Altamira paintings was, he said, overwhelming. The wealth of anatomical detail could not have been produced by any living artist; it demanded an intimate knowledge of the actual animals. The excavations proved that the cave had been unopened since Magdalenian times. The palette shells and the lumps of solidifed paint, ochre and charcoal mixed with animal fat had been found in the same levels as the Magdalenian implements and the bones of the very animals portrayed. Finally, certain of the paintings were covered with a layer of stalagmite which surely proved their age.

The assembled archaeologists were shaken: some even went to Altamira to see the paintings for themselves. But few were willing to change their minds. Professor Cartailhac remained adamant and even published a book that year which reinforced all his arguments against the Altamira paintings.

On a spring evening in 1888 Don Marcelino went back to his cave. He was alone. Maria was grown up now, and engaged to be married. For a while he stood at the entrance, remembering that first miracle of seeing the paintings. He looked at the long shadows of evening, and the mist over the high meadows, and wondered what this place had been like, fifteen thousand years ago. Cold, then, in the last ice age, but perhaps with spring then had come these blue skies, the eternal sunshine to warm the people who had expressed their feelings so vividly in their art. Perhaps they had used the pictures to teach, to instruct in some method of hunting; perhaps to capture the spirits of the animals, perhaps simply to express their appreciation of such strength and beauty. He shivered, suddenly. It was not that he himself was bitter at the rejection of the paintings, more that he felt he had failed those who had made them. What was it that someone had written? "Primitive man was little more than a gorilla..." He knew that now to be untrue. Silently, he saluted his ancestors, and walked back to his waiting horse to ride home.

He died a few days later at the age of fifty-seven. Five years later his old friend Don Juan Vilanova also died.

In 1902 Maria, now married with children of her own, received a visitor. She had been sitting in her father's old study in San Miguel. Outside, the fountain played as it had done on the morning they had found the paintings.

"Who is it?" she asked the servant.

"Professor Cartailhac of Toulouse University, president of the Prehistoric Society of France."

He was an old man, but he had lost none of his formidable presence.

"You may know, madame," he said bluntly, "that excavations have been taking place in the Perigord. They have found paintings similar to those at Altamira. They have also found incontrovertible evidence of their antiquity."

"And I know that they sent their findings direct to the Academy of Science in Paris, not to you." Maria answered.

"That is true. And I have to tell you that the findings have been accepted. I have therefore written a paper to be published in *L'Anthropologie.* It is entitled *La Grotte d'Altamira Mea Culpa d'un Sceptique.*"

"I see."

"Madame, I wish to make my apology not only in print but to

you, since I cannot make it to your father or to Don Juan de Vilanova. I must tell you that I am haunted by my great error, and it will weigh upon my conscience until my own death. Your father was a man of honour and discovered a great wonder of Europe. It is the Sistine Chapel of prehistory. I find my rejection of him, and my scorn of his work, very hard to bear."

When he had gone, Maria went out into the garden, and wept for her father.

19

Marriage

Al and I had two weeks' honeymoon in the Greek islands and then returned to his house in Stoke Newington. He had bought it three years earlier, very cheaply, despite the rise in house prices, because it was in need, as they say, of some refurbishment. It was also not in the smartest part of Stoke Newington, itself not exactly sought-after at the time. Nevertheless it possessed a garden, parking in the road outside, and the particular charm of all Victorian London brick terraced houses. Al had not done much refurbishing, but I was seized with enthusiasm and began a great programme of polyfilling and painting, although I was also busy with journalism. Al did some of the cooking. He took a keen scientific interest in it and was given to putting thermocouples in souffles to record the rising, or injecting pineapple juice into pork. (The latter is not a good idea, the enzymes turn the meat to blancmange).

Al and I were very happy, absorbed in our work and each other to the exclusion of the outside world, as is perhaps typical of newly married people. I did send two tapes to Mr Brouard but my interest in the Upper Paleolithic had slipped to the back of my mind. Perhaps he was sensitive to the change in my circumstances, for he sent only a short tape to say how glad he was that we were enjoying life, and that he was remaining in Boury for the time being.

The local GP said that as we were both so old (Al, at 36, was a year older than me) we should get on with it if we wanted children, so we did not bother with contraception. A few weeks later I realised I was probably pregnant. It was confirmed not only by the doctor but by the fact that when Al took me out for a celebratory meal I discovered that although I was very ready to gulp down a glass of Gevrey-Chambertin my body would not let me. I had never experienced this divergence of mind and body before. I did not like it at all and it presaged a continuing sense of alien occupation throughout the pregnancy, only relieved by finding that following the birth of our first child I was once more permitted to drink a glass of wine.

It was after Thomas was born that I began to think about the Neanderthals again. Tom was a good baby as babies go although at the time I did not know it. I spent a lot of time trailing miserably round Clissold Park while he wailed in a corduroy sling on my chest. I worried about his weight and eczema on his head and found other new mothers totally intimidating. When, in the spring of the following year, Mr Brouard sent me a long tape and said he had a feeling I might need some diversion, it was like being given a lifeline back to some kind of normality. I would put Tom in the old pram we had been given and let him sleep under the sycamore tree in the nature reserve we called a garden while I, observing him from the kitchen window, entered my other world.

20

Archeologie des Villages

Altamira was the first such discovery in Europe, but it was France that remained the early focus for the study of these ancient cultures. Some twenty-five thousand years ago, when the ice age was relenting a little, the valleys of the Dordogne were a paradise for hunting peoples. They were nearly five hundred miles south of the ice and it was possible to move north from the natural haven of the Gironde estuary almost all year. Moist winds, warmed by the Gulf Stream, encouraged lush summer grazing and attracted great herds of game. The narrow gorges provided easy hunting and the limestone cliffs were full of caves to provide comfortable winter shelter. Flints could simply be picked off the walls for making tools and spears.

I heard the tape click, stop, and then begin again, the sound of papers, the thud of some old book put before him, another voice – the cider-maker's? – speaking in the background. Then Mr Brouard's voice.

It was in the village of Aurignac in the Vezere valley that in the 1860s a workman found a skeleton hand in a rabbit hole. It was the start of excavations by two amateur archaeologists, one French, one English: they found several different levels of prehistoric occupation and classified them according to the bones of animals like reindeer and bison, and flint weapons. The earliest remained the Aurignacian, to which the cave paintings of Lascaux, discovered in 1940, belong: then there is the Solutrean phase, marked by very fine spearheads and a preoccupation with wild horses, and finally the Magdalenian. There were other phases of these cultures, overlapping, but sequential, and all named after small French villages where the finds were made.

In 1868, the same year as a hunter searching for his dog first came upon the caves at Altamira, navvies building a railway not far from Aurignac uncovered an old rock shelter and what appeared to be skeletons. The nearest village was called Cro-Magnon. Five adult skeletons and some fragments of infant and foetal bones were found, together with flint tools, sea shells, and fossil bones of mammoth, bison and wild horse. They were identified as belonging to the Aurignacian period of at least thirty thousand years ago – and they were modern *Homo sapiens*. Such people were the artists of Lascaux.

Since then more than fifty such sites have confirmed the existence of these new people. It was said – and indeed many still maintain it is so – that these people invaded Europe, that they exterminated the so-called inferior Neanderthals. But then what of our *sapiens* Swanscombe woman who died on the shore of the Thames three hundred thousand years ago? And if these people only appeared thirty thousand years ago – well, it does take some imagination to think they exterminated the Neanderthals so quickly, when the Neanderthals had been around for a hundred and fifty thousand years.

In 1947 there was another clue. Another French archaeologist was excavating a series of caves by a river in the Charente, near Angouleme, when she found a thick layer of stalagmite, separating the cave into two very different strata. The original excavation had found material with tools going back from Magdalenian to the Mousterian – pure Neanderthal – culture, but under the stalagmite layer were fossil remains not of ice age animals, but of such creatures as rhinoceros and tortoise that could only have lived in the warmth of the long interglacial period – about three hundred thousand years ago. Just the time when our Swanscombe lady met her end. It took Mlle Henri-Martin, the archaeologist, ten more years to discover two human skulls. They were in fragments, but enough to identify them as *Homo sapiens* – modern man. Mlle Henri-Martin gave them the name Taycian.

Later came finds in the Ukraine, where construction workers came upon piles of bones of mammoths that led to the discovery of sites dating from ten to seventy-five thousand years ago – inhabited by Neanderthal people up to thirty-five thousand years ago, and thereafter by our 'modern Europeans'.

What it all seems to mean is that there is no clear and simple line that can be drawn between Neanderthal and these new cultures. The combination of their particular skills, their traditions, their imaginations, resulted in the refinement of the age of the hunter, closely linked to the natural world, to place, to predator and prey. It was to last for thousands of years.

But as the last ice age came to an end, around twelve thousand years ago, it was already evident that a different world, a different way of living, had become established in that separate land known as the Fertile Crescent. If you take a pair of compasses and centre it on a point on the east coast of the Red Sea, you can draw a line in an arc from the north-eastern corner of the Mediterranean to Basra on the Persian Gulf. This was the place of the first real settlement. The ancient sea peoples had found a rich haven here in the Gulf, then in the great delta and the plains of the Tigris and Euphrates, up these rivers into the foothills of Anatolia.

It was here that they had continued to develop their dependence on their captive slaves. The trigger for what was to become our modern world. Slaves cannot be armed to hunt food for themselves. They cannot carry weapons. Yet they have to be fed. They must be looked after. They not only work for their masters, they are a symbol of his wealth. And the solution to that problem changed everything. It was agriculture.

21

Sowing the Seeds

"You're a farmer," I said to John, when we visited them in Cornwall.

"Not really," he said. "More of a peasant, perhaps."

It was the summer of 1983. John and Yolande seemed much the same as they had always been, not even appreciably older, although their children were now teenagers, each one very much an individual but all brown, beautiful and charming. John and I had left Al and Tom to be smothered by Yolande and two puppies in the garden. We had walked up to the meadow beyond the old wooden barn to look at a new foal. He might not be a farmer, but John had finally indulged his love of horses and had already bred a successful steeplechaser. He rarely rode himself, but was content to break the colts and fillies. I watched him now, calm and gentle as always, very still, as the white mare and then the jumpy little ginger foal came to him. Their thin coats, like satin over the delicacy of bone and vein, shone in the evening sun as they moved out of the shade of an oak tree, shadows long across the grass

"But you grow things."

"Yes, that is true. Potatoes, asparagus, strawberries, daffodils in spring: and a couple of fields of winter wheat. And grass, of course."

"And you have to thresh the wheat."

He smiled at me, that slow laconic smile he had perfected over years living with Yolande's loquacity. "Well, we have a contractor who comes in with a combine harvester, yes."

"It's just – well, Mr Brouard says that one of the things that made agriculture possible was the discovery of a rare mutant wheat. "

"Emmer."

One of his daughters was called Emma, so for a moment I was a little nonplussed: then he added, "*Triticum dicoccum.*"

"Yes, that's it – how did you know that?"

"Well, about a hundred years ago, I went to agricultural college."

"What I don't understand is how this mutant kind of wheat could be so important. How it could change things."

The foal reached out with quivering nostrils, like pale dewy velvet, to touch John's open palm. In it was a small handful of wheat grains. He let the foal consume them before withdrawing his hand and then, from his pocket, taking out another handful. "I used to wonder how it happened, too," he said slowly. "Wheat is a grass. It grows wild in Turkey, on the plains of Anatolia. People must have realised long ago that the seeds could be eaten. Taste these."

The grains were nutty, quite sweet, perfectly palatable.

"But they weren't easy to gather in any quantity. As soon as the ears of wheat ripened, so they split and scattered the seeds to the wind. But someone must have observed that some didn't open. I've often thought about it. Did a child, playing in the long grass, notice the dry heads of the wild wheat that stayed unopened on the stalk? Or was it a woman, perhaps given the task of attempting to gather the grass just as it reached the point of ripening? And did she then take a sheaf home with her, and lay it on some flat stone, and try to break open the ears to separate the seeds?   Was that the first threshing?"

I had never heard him give such a long speech. I said: "Mr Brouard says it was actually lethal – from the wheat's point of view."

Well, so it was, of course.   If the ears didn't split, the seed couldn't be scattered, and so that was the end of it. The wheat couldn't reproduce.   On the other hand, if the seeds could be threshed by hand, and gathered, they could not only be eaten and stored, but sown. It meant that people had control over it. They could begin to choose those plants that gave the best yields. They could apply the same techniques to other plants – barley, peas, flax. Your Mr Brouard is right.   It was the beginning of agriculture."

We walked back to the house, through the orchard, past the asparagus and strawberry beds and the three small cottages that John had built himself for holiday letting. We ate our evening meal round the kitchen table. Although they had extended the house, John and Yolande had never considered a formal dining room. The dogs sprawled on a threadbare Persian rug in one corner and every now and then a hen came pecking methodically through the open back door.   The late sun touched the mantelpiece, and all the assorted objects that Yolande's children had made or given or brought back from school trips over the years, and that she had never thrown away. There was a bowl of Mrs Sam McGredy roses on the massive old dresser, dropping coral-coloured petals. We were eating the last of the asparagus, roast teg lamb – ("last year's", said John) – and the first strawberries, with a bottle of chianti.   Upstairs Tom was fast asleep. I experienced one of those moments of pure happiness which people of my sort, brought up to fear the envy of the gods, do not expect to last.

"So you're still in touch with your old schoolmaster," Yolande said, adding bowls of peas and roast potatoes to the table.

"Well, intermittently. He has to spend a long time on research before he gets it on to tape."

"You don't mind this liaison, Alexander?"

"No," said Al with a shrug.   "Although I could wish he was working on something – well, something less barmy."

"Barmy?" I repeated, surprised.

"Well – I haven't read any of the transcripts, but I gather it disputes the fact that *Homo sapiens* originated in Africa and walked across the globe – "

"Well, yes, it does, but – "

"My point exactly," said Al cheerfully.   "I mean, he's a nice chap, and I admire him for carrying on with all this stuff despite his blindness.   And I admire you for doing it for him, I wouldn't dream of interfering.   But he's not a scientist, is he?   I mean – it's like ley lines, and Atlantis, isn't it?"

"No – and are ideas only valid if a scientist thinks of them?"

"Well, no, but at least one starts with a trained mind – "

"Mr Brouard has a trained mind."

"What was his degree?"

"Well, I'm not actually sure.   He was in the RAF in the last war, flying Hurricanes.   I think he went to university after that, but I'm not quite sure where, or what he did – classics, perhaps.   Or engineering.   I seem to remember he got two external degrees – "

"Classics or engineering?" said Al ironically. "Or one of each?"

"A nice combination," said John seriously.

"Well, anyway, I don't think anyone could say he hasn't got a trained mind," I repeated crossly.   "And an open mind.   Which is more than a lot of scientists have."

"Yes, but come on, you have to admit all this stuff about the sea and us going back to some sort of egg-collecting creature among the dinosaurs is just a little off the wall."

"Maybe it is.   I don't know.   I'm just a journalist with a completely untrained mind."

"I would have thought," Yolande put in at this point, "that being a journalist needs a rather particular kind of mind, able to absorb lots of different things, and able to see things from all points of view. My father was a scientist – "

"Really?" I said in surprise.

"Yes, he worked for ICI.   Something to do with molecular chemistry.   Anyway, he always said that scientists lived in separate worlds not only from the rest of us but from each other.   He said that often in science you would build a very tall hypothesis, like a carefully balanced tower of bricks, and then discover that one of the bricks at the bottom didn't actually fit the hypothesis. But if you removed that brick the whole lot would fall down. And the greatest temptation in science was to ignore the brick that didn't fit."

"Yes, but in old Brouard's case none of the bricks fit," Al said breezily. "He isn't building a tower – it's just a great pile of bricks."

I looked at him for a moment. He gave me a mutinous smile back. I had heard about love turning to hate but I didn't know it could happen quite so suddenly.

Hate turned back to love but for the first time we lay in bed as if we did not like each other, and I resented him the more because John and Yolande were aware of it.

Fortunately I began to like him again later, but I could not quite forget that moment. Was it true? But even if it was – how could I not go on with Mr Brouard's work? It wasn't just that I was fond of him, and was aware that he depended on what Yolande had called our liaison. For the first time I looked back over the story he had told me in the tapes and in our discussions. I thought of Rhea, surviving the cataclysm of sixty-five million years ago: of the first hominids on the island, the reed forests and the surrounding sea; the development of the mind, the brain, and the building of the first boat. I remembered the people caught in the ice age of the north, and those who had painted the bison in the caves at Altamira. I wanted to know the rest of the story. I wanted to know what had happened when someone discovered the mutant emmer wheat.

Things did change a little between Al and me after that. Such trivial things matter. I no longer talked to him about Mr Brouard's ideas, but kept them to myself. It was not difficult, for the tapes arrived at increasingly longer intervals, and my life was busy. There was Tom, and the house, and a steady if diminishing trickle of work from old newspaper colleagues. I started a new novel about two small boys and an old pony on Walthamstow Marshes. It did not help, perhaps, that Al was working long hours. There was a good deal of rivalry in his department at Imperial, and I did not know enough about physics – let alone the sensitivities of scientific colleagues – to discuss it with him.

I missed my old conversations with Geraint, and with other

friends, particularly men. I rarely went into a newspaper office now and lunches were usually with women friends, the worst being with those preoccupied with babies and children. I had been a careless gadfly of a journalist, rarely thinking of the future, always relying on a cheque in the post to pay the latest bill or a chance meeting to find another job. Al, who had followed a rigorous academic route from his Newcastle grammar school to Cambridge and thence Imperial, always conscious of his parents' sacrifices, saw life quite differently from me. Of course he was right: once there were children, you had to think of their security. But it was difficult.

In June, just as Mrs Thatcher was re-elected, I found I was pregnant again. We had wanted another baby but it was somehow unexpected. I was off the booze again. I turned the top attic room into my study and my study into the new baby's room. I wished there were not so many stairs in the house. I had dreams about Yolande's kitchen with the sun slanting through the open back door from the garden. Tom was very lively and I seemed much more tired than before. Only occasionally did I feel able to escape to the tapes, and Mr Brouard's deep and comfortingly familiar voice.

22

Slave Labour

"In 70 AD the Roman senator Cato wrote a recipe for keeping slaves. The gist of it was this:

"Rations: For the actual labourers four pecks of wheat in the winter months, and four and half in summer. For three months after the harvest, they should drink rough wine. In the fourth month, half a pint a day, or about two gallons a month. For the fifth, sixth, seventh and eighth months, the ration should be a pint a day or four gallons a month. For the remaining four months, give them one and a half pints a day, or six gallons a month.... Keep all the windfall olives you can. Then keep the ripe olives from which only a small yield could be gained. Issue them sparingly to make them last as long as possible. When the olives are finished, give them fish-pickle and vinegar.   Give each man a pint of oil a month.   A peck of salt should be enough for a man for a year.   Clothes: a tunic three and a half feet long and a blanket-cloak every other year.   When you issue a tunic or cloak, take in the old one to make rough clothes.   You ought to give them a good pair of clogs every other year."

"A hard man, Cato, but a respected farmer.   He was the very antithesis of the old sea people, the hunters and gatherers.   And he hated the Greeks."

Gazelle Girl

Most people did not like goats. The goatherd did not mind. He was a little like a goat himself: pale-eyed, hairy, and regarded with suspicion by the people of the village. He wanted no other companions than the scheming goats and the biddable sheep and his two dogs, tan-coloured shadows at his heels. Even now, as winter approached and snow fell in the mountains above the olive groves and the singing pines, he preferred to spend his days on the high slopes. In the village far below he could see a line of men cutting fields of wheat and barley, their sickles glinting in the sun. They were building a new canal to irrigate the upper fields now; there were new dusty roads from the lake, new houses, reed-thatched. He had never slept in a house. At night, when he brought the goats down to the fold he slept under a tent made from their rough hides. Out in the streets fires flared, food sizzled, torches lit the shining faces of the people for whom this was a kind of freedom after the hours of labour in fields and metalworking shops and raw building sites.   There was singing, storytelling, the sweet taste of honey cakes and resinous wine. Only when he glimpsed the parted lips and gleaming breasts of a young girl did he wish that he too was a part of them.

It was on a clear autumn morning that he first saw the girl on the ridge where the wild goats sometimes came, standing as if to call his herd back to them.   But his goats knew his call, and did not stray, although sometimes one would turn and look at him with its curved horns and yellow eyes as if considering the matter.   The sheep, these days bred not just for their soft underfleece and plump meat, but for their docility, always followed the goats.

He saw her several times after that.   And then, late on the sixth day, he was lying under a spreading mountain pine, watching his dogs quarrel over a dead hare, when he became aware that he was under observation.   He turned and saw her sitting in the level sun not three yards from him.   She was very thin, her breast bones prominent above the edge of a a soft tunic made from gazelle skin. Her arms were muscular.   She carried a spear and a slingshot.   Her feet were bare and calloused.   Her dark hair was very straight, like a river down her back.   Her eyes were narrow above high cheek bones.

"You are from the valley," she said at last. He could think of nothing to say, and did not know if she would comprehend him. But she spoke in his language, although differently.

"Yes," he replied.   "And you?   Where do you live?"

"Up there," she said, and gestured to where the forests and the high meadows climbed to the snows of the mountains.

He had known there were people who lived in the high peaks and the plains, living by hunting, for they sometimes spoke of them in the villages, and once he thought he had seen figures in the forest. On another occasion he had come upon the skins of wolf, gazelle, ibex and wild goat laid out on the rocks to dry.   Stories of such wild people abounded: they could not speak, they lapped water with their tongues, they could swim the widest rivers and leap across chasms.

"Why do you burn the forest?" she said then, as if it took courage to ask.

"To clear it – to make charcoal, to cook, to do many things. To grow other things upon the land, so that we may feed our people."

"And the goats – they eat the places you burn?"

"They eat everywhere. Everything."

She observed the goats, with their mad eyes and huge horns. The matriarch of the herd was almost as large as a male, her coarse brown coat faded to ochre in places, grey-white underneath. As if conscious of scrutiny, she turned her head from her browsing on a thicket of thorn and wild cherry and stared back at them.

The boy and the girl met again as the days passed. Each night he returned to his place in the goat pen and each morning went back up into the mountains, higher and higher, although now the wind was cold, hoping he might see her. She was not always there, and he never knew when she might appear, so silent, so elusive was she, appearing from the trees like the very gazelle she hunted. One day he offered her cakes made from ground barley, honey and goat's cheese. At first she would not take them, but when she did she seemed to find the taste good, and took more, as if indeed she was starving. So he brought more food for her: flat wheaten bread, olives and salt fish from the lake. She would try these delicacies, and smile at him. On one of these occasions he touched her arm, and smelt the strange sweet smell of her skin under the sun, and looked into her black eyes for so long that he wondered he was not sucked into her by that glance alone.

He did not know if it was the food, or something intangible that bound them, that at last made her come with him down from the high place towards the lake and the valley below. She simply followed him. As they approached the mud houses and the busy streets between, the barking of dogs, the traffic of ox cart and donkeys, people looked at the curious pair walking so calmly among them, followed by the herd of goats and the biddable sheep and the two tan-coloured dogs weaving at their heels. It was late. The sun was going down. The level rays from its red sphere glittered on the great lake, splintering through the still rushes along its shore. Long shadows spilled from poplars and cypress trees. The youth and the girl walked as if unaware that they were attracting any attention, but he was so fair, she so dark, both somehow different from those around them, that some, acquainted with him, called out in jest so rough there was a menace in it. She turned to flee: he caught her arm.

"Here," he said. "This is my place. Here we can be safe, and I will bring you food."

And she watched the goats and the sheep hurry in to the pen. In a corner of it was his tent, a wooden framework covered in goatskins, where his bed and a wooden table shared the beaten earth with the animals. She saw him begin to close the gate of the pen behind them. The trees rustled in the evening air, and there was the sound of the water licking round the nearby shore. Somewhere pipes played. He thought it a good place.

But she hung back.

"Come," he said. "You must not stray from here. Night is coming. I must be here with the animals at night."

"You must be here? Why? Could we not sleep out on the bank of the lake, or under the trees?"

"I have to guard the sheep and the goats."

"Why? Are they not safe here?"

"I think so – but it is what I do. It is why I am given food, why I am looked after by my master. That is what I am."

"Like a dog that is chained up at night. A guard dog." She stepped back, away from him. "No. No, this is not for me."

"But it is a good place – my master is kind, I have no need to ask for anything – "

"I have no master. I was hungry, and you gave me food, but I would rather starve than be chained."

"I am not chained – " he said.

She said nothing, but turned away, and all he could do was to watch her slip through the poplar trees and the people in the street beyond. She looked back once, but she did not smile.

In years to come, when he was so celebrated a storyteller that he gained his freedom, Aesop told this story. He called it The Dog and the Wolf.

A gaunt Wolf was almost dead with hunger when he happened to meet a house-dog who was passing by. "Ah, cousin," said the Dog. "I knew how it would be: your irregular life will soon be the ruin of you. Why do you not work steadily as I do, and get your food regularly given to you?"

"I would have no objection," said the Wolf, "if I could only get a place."

"I will easily arrange that for you," said the Dog. "Come with me to my master and you shall share my work."

So the Wolf and the Dog went towards town together. On the way there the Wolf noticed that the hair on a certain part of the Dog's neck was very much worn away, so he asked him how that had come about.

"Oh, it's nothing," said the Dog. "That's only the place where the collar is put on at night to keep me chained up. It chafes a bit, but one soon gets used to it."

"Is that all?" said the Wolf. "Then goodbye to you, Master Dog."

Better starve free than be a fat slave.

Farming Fire

Aesop's fables are very old. The ones we know best are the moral ones, but more of them actually attempt to explain particular natural phenomena. For example, one of them explains that weeds grow better than domesticated plants because they are the natural offspring of the Earth, and she favours them, as a mother will favour her own children, which suggests that the division between hunting and farming peoples must go back a very long way. Archaeological finds in Anatolia have shown the two systems co-existing there in very ancient time.

No one really knows who Aesop was. He is mentioned by early writers like Herodotus and Aristotle and Socrates is said to have passed the time awaiting execution by putting Aesop's fables into verse, but otherwise he is simply a figure out of ancient legend. There is a 'Life of Aesop', which may have been first written down as long ago as the sixth century BC, but no one knows how true it is. It does seem to be true that he was a slave. The Greeks may have invented democracy, but slavery underpinned it. Of a population of perhaps a quarter of a million in Athens about two thousand years ago, well over two thirds of men, women and children were slaves. Plato, for example, owned fifty slaves. One man owned about a thousand and rented them out. It was entirely accepted that the smooth running of society depended on slaves – children were especially useful in the silver mines. Manual labour and tedious bureaucracy were not for free Greek citizens.

Slavery has no parallel among other animals, save for certain species of insects. (Although I believe the African Blind Naked Mole Rat, which lives underground, has a similar system). Termites have brought it to a particularly refined stage of development. Sterile worker and soldier slaves build beautifully engineered cities and tend termite farms to feed the community, including a single gigantic queen and her vast quantities of infants. The idle but fertile termites of the elite reach maturity on a single warm night, taking flight on their first and last sexual adventure. Only one will succeed in becoming the tiny consort of a new queen. The rest will all be eaten. No one knows why so primitive an insect should have adopted a system which essentially depends on centralised food production and its rationed distribution to a working class. But it does bear comparison with what was happening in the Near East at the end of the last ice age.

The mutant emmer and einkorn wheats and the subsequent development of plant breeding provided increasingly controllable supplies of food for a subservient population. Its masters, descendants of the old sea peoples, knew about the way water worked: now they had the muscle power to put into practice designs for improved drainage, irrigation and hydraulic engineering. Canals and aqueducts could carry water to areas which had hitherto been the province of those who hunted wild animals and foraged for wild plants, nuts and fruit. Farming settlements were established throughout the area. The old skills in knapping flints for the weapons of hunting, barbed harpoons, spears and arrowheads, declined. Unskilled slaves could be given the time-consuming labour of grinding and polishing axes, sickles and agricultural tools. And it was these stone tools that gave their name to this new revolution: the Neolithic. From about 8000 BC it was already spreading beyond the cradle of the Near East.

Two other factors quickened that spread of the farming

revolution. Fire, once one of the prime tools of the Neanderthal people, was now widespread. It had many uses, not only for cooking but for charcoal burning and heating pitch. Bottle gourds had always been used to carry water, but one day someone probably smeared one with clay to make it stronger and more impervious. Imagine such a gourd being accidentally burned in a fire. The discovery that the clay alone could thereby create a waterproof, durable container was the beginning of pottery – just as the use of coloured metallic ores would lead to metallurgy.

But fire had another use, probably linked to that discovery of pottery. Forests covered much of the mountains and foothills of Anatolia at the end of the ice age. Burning could swiftly clear the land for cultivation of cereal crops and grazing. That might not have caused permanent damage, had it not been for the second element in the equation: the goat. Gazelles and goats had always provided a source of protein, but the wild bezoar goats were more amenable to domestication. More importantly, they could give milk. Their woolly coats provided hides, and their hair could be spun into rope. And goats eat anything. They could help in the domestication and protection of the wild sheep, like the argali, with its prized soft undercoat that was to be bred into valuable fleece. Goats were wealth on legs. Like slaves. Yet their ability to browse on any plant that might be trying to regenerate, perhaps after clearance burning, was literally devastating to the land – indeed, burning was hardly necessary where goats were allowed to roam.

The ownership of goats changed society. Those who would once have hunted and foraged for wild food, bringing back a deer felled by the throw of a single spear, now cultivated the land and looked after domesticated livestock. The natural world, of which they were once a part, became hostile. Wild plants became weeds and threatened crops. Insect pests had to be controlled. Wild animals were now predators of the farmed. Creatures with whom human beings once shared a common world, with all its dangers, could become enemies.

And farming made land valuable. Erosion, particularly by goats, meant that the maintenance of land, and the acquisition of more, was ever more imperative. Land could be owned. And ownership of property was a spur to that human instinct of family preservation which requires it to be increased. Family loyalties became tribal rivalries. Those who owned slaves began to extend their advantage of abundant, cheap and controllable labour over neighbouring tribes who had not acquired this particular working class. Slaves could not only work as agricultural labourers but provided the power to create weapons and build defences. They could build ships, maintain them and crew them. Their masters were still bound to water, to river, marsh and sea, and the desire for new and fertile lands was a constant pressure. So was the need to own more slaves. And the sea was still, as it had ever been, a route to new worlds.

The tape paused: I took off the headphones and listened for warning sounds of Tom. My mother was staying, taking great pleasure in looking after Tom although she did not like Stoke Newington at all. I could just hear their voices, though not the words. It was an ancient intermingling of a grandmother's loving admonition and a child's shrill recalcitrance. So ancient that no doubt it had taken place in just this way thousands of years ago. I thought I would just see what the next bit of tape was about before I joined them in the kitchen.

The old skills of the sea peoples to build and handle boats had not been abandoned. Water, salt or fresh, was at the heart of their technology. But because there is no evidence of boats, because reeds do not survive, boats are rarely included in any assessment of the spread of agriculture. The idea that such early peoples should understand how to negotiate rivers, estuaries, coastal waters – let alone open sea – is barely considered. Yet just look at the map. The pattern of the spread of agriculture is inescapable. Once you see how wave, wind and current are woven into that pattern, particularly at a time when the increasingly mild climate was causing a rise in sea levels, it becomes clear.

And remember - we aren't talking about years, or hundreds of years, but thousands. A thousand years ago in Britain we were in the Dark Ages. This is eight, nine – even ten thousand years ago. We are talking about a slow and gradual extension of farming methods, of a culture of agriculture and slavery, that was to spread across much of the world. But it took time. The boats of these seaborne farmers were unwieldy craft, seaworthy but not easy to steer and almost entirely subject to winds and currents. They had to make reasonably frequent landfalls for water, although no doubt the methods they employed for the collection of rainwater were as technologically adept as those they used to irrigate on land. The sea was still in some ways home to them, but now it had become primarily a way of extending lands, of finding new wealth. And remember – many of the coastal, estuarine and island areas of the world had long ago been colonised by the original diaspora from the Island. It had begun not just thousands of years ago, but over two hundred thousand years in the distant past, a gradual and continuing process of human movement across the globe. The lands discovered by the new farming tribes were not empty.

From the eastern Mediterranean and southern Iraq it was not difficult to sail to the Nile delta or east to where the river Indus joined the Arabian Sea. In both areas there is evidence of agricultural settlement. All round the Mediterranean were the estuaries of rivers which became the conduits for farming based on wheat and barley to spread throughout southern Europe and north Africa. Northwards, along the Rhone, they reached the Black Sea, then travelled further north up the Danube to the colder climates of the British Isles and Scandinavia.

Eastward from the Indus valley these practical people entered the tropics, too hot and wet for the now established cereal crops. They could either move on or adapt to local systems of hunting and gathering. And they employed their traditional expertise as plant hybridists to breed new cultivars of wild plants. In the hot, wet climate of the tropics, new kinds of rice were created from the wild forms. The first known example of such a cultivar is millet, yielding many times the weight of seed per plant than its wild progenitor. In northern China, many sites of settlement indicating the cultivation of millets and domestication of animals have been found. The sites of agricultural settlement can be traced on the map, although evidence of those on the plains of the Yangtze and the Yellow River has been erased by floods following massive deforestation. The Yellow River has long been called 'the ungovernable' because it has changed course several times since 600 BC.

Westward, the seaborne farmers could move out into the open Atlantic. Carried to the Canary Islands, they found themselves unable to rebuild their boats because there were no reeds, nor the flint and obsidian – sharp volcanic glass – required for making tools. When the Spanish arrived in the fifteenth century they found a complete Neolithic culture, as if frozen in time. The people were cultivating wheat, barley, beans and figs, their livestock included sheep, goats and pigs, and they made pottery – but they were isolated from the outside world, even from their immediate neighbours on other islands in the group, by their inability to build boats

Sailing ships which got as far as the Canaries risked being swept south and west into the open Atlantic by the Canary Current and the North East Trade winds. If they made it to a landfall, it would probably be in the Caribbean. The voyagers may have been killed or absorbed into that society. Some may have taken the winds into the south-west corner of the Gulf of Mexico, where they might not have encountered people but rather more dangerous enemies in the form of mosquitoes and other luxuriant creatures of the shores of rain forest and mangrove swamp. And some, in the end, might have found shelter in the great lagoons along that coast of southern Mexico, moving inland from the hot and hostile marsh and forest to the fresher air of the foothills beyond. It was in this part of central America that the Olmecs, creators of the earliest Mexican civilisation, were to flourish in about 1200 BC.

Traditional cereals would not have flourished there any more than in the valleys of the Ganges or the Mekong. But there was wild maize. Maize cultivation in this part of America goes back at least seven thousand years. Once again, it seems, the farming sea people used their skills in plant breeding. Maize became the staple of all subsequent American civilisations. But there's something else, too, that links the old world from whence they came to this new world of America.

I could hear in Mr Brouard's voice that note of speculative excitement which I had come to recognise as heralding some idiosyncratic point he felt might be disputed, but was nevertheless as important as a tiny detail of forensic evidence in a trial.

If we assume that people did make the voyage from the Near East, via the Mediterranean and the Canaries or the Gulf, then there are some anomalies which can be addressed rather than glossed over – as they so often are. Take the bottle gourd, for instance. It was dried and used as a container all over the Near East from the Gulf to northern Africa. It isn't native to America but it has been found to have existed there in all the ancient American cultures.

And then there's cotton. Wild cotton, Gossypium, is found all over the world. But the curious thing is that the cultivated American species is a hybrid. Genetically, the wild species in the New World are quite different from those of the Old World. It is impossible to spin wild cotton. The fibres have to be teased out of the seedhead, the fluffy cotton boll, to create fibres long enough to spin into thread, and in wild cotton the fibres – the lint – is too short. The cotton had to be bred and improved to form a long lint. Which is what they did in the Near East. And once the thread was formed it could be woven into cloth on a loom, just like wool or flax. Penelope – Odysseus's wife – worked on her loom, you remember, while she waited for him to return, unpicking her work every night to spin out the time and frustrate her waiting suitors. They were spinning cotton and weaving cotton cloth thousands of years ago. But the curious thing was that long before the Indians of Mexico and Peru, long before the Incas, they were also weaving cotton. Now, explain this: they could not have cultivated the wild American cotton, with its short lint, because it simply does not have the right chromosomes to enable it to be improved. They had to produce a man-made hybrid with a long lint. So how did they do it?

"Well, you tell me," I said out loud.

What seems to be the generally accepted explanation is that Old World cotton seeds floated across the Atlantic to South America.

There they germinated and grew on the east coast, somehow hybridising with a New World cotton, the result of this cross then being capable of improvement to produce a long lint.

At this point I telephoned him in Boury.

"I'm getting confused. Surely it is possible that it happened like that. I mean, seeds do get blown for miles. They could have germinated on a bit of weed in the Sargasso or an old log or something."

"It's possible," he said; "but then, consider this. Once you've bred your long linted cotton – and I may say the fine cottons produced by the early American Indians were extremely beautiful – you have to spin it and then weave it on a loom. Well, so they did. But they used a ceramic spindle whorl identical to that of the Near and Middle East – and a loom no different from Penelope's. Even the clothes made from the resulting cotton cloth have been described as almost identical to those worn around the Mediterranean and Egypt. I find it difficult to believe that the Indians of the New World not only spotted the importance of a new kind of cotton, but then bred it to produce a long lint, made a ceramic spindle, and wove cloth on a loom just like those already existing thousands of miles across the Atlantic. I'd rather go for the unacceptable explanation. That the cotton, and the knowledge of what to do with it, was brought by people. People from the Old World. By boat."

"Yes, but look – isn't it true that they never invented the wheel in America? Wouldn't that have been the first thing these Indian people would have adopted?"

I could hear him smiling. "Well," he said cheerfully, "for a start, they may not have invented the wheel, but they undoubtedly had wheels. Quite a lot of charming little pottery dogs were found when archaeologists started excavating Olmec sites I Mexico. They're rather like the wooden ones small children used to play with. They stand on two wheeled axles. They're similar to others found in ancient burial sites in the Near East and around the Mediterranean. I don't know why the wheel didn't become established – maybe because a moist jungle environment wasn't suitable for it, or because they didn't have horses or donkeys.

"The point is, technological development doesn't just happen. A new invention is not something a human being can simply dream up and create out of the air. Certainly it can be triggered by a leap of imagination, a sideways look, a sudden vision: but they are all built upon something that existed before. It may not even be tangible, although almost all inventions do emerge from a sequence of improvements on an original idea which itself sprang from something practical. The inventor may use an *intangible* analogy for his inspiration, but it is always based upon a real object.

" Everything we think has a basis in reality. Whoever invented the wheel probably saw a log roll down a slope. Empirical experiment, the testing of a hypothesis which is itself deduced from a practical manifestation, is the foundation of technology. But that is not all. The essence of technological development is that an invention must be capable of reproduction. Then, through the process of reproduction, comes refinement, adjustment, adaptation, perhaps rejection. Yet from that process comes the next leap of imagination. It is a continuing process, not an isolated moment of revelation.

"I find it very hard, therefore, to believe in the coincidental rise of agriculture along the coastal areas of the world. I would, rather, believe in the skills and endurance of those early people to survive, together with their cargoes of seeds, artefacts, and their own traditional skills - in a boat."

I said curiously: "Someone asked me the other day – what was your degree? I've never thought about it before. I suppose I just thought you knew a lot about everything. I took it for granted when I was ten and no one has ever asked me about it until now."

"Someone less than convinced by my theorising?"

"Mm. You could say that."

"Well, you can tell him I joined the RAF in 1942 instead of going to university, and then took two external degrees after the war: classics and mechanical engineering.

"Thank you," I said.

I could hear louder voices outside. Al was home.

"I must go," I said.

"Of course. Thank you for telephoning."

"Send me the next tape soon."

"That may be a little while. I have some more work to do. But consider this: not all the sea people of the Island went north along the shores of the Indian Ocean. Some went south towards Antarctica, into the grim gales that wind round that huge land mass. Most did not survive. But those that did were to change the human story yet again. The rigours they endured were to result in the origins of civilisation on the marshes of Mesopotamia. However, as I say, I may not be in touch for a while. In the meantime, there's a book you could read. *Sailing Alone Around the World,* by Joshua Slocum."

Argus Alone

My mother was telling Al, loudly, that it was about time we moved. Stoke Newington was not a good place to bring up children.

"Why not?" enquired Al, with the laid-back insouciance he knew infuriated my mother.

"It's half an hour at least to walk to the nearest park – then there's the traffic, the litter, the disgusting state of the front gardens."

"There are quite a lot of poor people round here," Al said.

"You don't need to be rich to keep a garden tidy," responded my mother crossly. "In fact if a few of these foreigners" (by which she meant Hassidic Jews, Moslems, Hindus, people who lived east of Dulwich and anywhere north of St Paul's) "started a horticultural society, everyone would get on much better, you mark my words."

I pointed out that I had only just finished doing up my study and the garden was beginning to look quite nice, I thought. Anything to keep the peace. My mother had promised to stay for the birth of the baby and I did not want her to go back to Bath just yet.

Penelope was born on Valentine's Day, 1984, and was very nearly called Jayne because I had been watching Torvill and Dean skate to Ravel's Bolero at the Winter Olympics about six hours earlier. Al wanted Margaret, which was his mother's name, but I persuaded him that Odysseus's wife was a good role model – beautiful, faithful and clever.

She was a delightful baby, even nicer than Tom, probably because I knew what I was doing this time, and Tom seemed to tolerate her quite well. But it was much harder work with two than with one and I secretly began to agree with my mother about the time it took to walk to the park and the general effort of getting about. I often thought about Yolande walking her children up the lane to the village school.

"We have to think about schools," I said to Al.

"Why?" he answered, surprised. "They'll just go to the school down the road, won't they?"

"Have you seen inside it? Or outside, come to that?"

He hadn't, of course.

Then one evening when Tom was four and Penny was two, Al came home and said he had been offered a research group in applied optics at Bristol University. I suddenly had to think not just about moving, but moving out of London. Al was due to take up the post in the January of the following year and it was already nearly the end of the summer. I had been doing very little work while I tried to finish my novel, which had become increasingly difficult as the children's lives became more sociable, mobile and demanding. My mother had given me a subscription to *Good Housekeeping* and I read about women who juggled careers as management consultants or interior designers with quantities of small children and exquisitely decorated houses. A friend of mine who was a successful journalist took me out to lunch one day to ask my advice about whether or not she should fit children into her future career pattern.

"Easily," I said. "Just make sure you get a good nanny." It had taken me most of the morning to arrange for Penny to go to one friend and for Tom to be collected by another, which would of course mean that I would have to return the favour.

"Why don't you, then?" she asked in surprise.

"Can't afford it, and we haven't the space," I pointed out.

"Oh. Well, of course I'd have to have one."

"Of course."

She went on to have four children, two nannies, and edit a London evening newspaper.

At least in Bristol I would be closer to my parents. We drove down on a fine September day and explored leafy suburbs, Georgian terraces and Victorian villas. I got lists of schools from the local education authority. Al talked to future colleagues. We put our house on the market and discovered that although prices in our bit of Stoke Newington had not risen like those in other parts of London, we could still make a reasonable profit. We bought a small Victorian semi on the corner of a road in Clifton, close to the Downs, within walking distance – just - of the university and a good primary school. There was an apple tree in the back garden.

We moved just before Christmas, which we decided to spend on our own among the packing cases. For me it meant a kind of new beginning. Al had chosen the house in Stoke Newington, but this was a joint choice, as much mine as his. Bristol was a good city to live in, especially so close to the generous green Downs with their secret grassy hollows, views across the Avon Gorge, daisies to pick and trim turf to run on.

"We could get a dog," I said to Al one day.

He would have preferred a cat but I found a whippet puppy which I said would be as good as, being quiet and fastidious.

"It's certainly not a proper dog," Al observed, when he first saw Whim, who was the colour of gunmetal and satin smooth to touch.

Once, on a visit to London that spring, I went past our old house. There was even more litter in the street than I remembered and the new owners had concreted the tiny front garden to make a parking space for a battered Ford Granada. The house looked forlorn. At home the cherry blossom was out in our road, the pink Clifton stone caught the evening sun and there were bluebells under the trees on the Downs.

It all meant that I rarely thought of Mr Brouard and only occasionally missed the tapes. He sent cards for the children's birthdays, however, signing them with his old signature which had always been indecipherable - sometimes, thinking back, I wondered if he had been dyslexic, even before his loss of sight. Dyslexia was becoming better known and when Tom got fed up with me trying to teach him to read, it was the first thing I thought of.

"Don't be silly," said Al impatiently. "It's called boredom."

In September I finished my novel at last and Tom started school. I telephoned Boury a couple of times. Once Mr Brouard was out and the second time he was apparently on holiday with Molly.

"She's taken him on a cruise," Freddie said. "All round the eastern Med – Istanbul, Constantinople, Greece. He wanted to see something called the Antikythera mechanism. At least I think that was it. In Athens."

I felt a sudden, unexpected, foolish pang of jealousy.

The Antikythera mechanism? What was that?

As instructed, I had read Joshua Slocum's *Sailing Alone Around The World.* Joshua Slocum was a New England sea captain who in 1895, at the age of 51, sailed single-handed round the world in a sloop called Spray. It took him three years. I had not really expected to enjoy his book, but I did, not just because Slocum could write with vivid directness but because he turned out to be such a modest and engaging narrator with a nice sense of humour.

Al read it too, and despite his dismissiveness about Mr Brouard's ideas he found himself liking this New England sailor as much as I did.

"It's the way he gets on and turns his hand to anything – I mean, he more or less built Spray himself from an old derelict hull, even cutting down his own oak tree for timber. He didn't even have a chronometer, but he could more or less calculate his position at sea just by using a sextant, the stars and a tin clock. I don't think I'd have believed it if he hadn't explained it so precisely."

"Well, you see, it is possible to sail the oceans in a small boat," I said, glad of this partial endorsement of Mr Brouard's judgement.

"As I understand it, Slocum was the first man to sail single-handed round the world."

"The first known man to do it. And he wrote a book about it. Lots of people might have done it before."

"He was also an experienced sea captain."

"Well, so might they have been."

He gave me one of his heavily ironic looks and suggested I ask Mr Brouard why he had suggested I read Slocum's book.

"I've tried to," I said, gathering up Lego. The children were in bed and I was going through my nightly ritual of restoring the sitting room to some kind of order. "Jean-Claude says he's away again. With his daughter."

"Perhaps he's got over his obsession."

I rescued a My Little Pony from under an armchair. "It's not an obsession."

"What would you call it?"

"Well – what about you and gravitational waves? Which may not even exist? Why is it all right to be obsessed with something if you're paid for being obsessed with it and not if you're not?"

"I'm not saying there's anything wrong with having an obsession. I'm just a little sceptical of your Mr Brouard's obsession with the origins of human beings. Especially as you're a bit obsessed about it too."

It was true that I was missing the tapes. My novel – which I had called *Joe's Walk* – had been turned down by the publisher of my first novel, and I was doing very little journalism. Not that I had much time for writing. Domesticity and children took up far more than I had ever imagined. I had always felt, and still felt, as if I was not quite part of this world of children and coffee mornings and discussions about asthma or not enough homework. I missed the gossip and camaraderie of London friends and colleagues, although many of them were similarly situated these days. I felt guilty about enjoying such idle pleasures as taking the children to the zoo or ambling along the summery roads with Penny and Whim to collect Tom from school. I did not make friends easily, never having been gregarious by nature. Fortunately Whim and I enjoyed each other's company. Al was engrossed in his work and I was absorbed at home. I was, I think, happy.

At the end of that year my agent found a small publisher willing to have a go with *Joe's Walk*. I was absurdly excited. I wrote to Mr Brouard to tell him. When I received only a Christmas card with his congratulations in return, I felt curiously crestfallen. Then, in the February of 1987, a colleague of Al's offered us the use of an old camper van for our annual holiday. I suggested we could go to Normandy and then call on the Melchiors – and Mr Brouard – in Boury-en-Vexin. Al was agreeable and we planned a week during Tom's half-term in June. My parents promised to look after Whim. I sent Mr Brouard a tape, giving him the dates and asking if it would be convenient to visit then.

Tom and Penny thought the camper van was magic, even though Penny was always sick if we set off too soon after breakfast. She was all right as long as she had her Sick Box – an old ice cream container – and they both thrived on French sticks and salami and frites. We ate vast amounts of mussels and bought ropes of garlic for sale along the roadsides. We fell in love with Honfleur and Trouville and and finally went inland towards Rouen. We visited Giverny, which was now crowded with tourists, before going on to Boury.

The house looked the same behind its high iron gates, creamy and grey stone, shuttered in the sunlight. A faded old golden retriever lay on the wide stone steps beyond the gravelled forecourt. As we hesitated at the gates, he lifted his head, as if aware of our presence there.

"Nuke," I said softly.

He seemed to look at us for a moment, ascertaining who we might be, and then dropped his head again between his shaggy paws, as if yet again his hopes had been dashed, and he was resigned to waiting there. I had a sudden memory of Odysseus returning to his palace, and finding his old dog Argus lying on the dung heaps outside the gate. "*But directly he became aware of Odysseus's presence, he wagged his tail and dropped his ears...*"

"He's not here," I said. I had not seen Trepidation for a while but now he hovered beside me.

"What do you mean?" Al said in surprise. "Look, ring the bell – "

"I just know he's not."

Al jangled the bell-pull in exasperation.

Jean-Claude did not look much older, his moustache still silky brown, his eyes gentle.

"It is true," he said. "He left a month ago. He has gone to live with his daughter in England."

"But he would have told me – "

"He has left you a tape. He felt he was imposing upon you, that with your husband and now the two little ones – "

"The fact is," said Freddie, as we sat in the garden and watched Tom and Penny playing with assorted other infants – grandchildren and cousins – "Molly didn't want him to contact you. She was always worried about his – his obsession – and he hadn't been awfully well, it's true. But I said she should contact you."

"Well, she didn't. But he – why didn't Mr Brouard?"

"I believe," said Jean-Claude carefully, "that he was assured that she had spoken to you, and that you had asked her to tell him you would really rather not keep up your old association, that your husband was not happy with it. Your life was very full with your work and les deux enfants – "

"But that's ridiculous – "

"I told you," Freddie said, turning on Jean-Claude. "I said she would never have hurt him like that – "

"But I sent a tape – "

"I suspect," said Jean-Claude, in distress, "that she kept it from him. He had become very dependent on her – "

"She'd made him dependent on her," Freddie said. For a moment we sat in silence: then she added, "he was finding it difficult to work without Roger. You know – no, you will not know, that Molly felt he wasn't – well – that he was trying to undermine her – "

"The cider-maker, you mean?"

"Oui, Roger Laurent," said Jean-Claude. "He would go through all the papers, the books, with William, reading everything to him, making notes – he is a cultured person, you understand, not young, but sympathique, and most – most thorough."

"Didn't you try to do something? To stop her, I mean? You must have known – "

"We did try," said Freddie. "But she – Molly is a very forceful person, and after all she is his daughter – "

"You're his sister."

"I know, although he never did take any notice of me...But we did try. Nevertheless his sight is very bad now, and life wasn't easy for him. She did more and more for him. He went to stay with her in London, they went on holiday together – I think he knew that she was probably as dependent on him as he was on her by then. He's in his sixties, now. But really I think what made him decide to leave Boury was – well, it was you, because he felt it might have been all right to send these tapes to you before you were married and a mother, but now – well, it wasn't suitable."

"Not suitable?"

"Well, it did seem a bit odd to me, as a matter of fact," said Al thoughtfully. "Now don't look at me like that – of course I haven't minded you transcribing all the stuff he sent you, but you do have a life of your own, now, without something like this hanging on from the past. After all, this has gone on since you were a child. And you've got your own writing. They want you to do another book – "

"Anyway," said Freddie quickly, "Molly said she would help him with his work."

"I thought she had some high-powered job in the Foreign Office?" I said.

"Yes, well, she has, but I believe she intends to devote her spare time to her father," said Jean-Claude.

"I don't think she's got a boyfriend," added Freddie.

Penny started to cry, over by the stream. I rose and went across to pick her up, hugging her plump little body. Over her shiny fair head I saw Jean-Claude walk across the grass.

"Is Nuke waiting for him to come back?" I asked him.

"Yes," he said. "He is a very old dog, now."

"No more eating peaches."

"He tries. He can only smell them, though. He is almost blind, too."

"You must give me Mr Brouard's address," I said.

"We promised we would not do that – "

"Promised who?"

"William. He left you a tape instead. He did not want you to contact him."

"I don't believe you. I don't believe him."

"It is true – je suis desolé – "

I looked wildly round at the quiet garden, the gate in the wall to Mr Brouard's part of the house. "You don't understand," I said. "This obsession of his – his ideas – I am a part of them too. He can't just cut me off. I am involved."

For a moment he looked at me with his kind brown eyes. "Listen to the tape," he said at last.

It was very short.

"Cherie – forgive me for not being here when you come to Boury. I thought it better we should not meet this time. For both our sakes. I realised some time ago that not only was I too dependent on you – just knowing you were there, always the same, always as you were even as a little girl – but that I was being unfair to you. Whatever you say, I was imposing on you and your family. And I was also unfair to Molly, for whom I have a special responsibility. You have your husband and children but she has no one, except me, and I can do very little for her these days except be with her, and let her feel she is needed. I wouldn't mind if she found someone else – I wish she would – but although she has her interests, her choral singing and her interest in dolls' houses, these don't seem to bring her many close friends. I don't really know what to say. I shall go on pursuing my ideas, and no doubt I shall continue to put them on tape, but I think we should have a space at least before I send you any more.

"Did you enjoy Joshua Slocum? Would that I could sail away, as he did, when he was old, and disappear for ever."

Uncivil Servant

Mrs Thatcher had won her third election while we were away.

At the Foreign Office they said they could not give me anyone's address but if I sent a letter to Miss Brouard, they would forward it.

She was not in the phone book.

I rang a friend on the Evening Standard and he found there was a Miss M Brouard working in the European Community department, but despite his best efforts over several beers in the Sherlock Holmes pub he could not find anyone who knew where she lived. However he did find someone who thought she sang in the choir at St Asaph's By The Wardrobe, in the City.

One weekend in late August I went to stay with a friend in Kensington. On the Sunday evening I went to evensong at St Asaph's By The Wardrobe.

The little Wren church was down a backwater off Cheapside, quiet and still as any church in the country at that hour on a Sunday.

Level sun was white on its Portland stone.   There were polished pews, sideways on to the aisle, and white-robed choirboys, and incense, which always made my eyes water.   I looked across through the wreathed smoke of it and saw Molly Brouard behind a line of choirboys.   She was absorbed in the music.   She did not see me.   I watched her pale face, the freckles, the red hair like his.   She must have been in her mid thirties by then.   All at once, in the prayers, she glanced up and round the church and saw me.   Our eyes met.   I could not tell what she thought.   There was no emotion in her face. Nor, perhaps, in mine.

I waited in the cooling dusk for her to come out.   When she did she tried to avoid me.

"Molly," I said.

"I'd really rather not talk to you now."

"Please, just let me see him."

"No."

"Why not?   Why on earth not?"

"He doesn't need you any more.   He has me to look after him, to do his work."

"But it's my work too," I said without thinking.

"What do you mean?"

"I just want to know – " For a moment I stared at her.   What did I want?   Then I said: "I only want to know what happens next. That's all.   Truly.   You see – it is my story too."

She said nothing, but stood there in the evening light, her pale eyes on mine.   "I'll ask him," she said at last.

"Thank you," I said.

"He is – all I have left," she said abruptly.

I did not know what to say to her, but I answered "I know.   I'm sorry.   I understand" as if I did.   Then I said: "how is he?   Is he – well?"

"Very well.   His blindness is a little worse, but he keeps very fit, and of course he has all the facilities he needs here in London. And we have each other for company."

"Oh.   Good.   Well – give him my love."

She said nothing, nor did she smile.   She said at last, "goodbye. I hope you enjoyed the service."

"It's a lovely church, but all that incense – not quite my sort of thing, actually."

"No."

She turned and walked away as if that was the natural conclusion of our conversation.   She did not look back.   After a while I walked away too, and hailed a taxi in Cheapside.

The Clock from the Sea

Something in me changed after that. Perhaps it was partly because something in England seemed to change in the last part of that year. A man shot fourteen people dead on a summer afternoon in Hungerford. In October Michael Fish dismissed the suggestion that a hurricane was imminent and a few hours later the worst storm of the twentieth century hit the south-east. Three days later the stock market crashed on Black Monday. In November eleven people died when a bomb exploded in Enniskillen and then thirty people died in the tube fire at King's Cross. You could almost taste the taint of violence in the air. But one becomes accustomed to a taste.

Joe's Walk came out in October, in time for the Christmas trade, and it seemed to appeal to people, particularly as the publisher had commissioned perfect little line drawings to illustrate the rather bleak landscape of the Lea river from Walthamstow to the City of London. Tom was old enough to like it too, and Penny, eager to catch up with him, spent what seemed like hours frowning over its pages and indeed apparently reading some of the words. Tom's primary school had opened a nursery class and she was one of the first in. I acquired a renewed sense of identity: I was asked to judge a children's writing competition.

Yet I was aware of a strange sense of hurt, like a wound somewhere inside me, not really painful, but which did not heal, as if I had lost some part of myself. Sometimes I opened the old Hong Kong wicker basket in which, among other things, I kept my copies of the transcripts of Mr Brouard's tapes. As time went on, less and less often.

Tom and Penny were growing up, becoming more and more interesting, giving me the chance to revisit my own childhood. I read books like *Treasure Island* and *Lassie-Come-Home* to them every day over tea, even at one stage tried to make them learn a poem a week (later, when Terry Waite told how he had drawn on such resources of memory when he was imprisoned in the dark in Beirut, they understood why). Every afternoon during the term Whim and I met them at the school gate and we went for a walk on the Downs, sometimes visiting the strange Victorian camera obscura that stood above Brunel's suspension bridge, never tired of its dim moving image of the world outside. Most holidays were spent with John and Yolande in Cornwall, but once we went to France again, and occasionally to stay with Al's parents in Northumberland.

One May we had a fortnight in Lindos on Rhodes. We had an apartment with a roof terrace and we lived mostly on bread, honey, melons, water and wine. In the evenings Al and Tom played chess under the lamplit trees at a nearby restaurant and during the day we often walked to St Paul's Bay with its little white chapel, white sand, shoals of fish and sea as salt and supportive as blue glass. Above it Lindos's own acropolis was etched against the hot blue sky. We went to Rhodes town on a bus that stopped at every village and went through dry river beds full of pink oleanders. Once we hired a jeep and went up into the mountains and across the island to a place called Monolithos. Ancient voices murmured like the crickets in the sun. And one day we took a boat to an island called Symi, where the deserted yellow and ochre and pink villas of sponge divers climbed the hillsides and the sea lapped the front stone steps of houses along the tree-shaded shores. Water and land seemed like one. We sat on the one with our feet in the other and watched an old woman in a headscarf hanging out washing on a line strung between two pine trees, with the idle turquoise waves beneath.

We found a café where we ate fried squid and chips and drank white wine, and Tom knocked a glass of orange juice over the man sitting at the next table. I mopped up with mineral water and Al's handkerchief but the little man was very kind and said it was an accident, please don't worry, in excellent English. I looked at him, then: he was dressed rather formally in a light suit and an open-necked blue shirt, wearing a slightly grubby white Panama hat. His eyes were pale and bright, his nose very short and snub, giving him an irresistibly impish look, as one might imagine Mole in *The Wind in the Willows*. And he was actually English. His name was Roger Milward and he was contributing to a travel book for Reader's Digest – "one of those beautifully illustrated and, I have to say, excellently researched books which look so good on coffee tables." And one of the objects of his excellent research was the Antikythera mechanism, which Freddie, long ago, had told me that Mr Brouard had wanted to see in Athens.

"Well," said Roger obligingly, "it is indeed a very extraordinary device. So extraordinary that a great many people believed it was some kind of hoax, or at best a mistake. It was found by the sponge divers of Symi in 1900, on the wreck of a ship which went down some time around 80 BC. By all accounts the ship was full of treasure – bronze statues, marbles, jewellery, wine, and all kinds of objects much affected by the centuries of sea water and marine animals. Among them was what looked like some kind of bronze gearing in four large pieces and a number of smaller fragments. At first they thought it was an astrolabe, a sort of navigational instrument, perhaps dating from the sixth century AD.

"And then, in 1951, a British physicist got involved," added Roger, enjoying his dissertation.

"Al, listen," I said, nudging him. "A British physicist."

"I know, I heard," he said. "What was his name?"

"Derek De Solla Price," said Roger Milward cheerfully.

"Never heard of him."

"You must have," I said.

"Not necessarily. Go on, then, Mr – What did this chap do?"

"Well, he analysed the mechanism. He published his conclusions in 1959. He said it was some form of intricate clock mechanism, contemporary with the ship – in other words, well over two thousand years old. It was thought so ridiculous that someone suggested some mediaeval sailor had dropped it overboard, coincidentally into the wreck."

"Possible, I suppose," said Al.

"Hardly," said the imp, with a touch of steel. "Besides, you might recall that Cicero wrote that a Greek friend of his had a globe which in its revolutions 'shows the movements of the sun, stars and planets, by day and night, just as they appear in the sky'. Perhaps you might not," he added, regarding Al thoughtfully. "Anyway, Price was not discouraged. In the 1970s he persuaded the Greek Atomic Energy Comission to let him shoot gamma rays into the clumps of corroded bronze, and thus was able to produce photographic plates that allowed him not only to reconstruct the device, but to ascertain that it was indeed constructed during the first century BC."

"Interesting," said Al.

"Well – what exactly was it?" I asked

"Now, I am not a scientist," said Roger. "But Mr Price is very clear about it. It is an arrangement of – now, wait a minute, I have my notes – ah, yes, here. 'An arrangement of calibrated differential gears inscribed and configured to produce solar and lunar positions in synchronization with the calendar year...with it one could predict the movement of heavenly bodies. It is believed, of course, that Rhodes itself was a centre for astronomical thought. We know very little about ancient celestial navigation, but we do know it existed, and it is worth noting that he man who invented trigonometry and first scientifically catalogued the stars' positions was Hipparchus of Rhodes. People do not like to admit that the impossible may exist, so there are those who still try to dismiss the Antikythera mechanism – it does not fit into their scheme of things – but to me it is quite manifestly true that the people of the ancient world did not simply think and feel as we do, but that their grasp of science and technology was equally akin to ours. And, indeed, a great deal better than most of us."

We sat there as the water lapped the quayside in Symi, and the sun glittered, and Penny was sick, and I thought of the man who might have made the Antikythera mechanism. I looked across at Al, sprawled in the shade with his baseball cap over his eyes, and thought that it was probably someone like him.

Then Roger Milward idly remarked: "I recall Sir Fred Hoyle once describing the ring of post-holes around Stonehenge as a kind of computer for predicting the date of lunar eclipses. Perhaps there is a link?"

"Hardly," said Al lazily. "Hoyle was always coming up with loony ideas."

"But he was at one time a respected Cambridge professor of astronomy and experimental philosophy, I believe?"

"Plenty of loonies among that lot. If there was anything in his ideas about Stonehenge, then prehistoric man must have been pretty bright. But what was the point of being able to predict eclipses? Seems like a lot of trouble to go to just to prove how clever you are."

I never saw Roger Milward again, but we exchanged addresses, and thereafter Christmas cards. He lived in a village in Worcestershire and some years later wrote a successful play about P. G. Wodehouse.

28

Scots and Stars

At home, family life and work absorbed me. I started another book, and managed to do some feature writing. Al was enjoying his work. Bristol was flourishing and the only slightly dark times in our lives were when Tom was found to be short-sighted, and had to wear glasses; Penny got pneumonia, although she suffered no lasting effects; and Al's mother had a stroke.

Nevertheless I could not quite let go of the story – Mr Brouard's story. I found myself noting every newspaper report of discoveries in palaeontology or archaeology. I read everything from Darwin and Alfred Wallace to the latest books on such subjects as finches in the Galapagos or aboriginal art in south Australia. When Al installed the internet on his computer I was one of the first to start surfing. There was always another new headline – "ape-man: origin of sophistication"; "fossil find may be missing link"; "DNA mitochondria proves our ancestry." Nothing really seemed to *prove* anything. Nothing, indeed, in the continuing saga of human evolution seemed to have changed very much since Darwin. We were all still climbing the ladder of life, progressing to perfection. In the meantime the Berlin Wall fell, tanks in Tiananmen Square squashed a few students, the Gulf War broke out, children starved in Africa and another rain forest was turned into garden furniture.

Sometimes I met people who shared something of my curiosity. I was not a very sociable person and not good at dinner parties, where I found it difficult to think of anything interesting to say. Al's friends and colleagues were all obsessional, but not about the origins of man – more, it seemed to me sometimes, about house prices. My friends were mostly the mothers of Tom and Penny's school friends, together with assorted fathers, so I knew we would simply recycle what we had talked about a dozen times before.

But then there was the lady who was doing research at an institute of molecular medicine and thought it was quite possible that redheaded Scots were descended from Neanderthals. She had been working on a particular gene called the melanocortin 1 receptor. "MC1R", she added helpfully as we demolished Rick Stein's fish pie. "The ginger version."

"The ginger version?"

"Yes – that is to say, the gene which causes red hair. It appears that it is older than the first settlers who came to Europe from Africa about thirty thousand years ago – actually at least seventy thousand years before *Homo sapiens* migrated into Europe. So this gene could be as old as a hundred thousand years. If you consider that ten per cent of Scots are redheads and another forty per cent with different hair colouring carry the same gene it seems to me quite logical to believe that many of today's human beings are descended from unions between the two species, Neanderthal and *Homo sapiens.*"

"You don't think they could actually be the same species – just different races?"

She stared at me. "What an extraordinary suggestion."

"Well - I mean, you're assuming that *Homo sapiens* came to Europe from Africa, for a start: and that they only arrived about thirty thousand years ago, after the Neanderthal people. What about Swanscombe Woman?"

"Oh – well, there are some odd fossil idiosyncrasies...The point is, the MC1R gene could not have originated in Africa, because its carriers are five times more sensitive to ultraviolet light, and therefore much more likely to contract skin cancer. It couldn't have survived the pressure of natural selection."

"But what if the people who interbred with the Neanderthals didn't come from Africa?"

She gulped her Chardonnay and turned thankfully to her neighbour, who was not mad.

I sent a bitter silent message to Mr Brouard.

At a school barbecue, I sat under a tree with a paper plate of sausages and baked potatoes and shared a bottle of red wine with a fellow of the Royal Geographical Society who was planning a study of the Mascarene plateau.

"You don't mean the Mascarene plateau in the Indian Ocean? The Mascarene plateau that was once an island?"

"Yes, that's right. Well, it was perhaps once an island. More recently, an archipelago. Fascinating place. We know it was once dry land, anyway, supporting plants and animals. Possibly even humans. It's extraordinarily rich in species of fish, gastropods, coral and amphipods – we hope to find the source for the nutrients that must feed this area."

"You really think there might have been humans there?"

"It's possible. You could say we are looking for a vanished world. A drowned testament to a vanished world."

"When will you start work?"

"Oh, this year. We'll probably report in about three years' time. I'll send you some information, if you like. Pity you can't come and join us."

"I wish," I said.

He was a young man, much younger than me, and he had nice eyes and a curvy mouth.

"Look," he said. "You should come to one of the lectures at the Royal Geographical Society. Let me have your address – I'll send you an invitation when something comes up about the Mascarene Plateau."

"Thank you," I said.

One day, visiting my friend Nicky in Kensington, I bumped into Geraint. I was taking Whim for a walk in Hyde Park before catching the train home from Paddington when someone behind me called my name.

"Hello," he said.

He looked exactly the same, tall, wearing his Murmansk greatcoat to ward off the April breeze (he was always in the first or last stages of flu). His nose was perhaps a little beakier, his red hair wispier, but his eyes were still bright pale blue.

"What is this?" he asked, stooping down to stroke Whim.

I told him her name and she flirted demurely with him, letting him stroke her ears. Her coat was still like grey satin although paler now on her muzzle.

"Very pretty," he said.

We went to Joe Allen's in Covent Garden for lunch and hid Whim under his coat.

His series of cave paintings had been very successful. They had been widely reproduced as cards and posters and he had made a considerable amount of money. Since then he had had several exhibitions and become increasingly established: he had won the Jerwood prize for painting and had been given some major commissions. Among several projects was a television series on the history of art. He was contributing to the first part: Art in Prehistory.

"The more you find out about it, the more fascinating it becomes," he said over his Tuscan bean salad. "It goes back further than I thought. And then there's the odd bits of research it throws up. There's a chap called Michael Rappenglueck who says you can identify maps of the night skies in cave paintings. For instance, there's a part of the Lascaux caves called the Shaft of the Dead Man, with drawings of a bull, a bird and strange creature that appears to be half-bird, half man. He reckons they actually mark the three stars we call the Summer Triangle – Vega, Deneb and Altair."

"What do you mean? How could they be a map of the night sky?"

"Well – " he took out a biro and his note book – "here, you

see, the bull, the man-bird, and the bird. Their eyes exactly represent this triangle of stars. Rappenglueck says that about seventeen thousand years ago, give or take a thousand, when the drawing was made, this part of the sky would have been permanently above the horizon."

"Seems to me Mr Rappenglueck has a lot of imagination."

"Ah, yes, but that's just one of his examples. There's another one – a painting of a great bull, with a map of the Pleiades just over its right shoulder, and other stars within the body of the bull, forming part of the constellation of Taurus."

"Really."

He was irritated by my scepticism. "Look, Rappenglueck is pretty sure about this. There's another one – a cave called Cueva de El Castillo in Spain – like the Altamira paintings – which shows a curved pattern of dots. He says it's quite obviously a drawing of the constellation called the Northern Crown. Quite extraordinary."

"Well – "

"No, look, you don't understand. What Rappenglueck is simply saying is that we are always underestimating our ancestors. We think of them as primitive people, although it's interesting how 'primitive' has been our response today to Hale-Bopp up there in the night sky... We can't acknowledge that they might have been capable of such sophistication that they could observe and reproduce maps of the night sky, even use them for some purpose we cannot yet understand. If we ever really acknowledged that, let alone examine how far we have really advanced from Chaucer's prose or Rembrandt's technique – well, then we would have to examine the question of whether we are really advancing at all. Your old fellow, Mr Brouard – didn't he think alone those lines? That we were deceiving ourselves if we thought we were really progressing up the ladder of evolution – that it wasn't as simple as that?"

"Well, yes, he did – does, I suppose."

"What's he doing now? Still sending you tapes of his great epic? Or has he finished it?"

"No. Well, no, he's not sending me tapes. I don't know if he's finished it or not. Sometimes I think he'll never actually finish it, because there are always new things to discover, there is always another piece of knowledge... Besides, it's about us, about who we are. So there isn't really an end. But I haven't been in touch with him for a long time."

"Oh? Why not?"

"He went to live with his daughter. Somewhere here in London, but I don't know where. She – and he, I suppose – decided he should stop sending me tapes. He felt he was imposing on me, especially now I'm married with children. And she – well, I think she wanted to take over the role. So that was it. I'm still interested in the subject, but I don't know what the next chapter was going to be. Or whether he's reached the last one. I just don't know."

He stared at me for a moment. "I'm sorry," he said at last. "You were fond of the old boy, weren't you?"

"Well, yes, I was. I mean, there wasn't anything – it was just – it was something that was a part of me. I miss it. I miss him." I shrugged. "But there we are. Life goes on. I'm very lucky."

At Paddington he said, without looking at me: "we could of course go back to my flat, if you like. I mean, for old times' sake."

"Thank you," I said in amusement. Images of Tom and Penny, like a threatening Greek chorus, rose up in my mind. "But I think it would spoil things, really."

"I suppose so," he said, without a trace of disappointment.

Are we so middle-aged, I thought on the train, that the pleasure is in the invitation and not the action?

The invitation to a lecture at the Royal Geographical Society as a guest of Mike Ridpath, the Fellow I had met at the school barbecue, arrived a month or so later. The subject of the lecture was 'The Future of Antarctica'. I wondered quite what its relevance might be to the Mascarene Plateau but I accepted.

"You don't mind, do you?" I asked Al. "Can you cope with the children?"

"Yes, sure," he said. "It'll do you good." Classic words, I thought. I felt like Celia Johnson.

I did not immediately recognise Mike Ridpath as I waited outside the Albert Hall in the evening sun. I rather wished I was going to a Prom instead. For some reason old Trepidation was there again. Then the man in the blue sweater and cords came over and said hello and I realised I was committed to the Antarctic.

"There isn't going to be anything on the Mascarene Plateau in the foreseeable future," he explained as we walked round to the sunlit red brick of the Royal Geographical Society in Exhibition Road. "But I'm afraid another of my enthusiasms is the Antarctic – so I thought perhaps you'd enjoy this one. It's being given by a member of the British Antarctic Survey. Should be interesting."

I had a sudden memory of Mr Brouard's last words to me, on the telephone from Boury – the last time I had spoken to him directly.

"But consider this: not all the sea people of the Island went north along the shores of the Indian Ocean. Some went south towards Antarctica, into the grim gales that wind round that huge land mass. Most did not survive. But those that did were to change the human story yet again."

We had a drink before the lecture, and I asked Mike about Antarctica.

"Well," he said, "yes, it is big – about fifty-eight times the size of the UK. The highest, coldest, windiest continent in the world. Its ice cap contains almost seventy per cent of the world's fresh water and ninety per cent of the ice. It affects the whole fabric of the Earth: in its ice sheet is a record of the last half a million years. And another thing: it links the Atlantic, Pacific and Indian oceans. Despite its icy temperatures it is biologically rich. And it wasn't discovered until the eighteenth century."

"Discovered by Europeans, you mean. By us."

Surprised at my interruption, he said: "well, yes, I suppose I do mean that. But I hardly think anyone else got there first."

The Royal Geographical Society lecture hall is a beautiful space. There must have been several hundred people taking their seats in a buzz of excitement and Fellowship. And then, about three rows in front of me, I saw Mr Brouard.

29

Don't Tell Molly

The seat next to him was empty.

"Um – would you mind – I've just seen someone I know – " I said to Mike Ridpath, darting away to scramble past people in Mr Brouard's row.

He looked older: his hair was grey, thinner, his beard more silvery, still trimmed. He was wearing a tweed jacket with a blue shirt and tie, neater than I remembered. But he had lost weight. He looked as if he had been tidied up. Diminished, in some way.

"Hello," I said, and touched his arm.

"Hello," he said. And then: "I'm sorry – I can't quite see – who is that?"

His eyes were still blue, but narrowed as he looked at me.

"It's me," I said foolishly.

For a moment he did not speak. Then he reached out and touched my face. "It is you. What are you doing here – where – "

"I'm here for the lecture on Antarctica," I said.

"But why? Why here – why this lecture?"

"I was invited. And I'm interested – "

"In Antarctica?"

"Well, yes – " It seemed to me that it was as if no time had passed at all, that at any moment we would be into some new discussion of his latest ideas. I had a resistible desire to take the empty seat next to him and listen. But time was running out. I said abruptly: "we ought to meet. To catch up."

"But I thought – you decided to end our association."

"Me? You did."

"No, I was under the impression – "

"Did Molly tell you I wanted to end it?"

"Yes, but it was perfectly understandable, I was disappointed, but of course I understood – "

"It wasn't true. I never wanted to end it. Look – give me your address. Please. Then I can get in touch. Wait a minute – I've got a pen – "

I wrote down my address and telephone number and gave it to him, then said: "now yours. Please – "

But I knew she was behind me even before she touched my shoulder and said coolly, "what a surprise. I think it's just about to start, Daddy."

"What about a drink afterwards?" I said cheerfully.

She looked at me over her large bosom. Her face was a freckled mask. "I don't think so."

There was applause. She suddenly said fiercely: "please – go and sit down."

But I knew that he had folded the piece of paper and put it in the inside pocket of his jacket.

I was not really surprised when he telephoned two days later. His voice was the same: the rich tone, the precise diction.

"Let us be clear," he said. "You did not want me to cease sending you tapes – you were happy to remain part of the project?"

"Absolutely."

"I see. But you didn't pursue it?"

"I pursued it. As far as I could. Which wasn't far, because I didn't know what to look for. But I didn't pursue you because I couldn't – no one would give me your address."

"Molly has been very – protective."

"Do you need protecting?"

"No. But I thought you did – from me."

"I think you need to talk to Molly."

"I think so too," he said judiciously. "But tell me - how things go with you?"

I told him about us, about Al's work, Tom and Penny both teenagers now and handling life like teenagers do. I had finished my book, a follow-up to *Joe's Walk* called *Joe Comes Home,* which had done quite well. I had done quite a lot of journalism since then and had begun a new novel. My parents remained in good health and I had become a parent governor at the children's school.

He said he was well enough, that he still retained a tiny area of sight – all the difference, he said, between staying in touch with the world and the totality of darkness.

"I have been told," he said, "that the fear of total blindness is worse than the reality, but I prefer not to test the hypothesis. At least there is still music. And here in London I have all the music I could want."

He gave me his address: he and Molly shared a large flat off the Old Brompton Road, close to the Natural History Museum. He said it had worked well enough, although she was indeed somewhat possessive, and he was anxious that she should have a life beyond her work.

"She has her singing, of course, and she is very involved with her work – she has been moved to the department of trade, and with the new government I suspect she will find things more congenial for her. But I wish she could find a few more friends. No, I suppose I don't mean that. I wish she could find a man. She's not getting any younger. I worry about the future for both of us – I have no intention of becoming a real burden to her. Sometimes I suspect I am a prop, a kind of excuse for not taking the risk of finding a real companion."

"Could you cope without her?"

"Of course."

"Why don't you go back to Boury?"

"Ah. Well, there are difficulties there. Jean-Claude has left

Freddie for a very charming occupational therapist in Le Vesinet."

"Oh," I said, thinking of Jean-Claude's brown eyes.

"But life goes on. Freddie has found consolation, I believe. She and Jean-Claude remain amicable. He retains the house, but she has found a cottage in Boury – she says she would rather stay there but in her own home. And they still share the flat in Paris, partly for Jack and Chloe."

"I'm glad...But look, what about your work? Have you progressed? Have you finished it? The last thing you said to me was about some of the Island people not going north, but south towards Antarctica – and you told me to read Joshua Slocum – "

"Did you like him?"

"Loved him. But why did I have to read him?"

"Because one should. And because he has a particularly modest and authoritative view of navigation."

"Navigation?"

"Yes. But to answer your question: yes, I have progressed, and no, I have not finished. It wasn't easy to do research at first, when I left Boury, and of course we have so much information now that simply discriminating between new work, new ideas, tracing sources, is in itself a longer job. I have, however, continued to put everything on tape. I was at that RGS lecture because Antarctica is currently being very thoroughly studied, and I wanted to hear the latest conclusions. So far, nothing has made me rethink my ideas – only reinforced them."

Whim suddenly rose from the kitchen sofa, making for the door. I could hear voices. The children were home.

"Look – at least let me know what happened to the Islanders who went south."

"Shall we resume, then?"

"Yes. Please. You needn't tell Molly."

"No, perhaps not."

"Agreed, then?"

"Agreed," he said, with the smile in his voice again.

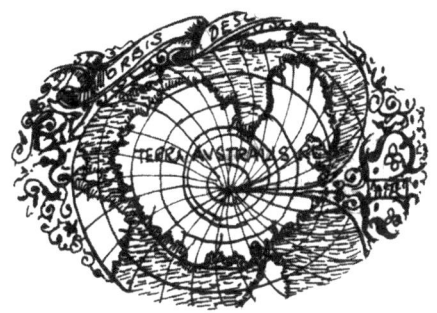

30

Charting the Unknown

Maps are strange things. Some, like the Mappa Mundi in Hereford Cathedral, bear little resemblance to any real world. Others are made to delineate territories, to define boundaries. Then there are those which can tell you where you are going, like road maps or maritime charts. And there are some that might help to tell us where we are coming from.

In 1956 a Turkish naval officer presented a copy of an ancient map to the United States Navy Hydrographic Office. The map was passed to a staff cartographer called Mike Walters, who mentioned it to a friend of his called Captain Arlington H. Mallery. Captain Mallery had combined a distinguished career as a naval engineer with a fascination for archaeology and, in particular, old maps. This one intrigued him. It had been found in the old Imperial Palace in Constantinople in 1929. It was painted on gazelle skin and dated in the Muslim year of 919, which is 1513 in the Christian calendar. It had caused a good deal of interest at the time because it appeared to be one of the earliest maps of America and was possibly linked to a lost map drawn by Columbus. It was signed by Piri Ibn Jaji Memmed, an admiral of the Turkish navy. The word for admiral in Turkish is "reis", and the map became known as Piri Reis.

Captain Mallery noticed something new about the Piri Reis map. It seemed to show part of the Antarctic coast now concealed under the ice. He suggested that somebody, some people, may have mapped this coast when there was no ice there.

Some scientists dismissed the suggestion as fantasy, but in the August of 1956 Mallery joined others in a discussion programme on the radio. The broadcast was printed verbatim and someone drew it to the attention of Charles H. Hapgood, Professor of the History of Science at the University of New Hampshire. Intrigued, he decided to investigate the Piri Reis map.

> "The investigation was undertaken in connection with my classes at the college, and the students from the beginning took a very important part in it. It has been my habit to try to interest them in problems on the frontiers of knowledge, for I believe that unsolved problems provide a better stimulation for the intelligence and imagination than do already-solved problems taken from textbooks. I have also long felt that the amateur has a much more important role in science than is usually recognised. I taught the history of science, and have become aware of the extent to which most radical discoveries (sometimes called 'breakthroughs') have been opposed by the experts in the affected fields. It is a fact, obviously, that every scientist is an amateur to start with. Copernicus, Newton, Darwin were all amateurs when they made their principal discoveries. Through the course of long years of work they became specialists in the fields which they created."

Ancient maps of the world were generally based on the Geographia of Claudius Ptolemy, who lived in Alexandria in the second century AD – then the centre of the scientific world. His work, including tables of latitudes and longitudes and the treatise on geography, was not discovered until the fifteenth century. For mediaeval cartographers the chief value in Ptolemy's maps was the basis they provided for the religious mappa mundi, but when Columbus excited all Europe by his discovery of the New World in 1492 the market in maps exploded. Cartographers struggled to meet the new demand. Old maps, kept because vellum and paper was always too valuable to throw away, were used to cobble together contemporary versions. Among these ancient maps were sea charts called *portolanos*, meaning 'from port to port', which were used by sailors in the Mediterranean and the Black Sea and were thought to have been based on an ancient chart discovered around 1300.

Like the Piri Reis itself, they were patterned with lines like those on a mariner's compass, radiating from centres on the map like spokes on a wheel, sometimes with sixteen spokes, sometimes thirty-two. They were decorated in a similar style to compasses, which first came into use at the time of the *portalanos*.

So the quest began to find the origins of the Piri Reis map. It involved scholars, mathematicians, the United States Air Force, cartographers ancient and contemporary, archaeologists and astronomers. Although Hapgood was the presiding genius of the search, he never shirked a challenge to debate both with his students or dismissive colleagues. The investigation was meticulous and painstaking and it lasted for years.

It was in the Library of Congress, working alone over one Thanksgiving, that Charles Hapgood came across one particular map. It had been drawn in exquisite detail in 1531 by a cartographer called Oronteus Finaeus. It showed the globe as seen from the South Pole and it was, essentially, a map of one great dominant continent: Antarctica. Yet no European was to set eyes on the coast of Antarctica for another two hundred and fifty years.

At first glance the map was uncannily true to the shape and position of Antarctica as we know it, but there were anomalies. The scale was disproportionately large. A circle of latitude, decoratively inscribed Antarctic Circle, was actually the latitude of 80 degrees south, but at some time a copier must have made an error with this figure. When put in its correct place at 66.5 degrees south, the continent became correctly adjusted. It also became clear to Hapgood and his students that the map had been made by sticking together fragments of accurate charts, but in the wrong place.   When adjusted to the correct longitude the match was almost perfect.   Yet still the coastlines did not match those of the most recent map of Antarctica.   The explanation for that was revealed in International Geophysical Year, 1958.

Until an international team surveyed Antarctica in that year, the only practical basis for maps were coastal and air surveys, and the precise line between sea and land was deep under the ice.   Seismic surveying during the International Geophysical Year revealed the exact boundary.   And it changed the previous map of Antarctica.   Not only that: it matched with the Oronteus Finaeus map.   It was Antarctica without the ice, where rivers ran down to the sea.

Yet surely Antarctica had been covered in ice for millions of years? Well, no, it seemed it had not.

In 1929 a United States navy pilot had become the first man to fly across the South Pole. Twenty years later Admiral Byrd gave his name to a number of Antarctic expeditions. On one of them scientists drilled deep into the Ross Sea to take cores from the sea bed. They were hoping to trace the climatic history of the continent. The resulting examples of sediment were examined by a new method of radioactive dating and showed that between twenty-five and six thousand years ago these sediments had been carried down to the sea not by glaciers, but by flowing rivers.   It seemed that for a period of thousands of years the coasts of Antarctica had been free of ice.

Charles Hapgood was persuaded that maps like the Orenteus Finaeus and the Piri Reis were based on much earlier charts of a continent thought to have been unknown to the ancient world. Which meant that not only was it possible to believe that the Antarctic was once a place of green and sheltered landfalls, but that the people who sailed its rich surrounding ocean were capable of calculating latitude and longtiude and drawing up accurate charts.

Hapgood died in 1982.   There were undoubtedly flaws in his interpretation of the mass of research, but he tried to face them and deal with them honestly. Many experts have dismissed his work as fanciful. Hapgood defined experts as "those who know everything, or nearly everything, and usually think they know everything important in their field, and if they don't think they know everything at least they know that other people know less, and amateurs know nothing." But others have been more cautious in their judgement, if only because the work is so thorough and meticulous.

> Mr Brouard commented at this point: "We are beginning to realise that the Chinese were one of the supreme sailing nations before Columbus. Their ocean going junks were often vast, and their fleets could quite well have circumnavigated the globe before Magellan. Not many of their maps and charts survive, but some do, and early European explorers – including Columbus – certainly had charts of their own. *We are always underestimating our ancestors.*"

31

The Navigators

I sat at my window in the room at the top of the house which I made into my study, looking down on the apple tree in the garden. It was September, and already the Worcester Pearmains were turning crimson. It was three o'clock in the afternoon. The country was still shocked by the death of the Princess of Wales. Tom and Penny were back at school. The hazy sunshine was mellow on the pink stone of the house beyond the apple tree. I wondered whether I should telephone Mr Brouard and ask what exactly was the point of all this stuff about Antarctica.

"Well?" I asked Whim, who was curled up on the old cane chair in the corner.

She lifted her grey snakey head and looked at me with blank dark eyes. She could tell I was not suggesting a walk so she was not interested.

He was there, at the end of the telephone, just as he used to be.

"Do you remember," he said, "that when the original Island people left to take their chances with wind and current, they gradually spread around the globe?   Over thousands of years, wherever they ended up – if they survived – they adapted to their different and shifting environments. Natural selection formed the Neanderthal people of the frozen north, just as had the Mongoloid seafarers.   Later it would produce the Caucasoid Europeans.   But what of the others, who went south?"

"Towards Antarctica."

"Well, certainly into the Southern Ocean.   Some would have been swept south on the Mozambique current into the westerly winds and currents that circle Antarctica.   They may have found shelter on the island of Kerguelen.   It lies in the path of the 'Furious Fifties' created by the meeting of warm Indian Ocean and icy Antarctic waters called the Atlantic Convergence, where winds often reach a hundred miles per hour.   The sea around its desolate coasts is full of life, but its land is barren, save for water, and such oddities as the Kerguelen Cabbage, which is so rich in Vitamin C that it saved many sailors from scurvy - including those of Captain Cook.   He named the island after the French admiral who had first discovered it.   Other Islanders probably reached the tip of south Australia, Tasmania, southern Africa – even southern Chile and Patagonia, caught as they were on the currents that ride eternally westward on the edge of the ice.   South of all of them was the vast coastline of Antarctica, surrounded by the powerful current and constant wind that revolve clockwise around the great land mass."

"But surely they couldn't have reached those places, in those winds, on their reed boats and wooden rafts?"

"Of course many would not have survived.   But reed boats and rafts are extraordinarily buoyant, chiefly because they allow for the sea washing over and through them rather than attempting to be watertight.   Our island people were by then extremely skilled in their construction and accustomed to the sea.   And once again we are talking of a very long timescale.   There is another element, too, which we who live on land never think of.   The oceans contain rivers, just like the land. Some of them are mighty rivers. We call them currents. We've all begun to hear about El Nino – a few years ago it caused a rise in the temperature of the Pacific which caused droughts in Australia and Indonesia and three hundred times the usual rainfall in Peru. The largest current in the world carries ten billion gallons of icy water from the Arctic into the North Atlantic every second – twenty-five times the volume of the Amazon. And the currents are cyclical, linked across the oceans. For the Islanders, as the first diaspora became many over succeeding millennia, they were the highways of the world."

"So what you're saying is that some of these people eventually settled on Antarctica?"

"That's right. Not at first. But then, about forty thousand years ago, in the warm interstadial, we know that something happen to Antarctica. The ice pack, the sea ice, and then the ice sheets that covered the coasts, melted. Some people have talked of shifts in the magnetic poles. Others that there was some distant explosion of a star, a supernova, that affected that part of the globe. What does seem to be certain is that although the ice returned to the north of the earth the Antarctic coast remained clear of it. I'm hopeful that the present surveys will reveal more, but it must have been inevitable that some of those early seafarers would have found many natural harbours along the apparently endless coasts of Antarctica, together with the finest fishing grounds."

"And these were the people you said would change human history yet again? Why?"

"Think a little. Antarctica is circular. The distance round it is less than half that around the equator. If you are caught in the constant wind and current that circulate round it, you will come back – with luck, and the chance to make regular landfalls in those green inlets that remain comfortingly always to starboard – to where you started. And what will you have done?"

"Well – I suppose you would have gone round the world. In effect."

"Not just in effect. You would have circumnavigated the globe. And in doing so you would have begun to realise how the brilliant constellations of stars that surround the Southern Cross would also move in circles in the sky: you could begin to see how sure a guide they were to follow.

"I read somewhere that birds use the stars to migrate."

"Well, that may be. Certainly, when blown off course by storms, they do seem able to calculate not only latitude but longitude from some kind of instinctive observation of the stars, giving them a known point of departure from which to plot their route home. Millions of years of evolution have probably perfected their methods. Just as thousands of years of conscious development may have given our ancestors similar powers."

"There was a book – oh, ages ago. Something about the Polynesian people who could navigate across the Pacific without charts or anything?"

"There've been several books. And the methods of the Melanesian and Polynesian islanders often seem to echo those of the Norse people who sailed between Norway and Greenland. Like the Chinese sea people, they believed their craft was a fixed point, and they could draw their destinations to them."

"Yes, but wait a minute. What about longitude? Harrison's chronometer – he didn't come up with that until the eighteenth century."

"True. It's comparatively easy to plot the latitude of a particular point and find one's north or south position by measuring the angles of the stars, or taking sunsights. Longitude, as you know, is another thing altogether, because it involves comparing local time with the simultaneous local time of some fixed meridian on the globe. That was Harrison's genius – before he worked out his chronometer, sailors were dependent on almanacks which contained sufficient information to calculate longitude by lunar distances, but even then only with great difficulty, and inaccurately. And they needed something else, too – something which could accurately measure angular distances between two heavenly bodies. That something was a sextant, originally designed by a country squire called John Haldey. Now – if we're talking about people circumnavigating the globe, we might as well look at the first man known to do so: Joshua Slocum."

"I know – he didn't have a chronometer, did he?"

"Well remembered," he said. I felt absurdly pleased. "He

decided he couldn't afford one. But he did have a sextant. So he used the ancient method of working out lunar distances, which he did extremely effectively. Wait a minute – I've got it here – " I could hear pages rustle.

"Slocum said: ...the greatest science was in reckoning the longitude.

"My tin clock and only timepiece had by this time lost its minute hand, but after I boiled her she told the hours, and that was near enough on a long stretch.

"It has to be said that Joshua Slocum was a genius. And mapping the stars is easy compared with measuring the moon's constantly varying elliptical orbit, which has a nineteen year recurring eclipse cycle. But it is – theoretically – possible. You can estimate longitude by predicting information about lunar eclipses. At the time of Columbus this was the only known method of finding longitude. Curiously enough we don't know much about how he did it. He wasn't a navigator, although he had once been an apprentice map-maker."

"But you're talking about primitive peoples – I mean, they didn't know anything about longitude – "

"Imagine for a moment that you are one of those people. You're on a boat: perhaps by now, in the southern hemisphere, where they are no reeds, a boat made of wood from the forests that would then have extended into Patagonia, to Antarctica itself. Logs of balsa wood from Ecuador, of notofagus from southern Chile. A boat based on a raft, which could sail to windward not by a steering oar but by an intricate system of streamlined centreboards such as those used by Inca sailors. They were known to navigate rich but dangerous cold currents like El Nino and the Humboldt – "

"On rafts?"

"The first report of balsa rafts was sent back to Spain by Pizarro early in the sixteenth century, when they described a merchant vessel carrying about thirty-six tons of cargo and a crew of about twenty men and women. In 1748 two Spanish naval officers made a study of the centreboard steering system and recommended it be tried in

Europe. Such rafts were observed until the end of the nineteenth century – by which time the centreboard had become well known in England and America. Thor Heyerdahl tried the system with his Kon-Tiki raft, and at first couldn't make it work – but in the end he proved it did. And there was Alain Bombard, a French doctor and marine biologist who had witnessed the results of a shipwreck at sea. He wanted to find out if it was possible to survive a sea voyage without any provisions at all, and in 1952 he took sixty-two days to cross the Atlantic in a small inflatable raft. He did survive – hang on – I'll find his book – "

I hung on: eventually I heard him return, and quote that young French enthusiast (who was later to become a minister in the French government).

> "...after half-catching and indeed wounding a number of fish and then seeing them wriggle off the end of my makeshift harpoon, I managed to catch my first dolphin (or, to be correct, dorado. This is a fish, not a mammal, but I shall use its more common name). I was saved, not only did I have food and drink, but bait and hook as well. Behind the gill cover there is a perfect natural bone hook, such as has been found in the tombs of prehistoric men, and which I think I can claim to have adapted to modern use. My first fishing line was at hand. From then on I had all the food and liquid I needed every day, and was never in danger of starving. That was probably the most heretical aspect of my self-imposed role of castaway."

Mr Brouard interjected: "He drank very small amounts of seawater too, and thus proved his point – although he was very emaciated and pretty sunburnt by the time he reached Barbados. And it was very much due to Bombard that life rafts then had to be carried on all ships at sea.

"Well. All right, so I'm on my boat. My raft."

"At night, lying on deck, you would look up at the same

southern constellations that we see today. You might observe how the stars, the sun and the full moon described circles in that vast sky, and relate it to that very circle you were following around the shores of Antarctica. Today you could leave a camera on deck all night with the shutter open, pointed at the Pole Star, or the Southern Cross, and find that the stars have described a pattern of concentric circles on your film. But then you had time to observe, to follow those patterns in the brilliant sky. And you had a mind, a curious, enquiring mind."

"So one day, in one of those wide harbours of Antarctica, whilst others repaired the boat or fished in those rich waters, you stared down at the sand. It invited some inscription, for it was damp, hard and smooth in the sunlight. You took a stick and drew a circle, like the circles you had observed as the stars drew circles in the sky, those circles that somehow seemed to connect with the circle you drew around the earth. You wanted to make the circle perfect. So you found another stick with a bit of broken branch at right angles to the end, making a kind of peg. You stuck the peg in the sand and moved the stick round so that it drew another circle. A perfect circle. And when it was a perfect circle, the impulse to divide it with other perfect circles, using the stick, was impossible to resist. By this method you could reproduce the divisions of the heavens themselves."

Then he told me to go back to the tape, and so I did, before the children came home from school. But before that I looked up something I remembered in one of the books written by Alfred Russel Wallace. *The Malay Archipelago* was an account of his travels among those remote tropical islands. It had been published in 1869. Eleven years earlier he had written to Charles Darwin, enclosing the ideas that had come to him in a bamboo hut while he endured another bout of fever. He accompanied it with a letter in which he said he hoped:

> "that the idea would be as new to him as it was to me,
> and that it would supply the missing factors to explain
> the origin of species."

But it was not that long-ago meeting of minds that resulted in Darwin and Wallace sharing the publication of their papers on the *Origin of Species* that intrigued me now. It was something else in Wallace's adventure. Something about a boat.

He had managed to get a passage from Celebes to the Aru Island on a trading vessel, called a prau, which would take advantage of the west monsoon for the outward voyage, and the east monsoon for the return.

> "The prau was a vessel of about 70 tons, shaped something like a Chinese junk. The deck sloped considerably downward to the bows, which are thus the lowest part of the ship. There were two large rudders, but instead of being placed astern they were hung on the quarters from strong cross beams, which projected out two or three feet on each side, and to which extent the deck overhung the sides of the vessel amidships. The tillers were not on deck, but entered the vessel through two square openings into a lower or half deck, about three feet high, in which sat the two steersmen."

Wallace was rarely phased by anything, but about ten days out in a heavy swell he noticed something that gave him pause for thought.

> "I made a discovery today, which at first rather alarmed me. The two ports, or openings, through which the tillers enter from the lateral rudders, are not more than three or four feet above the surface of the water, which thus has a free entrance into the vessel. I of course had imagined that this open space from one side to the other was separated from the hold by a watertight bulkhead...To my surprise and dismay, however, I find that it is completely open to the hold, so that half a dozen seas rolling in on a stormy night would nearly, or quite, swamp us. But our Captain says all praus are so; and though he acknowledges the danger, he does not know how to alter it – the people are used to it; he does

not understand praus so well as they do, and if such a great alteration were made, he should be sure to have difficulty getting a crew."

In fact the voyage was entirely smooth and Wallace became very fond of the prau, praising the comfort of his tiny cabin on the deck – "the snuggest little place" he had ever enjoyed at sea.

"No paint, no tar...no grease, or oil, or varnish; but instead bamboo and rattan, and coir rope and palm thatch, that recall quiet scenes in the green and shady forest."

The prau, like the others they met on the voyage, had no compass. During the day they were seldom out of sight of the mountainous islands, but even at night they kept a true course. And Wallace was charmed with a water clock they carried:

"It is simply a bucket half filled with water, in which floats half a well-scraped cocoa-nut shell. In the bottom of this shell is a very small hole, so that when placed to float in the bucket a fine thread of water squirts up into it. This gradually fills the shell, and the size of the hole is so adjusted that, exactly at the end of an hour, plump it goes to the bottom. The watch then cries out the number of hours from sunrise, and sets the shell afloat again empty. I tested it with my watch and found that it hardly varied a minute from one hour to another, nor did the motion of the vessel have any effect upon it, as the water in the bucket of course kept level."

As often happened when I had been alone for most of the day, sitting at the computer and doing the ironing, I had the feeling I couldn't speak properly for quite a long time after Tom and Penny came arguing through the door. They made themselves Marmite and toast and brought me a cup of tea but it took me a little while to return to the real world.

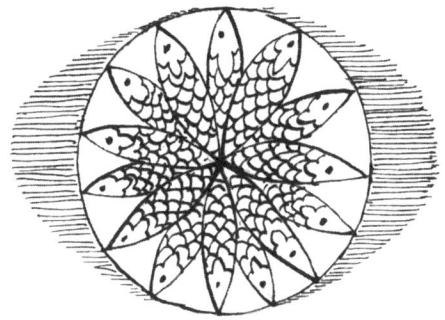

32

Magic Numbers

He must have been one of those whom men may call mad. A genius. We could give him the name Alcinous, whom Homer described as the King of the Phaeacians, lords of the sea and the greatest seamen of the ancient world. The goddess Athene told Odysseus: "They put their trust in fast ships that carry them across the far-flung seas, for that is a privilege granted by Poseidon, and these ships of theirs are as a swift as a bird or as thought itself."

To his own people he was an oddity, for his obsession with drawing on the sands seemed to them beyond reason. But he was not harmful. He was as skilled a sailor and fisherman as any of them, with all the instincts of ancient tradition. And there were times when his understanding of the stars, of the ways of the sun and the moon, had been their salvation on the dark seas. So they left him alone, a solitary figure, with his bits of stick, one end pegged in the sand, the other scribing his endless circles and the curious elliptical segments within them.

The segments were in the shape of fish. So he called them fish. Sometimes people, women and children among them, came to watch him, squatting on their haunches and eating shellfish in the sun, and one or two would ask what he was doing. He would attempt to explain, demonstrating his circles, showing how he could divide the circle into six fish by drawing more circles, circle upon circle; how he could divide and divide again. He tried to make them see that by doing so you could follow the way in which the circles of stars moved in the night sky. A complete circle was formed from three hundred and sixty very small segments – degrees. Sixty degrees made one fish. So six fishes formed the circle. Within a degree one might make sixty minutes: within sixty minutes, sixty seconds. Six was a magic number. So was twelve: twice six. There were twelve periods of new moon to new moon between consecutive midsummer days, the synodic months. He drew symbols for these on the sand.

Twelve could be used for linear measurement, too, all based upon the same pattern observed in the sky. There were twelve seconds to an inch, twelve feet to a foot, six feet to a fathom. At the summer solstice daylight could be divided into twelve parts. The night sky itself divided into twelve segments, each marked by a constellation of stars.

Many among his audience, hitherto attentive as long as the sweet shellfish lasted, had by now risen to return to work upon their boats, to gather firewood or food. But gradually more remained, grasping the concepts, adding their own interpretation. To do so they too drew upon the sand, following the patterns made by Alcinous. They marked the signs of the zodiac, using pictures, so that all might learn them, and to memorise the positions of the stars in the sky at different times and days they marked them on the sand diagrams with other pictures, symbols, each one different.

Twenty-four such symbols would be sufficient for an alphabet from which all spoken words might be written down. And as the sea washed the sand, so those who now began to follow Alcinous, to understand how they might employ such knowledge, could engrave pictures and symbols on wet clay, or carve them upon rock. In this way they might keep the knowledge, and pass it on.

For perhaps twenty-five, thirty thousand years in that remote but vast land of Antarctica and its surrounding interlinked oceans, so these seafaring fishermen learned the science of navigation, and with it an understanding of mathematics. They created the crafts of writing, and of reading the complexities of the symbols upon which each succeeding generation might build. They could use such knowledge in building ever finer boats, in charting the skies and the seas, in becoming masters of their own environment. No longer must they remain at the mercy of wind and current. And those who now possessed such knowledge also acquired its power. In his own time, their Alcinous was given the respect due to a king. Or a god.

But once again there was to be a shift in the environment of these increasingly literate, numerate sailors. The climate of Antarctica was changing, as it was all over the world.

Climatic change has always influenced human development, but its fluctuations over the past millennia in different parts of the globe are almost impossible to ascertain. What does seem clear is that the ice began to return to the shores and surrounding seas of Antarctica several thousand years ago, when the northern hemisphere was enjoying – or in some cases enduring, so turbulent were some of its effects – the new warmth of our interstadial, with its corresponding rise in sea levels.

This was the time when the seafarers who had made their home in Antarctica and the southern hemisphere found themselves forced into a new diaspora. But this time the exodus could be planned. The people had control over their enforced migration. They could navigate: they could steer. Some took the route from Australia into the Indonesian archipelago and the China Sea and found that forests of bamboo provided buoyant and durable materal for building rafts. Other established cultures provided new knowledge of boat construction: the Chinese, with their great ocean-going junks and sampans, were almost self-sufficient and controlled much of the coastal waters of the Far East for millennia yet to come.

The summer winds of the south east monsoon took some of the seafarers to Japan, warmed by the Kuro Siwo drift. In recent years traces of human activity have been found dating back some fifty thousand years. And there is evidence that twenty thousand years ago settlements in Tokyo Bay were trading in a form of obsidian –

the hard volcanic glass so important to early peoples – with an island called Kozushima, two hundred miles away in the Pacific. It was the only source available. To trade routinely with such a distant island would have required a considerable standard of navigational skill.

We also know today that despite the Australian aboriginal people being almost completely dismissed from prehistory only a few years ago, they must have occupied that continent for some sixty thousand years. The earliest evidence of their settlements are all in the south, and in Tasmania. Yet it has never been possible to walk to Australia. Even when sea levels were at their lowest, that continent remained surrounded by water. The aborigines had to cross at least sixty miles of open sea to reach it. There is, of course, no record of what craft they might have used. The only clue to their way of life was that all around the coasts were huge mounds of shells, some thirty feet high and covering half an acre. Otherwise the early Australians were regarded by their European successors as simply in the way. Until 1967 they were not even included in national censuses. Darwin, visiting Tasmania in the Beagle, regretted having missed the sport of hunting the natives – all of whom, as it happens, are now extinct.

But some of those Antarctic sailors went north across the Indian Ocean. Eventually they made contact with the coastal peoples of western Asia, the slave-owning, farming sea people of the Persian Gulf. Their light and navigable craft met the great papyrus ships berthed in stone docks or along quaysides in trading ports and harbours. The traditional land-based skills of the mason, the engineer, the metalworker, met the new elusive arts and mathematical skills of the seafarers from the far south. On the salty swamps of southern Iraq, the desolate flood plains of the Tigris and Euphrates, these two cultures formed a new symbiosis. And out of it, in this unstable land, liable to both drought and flooding, was conceived the first urban, literate civilisation in the world: Sumer. It was the beginning of history.

33

Tel a Story

It was the damn sweat that was the worst. Despite the band round his head, trickles kept running down into his eyes, and he could only make the merest swipe at it with his wrist for fear of dropping the pencil – or, for that matter, falling off the bloody ladder. He could hear somebody shouting up at him to come down, he had been up there over two hours, but there was at least half an hour of reasonable evening light left. And this was the best light. Low, slanting like this, it etched into the strange indentations on the rock as if they had just been made – instead of over two thousand years ago. He wiped his forehead again, steadying himself on the ladder, momentarily terrified that he would drop the pad of paper on which he was so meticulously copying the inscription. He was aware of birds circling above him, of the immensity of shimmering air between him and the remote ochre landscape below, of the red sandstone cliff that towered implacably above him, but it was the writing that absorbed him. It was already an obsession.

In 1827 the younger son of a middle class English family had little choice of careers. For Henry Rawlinson, service with the East India Company, that curiosity of Empire which was both larger and probably better organised than the British Army and doing much of its work, was the best option. He was already interested in linguistics, and as 'John Company' was based in India he could pursue his fascination with ancient languages of the Near East. At twenty-three he was reorganising the Persian army, which had got itself involved in some dirty work with Russia in Afghanistan. At the same time he had begun to research the baffling cuneiform script found on fragments of clay tablet and brick all over southern Iraq – Persia, as it was then. They turned up out of the mysterious mounds called *tels* which littered the arid desert around the Tigris and Euphrates, and already more formal excavations were being planned. For this was ancient Mesopotamia, 'the land between the rivers' and tales of Nineveh and the hanging gardens of Babylon had long surrounded it.

Besides, interest in the ancient world was in the very air. It had been, perhaps, since Napoleon's soldiers had found a black basalt slab, inscribed with some kind of writing, in an Egyptian village called Rashid. The soldiers called it Rosetta. Captured by the British, the stone ended up in the British Museum, and the three languages it bore were finally to be deciphered in the 1820s. But now the race was on to decipher those other strange languages – like those on the Rosetta Stone, often found as three variants together – which still eluded scholars.

Without writing there could be no history. Without understanding written text the past remained mute. And writing could mean many things. It might be pictures, simplified into pictograms, inscribed on a Mesopotamian clay tablet the size of a postcard. A variant of pictograms was the system of Egyptian hieroglyphics, written on papyrus. It could be the cuneiform writing which so fascinated Henry Rawlinson on his ladder – so called because it turned the pictures into tiny wedge-shaped marks made with a reed stylus, and the Latin word for wedge was *cuneus.* Yet again, writing could be based upon a system of symbols representing sounds – an alphabet.

Henry Rawlinson's problem with deciphering the Sumerian cuneiform writing was that so many tablets were in fragments. Then someone mentioned to him that there was a large and complete inscription in these three languages, together with some sort of relief sculpture, on the Rock of Behistun, about two hundred miles east of Baghdad.

"Something to do with Darius the Great, King of Persia," added Rawlinson's informant. "But you'll need a bloody long ladder to get up there."

Which was why Henry Rawlinson was on a ladder, three hundred feet up on the sheer face of the Rock of Behiston (the ladder resting on a ledge below), copying out an account of how Darius the First came to the throne of Persia and overcame those who threatened to destroy the unity of his empire.

Unknown to him, a scholarly German linguist called George Grotefend had already managed to decipher some of the three forms of writing on some Mesopotamian clay tablets. In 1802 he had written a paper on his work and conclusions, but the Gottingen Academy refused to publish it. His ideas about the early date of the inscriptions were thought absurd. Ninety years later, by then superseded by the work of Rawlinson and other scholars, the paper was eventually published and acknowledged as proven. By then Grotefend was dead.

Even when Henry Rawlinson finally deciphered the Darius inscription in 1846, together with like-minded colleagues, few believed that these really were the writings of an ancient world, thousands of years old. Then, in 1857, a new clay cylinder similarly inscribed in cuneiform writing was brought back from Mesopotamia. It was given to Rawlinson and his three scholarly colleagues for independent translation. Each returned a matching version of the story of the Assyrian king Tilglath-Pileser the First. It was finally accepted that the ancient cuneiform writing of Sumer had at last been translated.

By then – in 1842 – the French consul in Mesopotamia had already started to excavate one of the great *tels*, the mounds thought to be the site of Nineveh. He did not discover Nineveh, but he did unearth the great palace of the Mesopotamian king Sargon the First. It was almost five thousand years old. It was the first of a continuing series of excavations in southern Iraq which was only temporarily to end with the reign of Saddam Hussein at the end of the twentieth century. The unfolding of the story of the earliest civilisation had finally begun.

34

Fish Men

The first of the great temple cities of Sumer was Eridu. It was about a hundred miles west of the city of Basra in modern Iraq. Eighteen separate layers of excavation displayed a sequence of urban development centred on buildings that appeared to have a religious purpose. The topmost layer was contemporary with the last of the curious terraced towers that dominated the flood plains, the ziggurats (meaning to be high and pointed), and was dated about 2000 BC. In the deepest stratum was a simple temple from around 5000 BC. Dedicated to Enki, all-powerful god of the sea, it was floored with fish scales and contained a clay model of a boat.

What was the significance of that small chapel, built on the shore and above the normal level of the cyclical floods? Was it built to placate, to ask for his help in combating the risks of trade and travel up the mighty rivers from the sea?

For thousands of years agriculture had been expanding in these hundreds of square miles of alluvial plain, bordered in the north and east by vast mountain ranges and in the west. Yet its people had remained largely dependent on the sea and the rivers for trade. Economic expansion depended on slaves. The Sumerian word for slave also meant foreigner. They became ever more necessary, not only for building and crewing ships, but for constructing the means with which cargoes could be loaded and unloaded, transhipped and distributed.

Many types of trading vessels are listed in Sumerian records and they traded at least as far as Egypt and Ethiopia. Wharfs, piers and docks to take large ocean-going vessels were essential to this trading economy. Anyone who has ever tried to come ashore in a small boat in any kind of a wind or swell, will realise how impossible it can be, and how vital, therefore, was the construction of such shore support for commercial transport. And the dangers did not cease as smaller craft travelled upriver. The gods must always be involved. The chapel to Enki was simple insurance.

Eridu was the blueprint for the city states of Sumer. At the height of this first civilisation there were twenty. Each had its own deity: Nippur was dedicated to Enlil, god of the winds; Uruk, destined to become the largest of the twenty city states of the later period of Sumer, was dedicated jointly to the sky god Anu and Inanna, goddess. And Ur, comparable in size with a city of the twenty-first century, had as its deity the moon god Nanna.

Ur began as a small settlement in the marshes, and indeed suffered disastrous floods; but it was to become the capital of a Sumerian empire that stretched to the highlands of Anatolia. At its height it may have had a population of about several hundred thousand. Contained within massive brick walls were some four square miles of houses, streets, offices and warehouses. Two wide canals encircled the city and another bisected it, with the wharves and docks to accommodate trading vessels from all points of the compass. Cargoes included the precious metals, timber, ivory, pearls and gem stones for the workshops of metalworkers, sculptors, cabinetmakers and jewellers, whose glittering workmanship still fills with awe those who gaze upon it in the galleries of the British Museum. They also produced musical instruments, flutes, horns, the harp and the lyre. Librarians collected and catalogued not only administrative but scientific and literary texts – like The Epic of Gilgamesh, earliest of all great ballads. Sumerian legal and political systems seem to have been consensual and fair – even slaves had rights. Life was to be enjoyed, for death, it seems, was not a comforting prospect.

The city was dominated by the sacred enclosure in the centre of the city, whose massive terraced ziggurat temple was always visible, towering above everything else. This was the heart of the city, ruled by an elite of wise men, the priests who held the secrets of knowledge. It was they who governed and protected the land, who understood and interpreted such mysterious phenomena as the sun and the moon, drought and flood, sowing and harvest. The Sumerians possessed an accurate lunar calendar, adjusted to movements of the sun and stars. Astronomy was important both for ships and agriculture. Detailed instructions on farming activities throughout the year were written on a tablet called The Farmer's Almanac. Numerical computation was based on positional numeration and sexagesimal system of mathematics, which we still use for calibrating clock faces, latitude and longitude and general angular measurement. Complex mathematical calculations were required for surveying and building complex engineering projects.

I heard Mr Brouard chuckle at this point, and interject:

"Other duo-decimal systems of money and measurement have been superseded by the ten-finger counting decimal system – enforced by Napoleon, of course, and which is undoubtedly more easily mechanised."

Secular rulers and kings had their place, but it was the guardians of ancient knowledge who preserved the traditions of arts and science and effectively made the laws that regulated society. They still echo in our own. Families were patriarchal, but all women were considered individuals with their own rights - even the slave mother of a free man's children had rights of her own. And children went to school. A Sumerian schoolteacher wrote the following, probably for amusement, to describe a typical pupil:

"Arriving at school in the morning I recited my tablet, ate my lunch, prepared my new tablet, wrote it, finished it, then they assigned me my oral work...When school was dismissed, I went home, entered the house and found my father sitting there. I told my father of my written work, then recited my tablet to him, and my father was delighted. When I awoke early in the morning, I faced my mother and said to her: 'Give me my lunch, I want to go to school.' My mother gave me two rolls and I set out. In school the monitor in charge said to me, 'Why are you late?' Afraid, and with a pounding heart, I entered before my teacher and made a respectful curtsey."

The tape paused, and then Mr Brouard added: "By the way, this is the sort of mathematical problem that schoolboys would have had to solve...This is from a text of about the same date, 2000 BC:

"An area A, consisting of the sum of two squares, is 1000. The side of one square is two-thirds of the side of the other square, diminished by ten. What are the sides of the square?"

I was never any good at maths.

"You could do it by using equations – and then solving a quadratic equation – but in the actual cuneiform text it's answered by a simple enumeration of the numerical steps that must be taken. They could actually work with quadratic equations in two variables, as well as with cubic and biquadratic equations. Ah. Well, anyway, they were pretty good at mathematics."

Outside the city walls the surrounding fields grew barley and wheat, staple food for slaves. Barley was important for ale – forty per cent went into brewing. There was a goddess of brewing, as indeed there was a deity for almost every human activity. There were date palms, orchards, vineyards and vegetable gardens growing the contemporary equivalents of onions and lettuce. Dairy cattle and goats provided milk, cheese and yoghurt and donkeys were a universal means of transport. And every farmer, every slave in the fields, straightening his back from his hoeing, would see the sun glinting on the tower of the ziggurat, perhaps ten miles away beyond the city walls, and be reminded of the gods and their priestly chief executives. Kings might impose their rule, but even they were subservient to that central religious power.   The very wheat, when ripe, would be delivered to the temple.   Seed would be given to the farmer at the due time.   Every object made within the city, and every cargo imported to the wharves and warehouses, whether copper, timber, pearls or ivory from Asia, had to be offered to the god.   And every item, every delivery and consignment, was meticulously accounted for on his behalf.

Bureaucracy was a cornerstone of Sumerian life and the knowledge of writing and arithmetic was central to it. The earliest writing was simple picture writing, which could be elaborated to cover all administrative needs.   It was to develop into the cuneiform writing of later periods.   Inscribed tablets were sealed with innumerable little cylinders of stone or metal, used to identify and protect property, and some of them are engraved with extraordinary delicacy both with writing and pictures.   Thousands have been found but they are probably a fraction of those that were made. There was also a form of printing, carving 'negative' images on to stone cylinders and then rolling them over fresh clay to produce a 'positive' inscription.

The Sumerians seem to have loved life – and feared death. One description of the afterlife is bleak enough:

> *"...the Dead shuffle*
> *Under their black plumage...Where the food is clay*
> *And the drink ashes...whence there is no reprieve..."*

Yet when Sir Leonard Woolley made his celebrated excavation of what came to be known as the royal tombs of Ur in 1823, he found an extraordinary mix of wealth, art and poignant acceptance of death in the orderly rows of corpses.   These men and women were well-fed and exquisitely dressed: some were probably musicians, others perhaps simply servants of these dead rulers of Ur.

They appeared to have gone calmly to their deaths, perhaps to take some drug from the small cups that lay beside the bodies. Whatever religion or authority demanded such submission from them was indeed powerful.

The Sumerians were one of the most creative peoples who ever lived. But why? Why – and how – did such a phenomenally gifted people arise here? What was the stimulus that created this literate, numerate, artistic, urban civilisation in such a place – marsh and desert, riven with wind, drought and flood? It lacked the resources of metals, timber, even flint or the obsidian for agricultural implements. Yet here in Sumer, in Ur itself, was found the first potter's wheel that was to drive a vast industry: here too they invented glass, and learned to cast in bronze.

The Roman historian Thucydides used the Greek term *synoecismus* to describe the amalgamation of several towns and villages into a single city. But nothing just happens. Wherein lay the stimulus? The Sumerians might have been creative but their culture and ideology was rigidly traditional. Their educational system was not a forcing house for new ideas, but consisted of careful copying of ancient legends – which, as it happens, may hold the clue to the mystery of this sudden flowering of civilisation in this particular place. They tell of an invasion by a strange new people who brought with them the secrets that were to become the heart of the new city states of Sumer.

The legends of Sumer and Babylon were written on clay tablets but they were also sung to the music of the harp. Like The Iliad and The Odyssey, The Epic of Gilgamesh, the stories of the Old Testament, they were handed down in song. The first books to be written about the creation and early history of the world were the work of a Babylonian priest in the third century BC. Only authenticated fragments remain, but Berosus was quoted by several sources, including a disciple of Aristotle and the philosopher Apollodorus of the second century. When Babylon was conquered by Alexander the Great Berosus went to the island of Kos, near Rhodes, where he set up an observatory and a school of astronomy. People at the time were interested in their early history, as people in every age have been.   Berosus visited Athens, and his writing was held in such high academic esteem there that a statue was erected in his honour.

According to the legendary histories recorded by Berosus, the people of the great plains of the Tigris and Euphrates had been presented with the arts and sciences – writing, astronomy, mathematics – by an invasion of godlike 'fish men'.   Their leader was called Oannes.

"All the things that make for the amelioration of life were bequeathed to men by Oannes, and since that time no further inventions have been made".

The invaders were vividly described:

"The whole body of the animal was like that of a fish; and had, under a fish's head, also feet below, similar to those of a man, subjoined to the fish's tail. His voice too, and language, was articulate and human.   When the sun set it was the custom of this Being to plunge again into the sea, and abide all night in the deep; for he was amphibious".

Some subsequent versions of the legend said that Oannes came out of a great egg, hence his name; others that he was actually a man, but only seemed a fish because he was clothed in the skin of a sea creature.

"And it has to be said," put in Mr Brouard at this point, "that the portraits of this legendary figure on Assyrian cylinder seals in the British Museum do resemble a Victorian admiral making a formal call in a full dress sharkskin frock coat... But do you remember when I told you how I had stood at the mouth of the Shatt Al Arab and the world seemed to be unmade, as if sea and land were one?   That is the way another legend begins, the legend of the creation of Sumer inscribed on clay tablets:

"All lands were sea
Then there was a movement on the midst of the sea;
At that time Eridu was made...
Marduk laid a reed on the face of the waters,
He formed dust and poured it out beside the reed
That he might cause the gods to dwell in the dwelling of their hearts' desire
He formed mankind
With him the goddess Aruru created the seed of mankind.
The beasts of the field and living things in the field he formed
The Tigris and Euphrates he created and established them in their place:
Their name he proclaimed in goodly manner
The grass, the rush of the marsh, the reed and the forest he created,
The lands, the marshes and the swamps;
The wild cow and her young, the lamb of the fold,
Orchards and forests;
The he-goat and the mountain goat...
The Lord Marduk built a dam beside the sea...
Reeds he formed, trees he created
Bricks he laid, buildings he erected;
House he made, cities he built..."

There are other such creation legends. And of course there is the opening chapter of Genesis in the Bible. The ancient texts of Hindu literature, the Veda, describe the bringers of new culture as having come from ice-bound frozen regions. It was assumed that this meant overland from the Arctic – not strictly practical.

There is another enigma. Sumerian writing was essentially picture-writing, even the later cuneiform. Alphabetical writing – that is, the concept of using a certain number of representative symbols of the sound of spoken language – was not discovered until a French archaeologist called Claude Schaaeffer began to excavate the ancient city of Ras Shamra in Syria in 1929. Among his finds was a library. It was about five thousand years old. It contained clay tablets on which were written diplomatic communications, personal and official letters, tax accounts, temple records, a treatise on veterinary medicine, a shipping list, business records and trading accounts. They were decoded by Charles Virolleaud in Paris. And he found that the alphabet with which they were written was virtually the same as that we use today. It was to be the basis of the Phoenician language. It was the alphabet rediscovered by the Greeks in the eighth century BC: the alphabet that provided Homer with the means to write *The Iliad* and *The Odyssey*.

So where did it originate? We now know that Ras Shamra was the ancient city of Ugarit, and that this was also the land of Canaan, from where Abraham is said to have come, and a base for the Phoenician sailors. Here, too, was the great port of Byblos, one of the wealthiest cities of the ancient world. But the roots of its language remain a mystery. It is perhaps easy to overlook the fact that the only evidence we have is written on clay tablets, although papyrus was undoubtedly also used for writing. But clay survives: papyrus, except in the dry air of Egyptian tombs, does not. Many of the texts of Homer are written on papyrus, but all come from Egypt. None survived in Greece, with its wet winters. It seems that the origins of our written alphabetical language lie with the peoples of the sea, but like so much else of their cultures, only clues remain.

The rulers of Sumer expanded their city states, squabbled with their neighbours and endured drought, flood and tempest, but it was probably the eventual salination of the soil due to the effects of long-term artificial irrigation that forced them to abandon their cities. To the old internecine warfare, the arguments over irrigation and trade routes, was added incursion from tribes in the mountains and beyond the desert. Ancient differences between farmers and hunting peoples became conflicts. Dissatisfied mercenaries, disaffected slaves and a fearful middle class provoked resentment and resistance to any code of law. New states, new kings would arise, north on the Euphrates Sargon of Akkad, Hammurabi of Babylon, but despite attempts to impose order there were increasing tensions.

The elusive influence of the Antarctic seafarers had once exercised a unifying authority like that of the Pax Britannica of the nineteenth century, in that there had been no need for a formal organisation of defences against external threat. But it had begun to wane. The land, not the sea, was becoming dominant. The resources of the land were ever more important. Metal, which had for so long been used for beautiful ornaments or practical implements, was increasingly used for weaponry. The technology of metalworking was to give civilisation perhaps its most distinctive and enduring element, the one which in the end always determines the way history is told. That element is *war*.

The seafaring peoples of the oceans and archipelagoes did not disappear. As Sumer declined, so some of them went on to sail up the Red Sea to the wild marshes of the Nile delta. Here the great river was predictable. The earliest inhabitants of this circlet of green in the Arabian Desert could tell precisely when the benign flood would come. They left little trace of their existence, but as centuries passed so there arose new kingdoms on the Nile, the death-obsessed dynasties of Egypt. Others of the seafarers, perhaps who found the slave-based dark world of Egypt too oppressive, sailed north west across the Mediterranean to found another civilisation. It too would last a thousand years, although nothing was known of it, save in legend, until the beginning of the twentieth century. It was, perhaps, the very zenith of what we mean by civilisation. The Greeks were to look back upon it as a golden age. It was, in fact, the age of copper alloyed with ten per cent tin: the Bronze Age.

35

Floating Factories

In 1807 the British Fleet bombarded Copenhagen in an effort to prevent neutral Denmark from providing a haven for Napoleon. Denmark surrendered, but before it did, a Dane called Christian Thomson managed to save many of the city's antiquities from destruction or capture. When the war was over, the objects he had collected together became the basis of a museum. Many of them were from prehistory, and he had no means of dating them, save that he knew that stone tools and weapons were made before metal ones, and that bronze was smelted earlier than iron. So he arranged his exhibits in three glass cases labelled chronologically Stone Age, Bronze Age, and Iron Age. His system of classification is essentially the one we use today.

The Bronze Age began when someone found that when pure copper is contaminated with tin it produces an alloy that does not rust but which is as hard and tough as steel. Copper had been found in various parts of the world for thousands of years, and although it was too soft and malleable for much practical use craftsmen employed it for jewellery and ornament. It is likely that someone then discovered that the green malachite used for decorating clay pots turned to molten copper if the pots were overheated – to a temperature of 1100 degrees Centigrade – in a wood-fired kiln. Molten copper could be cast, and when it cooled, natural impurities like arsenic made it harder. Annealed and then beaten, it could be used for tools.

The seafaring peoples dominated the trade in copper ore, and it made sense to build simple improvised furnaces for smelting the cargoes where they were unloaded, on the shores of estuaries and rivers. In Thailand and Malaya the gravel banks of rivers are rich in tinstone-cassiterite, tin dioxide. Copper thus contaminated was found to produce bronze. The art of smelting and working bronze probably then spread north-east from the Mekong to the China Sea and westward to the Indus Valley and beyond. By the third millennium it was being traded into the Mediterranean. Copper ore and tin were suddenly precious cargoes, and they were the preserve of the people whose ships crowded the seas.

There are hundreds of known ancient wrecks in the Mediterranean, and in 1959 two Americans, a marine historian called Peter Throckmorton and a young archaeologist, George Bass, decided to excavate a ship that had sunk off the coast of southern Turkey about three thousand years ago. It was the first such scientific excavation of an undersea wreck – and George Bass had to learn to dive first.

The ship was about eleven metres long at the waterline. In its hold Bass found ingots of hallmarked copper and bronze. Broken bronze tools, knives, bowls, spearheads and other apparent scrap metal had been packed in baskets. There were newly-cast, unsharpened tools. There was waste metal from casting, ingots of tin, raw tin ore. In addition there was a stone anvil, hammers for beating bronze into sheets, whetstones, polishers. In what appeared to be the living quarters of the captain or crew were traces of food (olive stones and bones), a cylinder seal for stamping official documents, a merchant's accurate set of weights and an oil lamp. The ship was a vehicle for collecting mined ore, smelting it and casting the copper into ingots on any convenient shore, before shipping the refined metals on board to trade.   It carried everything required for metal working, dealing and trading.   It was a floating workshop. In the 1980s Bass began work on another ship off Uluburn in Turkey, with a similar cargo, and even earlier in date.

Such practical, pragmatic working ships were the mainspring of the Bronze Age, and of the great civilisation that from its centre on the island of Crete was to dominate the surrounding world of the Near East and the Mediterranean. It was, wrote Homer, "a rich and lovely land, washed by the waves on every side...and boasting ninety cities."   The Greeks had long told the story of Theseus and the Minotaur, and how he had escaped with the help of his beloved Ariadne and her ball of thread. Theseus, returning home in triumph after slaying the Minotaur, forgot to hoist the white sails that were the pre-arranged signal of his success in Crete.   His stricken father, King Aegeus, seeing the black sails, believed him dead.   He threw himself into the sea that was ever afterwards called the Aegean.

It was a magical legend. No one thought it could be true. Then, in 1899, a man called Arthur Evans did.

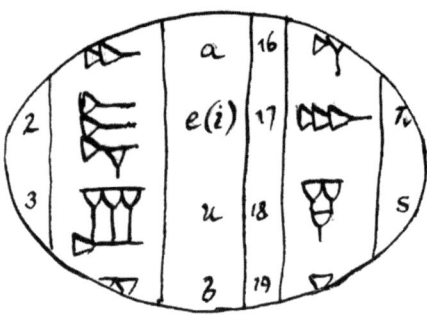

Secrets of the Lords of the Sea

Arthur Evans was only thirty-three when he became Keeper of the Ashmolean Museum at Oxford. He was already not only a scholar but a war correspondent. He was also a political activist on behalf of Bosnia and Herzegovina against their Turkish occupiers. A complex and forceful individual, he also possessed remarkably acute eyesight.

Among the trinkets sold in Shoe Lane in Athens were tiny bead seals. No one else seemed to have noticed that they bore minute carved squiggles. When Evans asked the dealer about them he was told they were from Crete. They were called 'milk stones', because Cretan women wore them round their necks as charms while they fed their babies. Perhaps that had a resonance for Evans: his much-loved wife Margaret died in that same year. After her death he decided to go to Crete. When he did, he fell in love with it. In 1900, with two archaeologist companions, he began a dig. Almost at once he began to uncover a vast labyrinth of buildings. He was to devote the rest of his life to the excavation and interpretation of the civilisation to which he gave the name Minoan, after King Minos, whose great palace had been hidden for so long beneath the little Cretan village called Knossos.

I heard the tape click, and then restart, and for a moment there was no sound except the liquid notes of Beethoven's unmistakable sixth symphony, and the low murmur of London traffic. Then Mr Brouard's voice.

It is a beautiful day. I can see the brightness in the sky, the sun on the red brick of the buildings across the street. Thinking of the Minoans makes one reflect on the nature of civilisation, for theirs was to be the first of a succession, sometimes contemporaneous, but on the whole following one another, in and around the Aegean and the Mediterranean, in Syria, Egypt and Anatolia. We have learned to believe much of what the Greeks said of their forebears, but still we know very little of these peoples save from what they left us of their art and architecture. Arthur Evans never did decipher the squiggles on the Cretan seals. They were in the language we call Linear A, which is found only on Crete and which no one has yet managed to translate. And he died before its apparent successor, Linear B, was deciphered by a young English architect called Michael Ventris.

As a boy Michael Ventris had heard Evans lecture on the Minoans. Since then he had been determined to break the code of Linear B. In the end he managed it, proving that it was an early form of the Greek language. It was a major achievement – although it has to be said that no great literature in Linear B has been found, only business and administrative records. It was a tragedy that Ventris was killed in a road accident just before his book on deciphering Linear B was published in 1952. He was only thirty-four.

But even without the knowledge of their language, we can appreciate the sophistication and beauty of Minoan art and culture. By 2000 BC their civilisation was established in the Aegean with colonies throughout the Mediterranean, their ships trading across the seas – including to Britain, a valuable source of tin and copper ore. On their great island home they needed no fortifications: they had no slaves. Their palaces were beautiful and open and they delighted in the natural world, in the sea and the air. Arthur Evans was a romantic and no human society is without its darker side, but somehow the Minoans portray a world of such sensitivity and freedom, such exquisite craftsmanship, such sensual pleasure and joy in their very being, that one can understand why they remained in the imagination of those that came after them.

There's a passage in *The Odyssey*...it's a description of the island of Phaeacia, where Odysseus is shipwrecked and meets the king's daughter, beautiful Nausicaa, daughter of Alcinous. I always had a bit of a yen for white-armed Nausicaa. It always makes me think of Crete, and it may be that Homer had that legendary island in mind. He describes the Phaeacians as famous seamen – as were the Minoans – and Odysseus marvels at the harbours with their trim ships, the meeting-place of the sea lords. King Alcinous's palace is famous...listen to this:

> "A kind of radiance, like that of the sun or moon, played upon the high-roofed halls of the great King. Bronze walls, topped by a frieze of dark blue enamel, ran round to left and right from the portals to the back of the court. The interior of the well-built mansion was guarded by golden doors hung on posts of silver which were set in the bronze threshold. The lintel they supported was of silver too, and the doorhandle of gold. On either side stood gold and silver dogs, which Hephaestus had made with consummate skill, to keep watch over the palace of the great-hearted Alcinous and serve him as immortal sentries never doomed to age...Golden statues of youths, fixed on solid pedestals, held flaming torches in their hands to light the banqueters in the hall by night.
>
> "The house keeps fifty maids employed. Some grind apple-golden corn in the handmill, some weave at the loom, or sit and twist yarn, their hands fluttering like the leaves of a tall poplar...For the Phaeacians' extraordinary skill in handling ships at sea is matched by the dexterity of their womenfolk at the loom, for

Athene has given them outstanding skill in beautiful crafts and such fine intelligence.

"Just outside the entrance to the courtyard, surrounded by a wall, lies a large orchard of four acres – pears and pomegranates, apple trees with glossy fruit, sweet figs and luxuriant olives. Their fruit never fails nor runs short, winter and summer alike. It comes at all seasons of the year, and there is never a time when the West Wind's breath is not assisting, here the bud, and there the ripening fruit; so that pear after pear, apple after apple, cluster on cluster of grapes, and fig upon fig, are always coming to perfection.

"In the same enclosure there is a fruitful vineyard, in one part of which is a warm patch of level ground, where some of the grapes are drying in the sun, while others are being gathered, or trodden in the wine press, and on the foremost rows hang unripe bunches that have just dropped their blossom or show the first faint tinge of purple. Beyond the furthest row, vegetable beds of various kinds are neatly laid out, luxuriantly productive all the year round. In the garden are two springs; one flows in channels to all parts of it; the other, starting next to it, first provides a watering-place for the townspeople and then runs under the courtyard gate towards the great house itself.

"And then... Alcinous says:

"...we can run fast, and we are first-rate seamen; but the things in which we take a perennial delight are the feast, the lyre, the dance, frequent changes of clothes, hot baths and our beds."

I find that particularly alluring. And then there is something Nausicaa herself says:

"There is no man on earth, nor ever will be, who would dare to set hostile feet on Phaeacian soil. The gods are too fond of us for that. Remote in this sea-beaten home of ours, we are the outposts of mankind."

Phaeacia was supposedly imaginary, but to me it speaks of that hunger for a vanished Eden which runs through all civilisations...And this one of four thousand years ago, on Crete, was perhaps the closest we have ever been to it.

I stopped the tape and sat for a while, finding the passages in *The Odyssey*. The sea pervades it. I saw not the back garden and the apple tree but the wine dark sea and the white-sailed ships upon it.

37

The Hand of David

I did not hear from Mr Brouard for some months after that, and I did not like to telephone.   Besides, my life was full with work, children and some problems with my and Al's parents, none of whom were getting any younger.   I had been given a monthly column to write in a magazine and it took up more time than I had expected. We spent Christmas with my parents and New Year with Al's in Northumberland.   In April Al was invited to take part in a conference on astrophysics and he suggested that the children and I went along too: the conference was in Florence and he had been offered an apartment to rent for the week.   April was also the month of my fiftieth birthday and until then I had not been looking forward to it.

The apartment was in a narrow guano-encrusted street near Santa Croce, and had a small roof terrace from which we could see the Duomo and the hazy blue hill of San Miniato across the Arno. We ate *bistecca alla fiorentina* in the local trattoria on the corner, sauntered through cobbled streets in the evening passeggiata and drank endless cups of liquid chocolate with teaspoons in the Rivoire café in the Piazza della Signoria.   We did the Uffizi and the Boboli Gardens and stared up at half a dozen church ceilings and frescoes and climbed the four hundred and sixty three steps up into Brunelleschi's dome. We went to see Michaelangelo's David in the Accademia, and I was strangely reminded of the description of Odysseus, when in front of Nausicaa he scrubbed his head "free of the scurf left there by the barren sea" and the bushy locks hung "thick as the petals of a hyacinth in bloom".   And David's beautiful great hand upon the slingshot made me think of those early sea people, for whom weapons had been no more than this, yet as accurate.

On the last day we went to Fiesole in the hills above the city, and had iced tea and cakes overlooking the blue distance.   It was a day of crystalline sunlight, and under the silvery olives of the Roman and Etruscan ruins a breeze rippled through shining grass and wild flowers. We watched a tortoiseshell cat crouching on a warm Etruscan wall and staring, transfixed, at a bright green lizard. So must cats and lizards have been for three thousand years.   In the exquisite little museum we looked in entrancement at the delicacy and love that informed the paintings, the decorated vases and bowls, the tiny figures, the wine jugs and jewellery and glass.   It seemed to me that in those three thousand years we had achieved nothing more beautiful, no craftsmanship more immaculate than this.

I bought a tiny bronze lizard as a souvenir, like the one we had seen on that warm Etruscan stone.

38

Black Sand

The end of the Minoan civilisation was not without warning. The first rumblings came in the fifteenth century BC. But when it came it was sudden and violent. Around 1470 BC the volcano on the island of Santorini, one of the Minoan bases in the Mediterranean, erupted. Fifteen cubic miles of rock were blasted into dust with over a hundred times the power of a hydrogen bomb. Mountainous waves swept the Mediterranean. The palaces and cities of Crete were destroyed. Some survivors did reach the mainland of Greece. Life always proves to be extraordinarily resilient, and within a generation normality began to return. A new force was to arise in the Aegean as the survivors of Crete met other peoples from the north. The warriors of Mycenae were soon to build their own golden empire.

But the supremacy both of bronze and maritime power was almost over. The Bronze Age was to be replaced by the Iron Age – although perhaps it would be more accurately called the Steel Age. Wrought iron is strong, workable and rustproof when it is burnished, but it is too ductile, too easily moulded, to retain a cutting edge. As copper required smelting to produce bronze, so iron ore had to be smelted to produce steel.

The first commercial smelting of iron almost certainly took place on the southern coast of the Black Sea, where the black sands of the estuary of the Kizil Irmak river are so rich in iron ore that crude iron can be derived simply by smelting sand in a primitive furnace. In his great poem about Jason and the Argonauts, Appollonius Rhodius described the people of the region:

> "They dig for iron in the stubborn ground, and they
> live by selling the metal they produce. To them no
> morning ever brings a holiday. In a black atmosphere
> of soot and smoke they live a life of unremitting toil."

Iron ore is much more common than either copper or tin, but its extraction is more difficult. Part of the technique would have been discovered in the course of copper smelting, since the waste part of the ore from copper or tin, and limestone flux, may contain a high proportion of iron. It is de-oxidised by the charcoal, together with the copper and tin, but the result is not a pool of molten iron because its melting point is much higher – 1540 degrees Centigrade. Instead there remain 'puddle balls' of slag and pure iron, intimately mixed together. By heating these balls again in a furnace and hammering them briskly while still hot – an extremely exhausting form of labour – the iron can be squeezed out of the spongy mixture and shaped into 'muck bars'. When the process is repeated, billets of wrought iron – pure iron with less than five per cent of slag – can be produced. If these billets are then cooked between layers of charcoal in a furnace, which need be no hotter than that required for smelting copper, the carbon from the charcoal starts to soak into the surface of the iron billets, converting them into 'cement steel'. It takes only two or three days and produces a much better material for making weapons and sharp blades than bronze. But it has drawbacks.

Whereas bronze could be produced by fleets of small ships, picking up tin and copper ore from widely dispersed sites, iron needs a fixed site with plentiful iron ore, wood for charcoal burning, and a supply of fit workers.   And steel, which was suited to large scale production, depended chiefly on slave labour.   But the recruitment of suitable young slaves required armies – and the armies needed steel weapons.   The great empire of the Hittites, ruling the hinterland of Anatolia and beyond, was built upon steel production.

Centuries later, when Homer wrote down *The Iliad* and *The Odyssey*, iron had long been established as the metal for everything from axes to door handles, but bronze was still the stuff of heroes. Rarely does he mention iron, as when the disguised Athene says to Telemachus "we are bound for the foreign port of Temesa with a cargo of gleaming iron".   More significantly, Homer uses what must by then have been a well known proverb: "iron of itself draws men on to fight".

Yet the final end of the seafaring Bronze Age was accomplished not by men, but by the violent meterological, volcanic and seismic turbulence that afflicted the area of the central Mediterranean early in the second millennium BC.   Quite what caused these natural phenomena continues to be debated, but what is certain is that memories of the old holocaust of Santorini were sufficient to spread panic among the surviving sea peoples.   The Old Testament describes the wrath of God being manifest in the contamination of the Nile, plagues of frogs, hail mingled with fire, darkness during the day and pestilence brought upon the land.   Six hundred thousand Hebrew slaves, employed in Egypt on the construction of the great temples of Abu Simbel, were released through Moses' intervention.

On a warm summer night in 1926, Arthur Evans had some inkling of the fears that people had experienced nearly four thousand years before.   He was in his villa on Crete:

"In the evening of calm, warm day, the shocks began. They caught me reading on my bed in a basement room...and, trusting to the exceptional strength of the fabric, I chose to see the earthquake through from within...The movement, which recalled a ship in a storm, though only of a minute and quarter's duration, already began to produce the same physical effect on me as a rough sea.   A dull sound rose from the ground like the muffled roar of an angry bull; our single bell rang, while through the open window came the more distant jangling of the chimes of the cathedral...It is something to have heard with one's own ears the bellowing of the bull beneath the earth."

'The Peoples of the Sea', as the Egyptians described them, dispersed across the seas, and wherever they appeared, quite literally 'out of the blue', they spread fear. They sacked the empire of the Hittites, together with the old port of Ugarit and the fortress of Troy. Neither was ever restored or reoccupied.   Those who invaded the coastal lands of Palestine, Lebanon and Syria, established originally by the Canaanites and the Phoenicians, were to be called Philistines. The smoke from their furnaces and weapon foundries darkened the skies. Had their amphibious operations against Egypt succeeded, it is likely that none of us would have known of them; but Ramses III repulsed them and commemorated his victory with a temple at Medinet Habu on the Nile.   On its walls the invading Peoples of the Sea, with their high-prowed boats, come vividly to life.

Included among these various seafarers were those who had long ago settled on the coasts of Tuscany, and become famous for their elegant, ocean-going fleets of ships.   For a time they had been contemporaries of the Minoans of Crete, likewise prospering through the Bronze Age, commanding the Tyrrhenian Sea and exploiting the tin and copper ores of the hills inland from Elba and Piombino. They too fled the turmoil of earth, sky and sea in that second millennium, obliged like all the survivors to adapt to other ways of living, to other cultures and traditions. They learned how to organise slaves, how to adapt their maritime skills to land-based hydraulic engineering and building in stone.   And when, in the end, they returned to Tuscany, they found that not only had its green and fertile land become renewed, reforested with mature oak and pine, but that the 'metal hills' from which their ancestors had extracted copper and tin were also rich in high grade iron ore.

D. H. Lawrence called Etruria "the best integrated civilisation of the ancient world", and indeed it surpassed Crete in its industrial development.   Forests were skilfully coppiced and maintained to feed the beehive smelting furnaces for steel production. Slaves were rounded up by seaborne raiding parties. The wind itself was used to funnel air, economising on slave power. A pall of smoke hung permanently over the strait between Elba and the coast: highly productive farms were terraced out of the hillsides to feed the labour force, with subsoil irrigation systems we might consider recent technology. And arms were sold to other empires in exchange for consumer goods and luxuries. Within a few generations the Etruscans were increasingly reliant on seafaring mercenaries, whose nautical expertise was also used to improve hydraulic engineering – to this day Tuscany has a subterranean network of ancient conduits, drains and sewers.

The Etruscan civilisation had echoes of the Minoan in its delight in life. Its art is full of a sensuous appreciation of beauty, both of the human body and the natural world, of dance and music. (Aristotle said they beat their slaves to the sound of the flute – or so he was quoted). D. H. Lawrence described them thus:

> "This sense of vigorous, strong-bodied liveliness is characteristic of the Etruscans, and is somehow beyond art. You cannot think of art, but only of life itself, as if this were the very life of the Etruscans, dancing in their coloured wraps with massive yet exuberant naked limbs, ruddy from the air and the sea-light, dancing and fluting along through the little olive trees, out in the fresh day."

Yet harsh winds were blowing. There had long been rivalries between the Etruscans, the Greeks, the Carthaginians and the Phoenicians, but accommodations had been made and the shifting territories on land and sea had continued over hundreds of years. Etruria was never a united empire but a loose federation of independent city states of which twelve formed what was known as the League. Thousands of years later they were to become such Renaissance city states as Bologna, Florence and Milan. In the seventh century the Etrurian dynasty of the Tarquins chose to develop the seven hills that rose out of the Pontine marshes, south of the river Tiber. The people of Latium were poor, augmented by runaway slaves and their families, speaking what to many seemed a barbaric language called Latin. The area was ripe for a new town. The world had been shaken by the fall of the Assyrian empire to the east, and young men were excited by militarism, by new weapon technologies and the prospect of personal power. Etruria's ease and unprotected luxuries were a prime target.

During one such skirmish Tarquinius of Rome was killed, to be succeeded by his adopted son, Servius Tullius, reputedly the son of a slave. Servius Tullius was an admirer of efficient administration, like that of Assyria, and he introduced rigorous reforms. Censuses of population and property were taken, dividing the people into five classes – not, of course, including slaves. Each class had statutory obligations to pay taxes and make direct contributions to the defence of the city state: the highest class had to provide cavalry regiments, while the fifth and poorest were obliged to arm themselves with slingshot.

The old comfortable way of life of a typical Etruscan city was turned into the Roman ideal of a rigidly organised state. It was to be dedicated not to a pantheon of deities of the natural world but to Mars, god of war, and two-faced Janus, whose temple doors remained forever open as a reminder that war, not peace, was the right direction. Only industries which served that purpose were permitted. Only martial music was tolerated. Recreation was for young men to practise war, with spears and javelins. Women, like slaves, did not qualify as citizens. From the rich legacy of Etruria the Romans took what they wanted, including the toga, the colour purple, engineering, infantry formations, roads, metallurgy, skills of divination and craftsmanship, social customs - and then destroyed everything else. It seems that a dark fatalism gripped the Etruscans who tried to combat this new and ruthless nation state. Gradually, by burning, by destruction, by propaganda, the Romans virtually erased them from the face of the earth.

I stopped the tape then, remembering the great stones of the Etruscan temple in Fiesole, buried so deliberately and for so long beneath its Roman successor. By all accounts the little Etruscan town had been a good place to live, up on its hill above the valley of the Arno. The Romans had killed all its inhabitants and burned it to the ground. So fierce had been the fires that the black earth was still there. And as they had burned Fiesole, so they had burned Carthage, with its library of half a million volumes, works on science, on history and literature; and Alexandria, into which had been gathered almost the entire knowledge of the ancient western world.

39

Unexpected Callers

After Tom's GCSEs in June I realised it had been a long time since I had heard from Mr Brouard. I telephoned him three times, but there was no reply. At the fourth attempt I got Molly.

She sounded different. Less brusque, not as hostile.

"He's in the library," she said.

"Oh – "

"The British Library. I'd normally go with him to read but they do have a special gadget he can use with most of the books. I'll tell him you rang."

"He's well, is he?"

There was a brief pause. Then she said: "As well as you might expect. We've been away for a while and he's been rather tired. A touch of angina, the doctor says."

"Oh."

"I'll tell him you rang," she repeated.

"Yes – please do – "

And that was that.

A week or so later Tom, Penny and I decided to spend a few days in London. I did not trust Al to look after Whim, he was quite likely to forget her altogether, but my parents said they would be happy to have her. My friend Nicky said we could stay if we could all sleep in the same room, and as her spare room was vast I said that was fine. We did all the usual things, the Science Museum, the Natural History Museum, the Tower, and went on a boat up the Thames to Hampton Court. For Tom's sake we rode on the Docklands Light Railway, walked under the Thames from the Isle of Dogs to Greenwich and went to the National Maritime Museum, and for Penny we did Camden Market, Oxford Street and a concert at the Wigmore Hall. And we spent one day trying to find Mr Brouard.

"Look, I'm OK on my own," Tom said cheerfully. "I'll meet you back at Nicky's this evening if you like. If you can let me have some cash – "

I had already telephoned Mr Brouard twice, but there was no reply. Penny and I walked round to his address in Denbigh Street. It was one of those handsome, anonymous red brick terraces off the Brompton Road. I rang the bell that said 'Brouard'. No one answered.

"We'll try again later," I said.

We had lunch at a café nearby and watched people, and then tried again without result.

"He might be out, and she's probably at work," said Penny practically.

"Yes, I suppose so."

Then we went to Knightsbridge, and Harrods, and went upstairs to the piano department where Penny asked if she might try a few pianos. I tried to look wealthy, in an understated sort of way, as if I might be considering buying a Steinway for my fourteen year old prodigy. The assistant gave Penny a sheaf of music and said wistfully that although she herself played the piano she was not allowed to, which seemed very short-sighted, I thought, for pianos were meant to be played. I always liked listening to Penny and so it seemed did everyone on that floor of Harrods, because a small audience accumulated, and surprised Penny with their applause.

We had tea and cakes in Harrods and then tried Mr Brouard's address again.

It was almost half-past five. I rang the bell and we waited. It was a grey evening and Denbigh Street was busy with traffic and people going home. We were both startled to hear a voice, a male voice – speak to us from the entry phone. It was not Mr Brouard's voice. He asked who we were and I explained. There was a moment's hesitation. Then the voice asked us to wait a moment. I looked up at a pigeon on one of the window ledges above. It reminded me of Florence. The voice spoke again: said we had better come up. The door clicked, and we pushed it open.

He was waiting for us at the door to the flat on the second floor landing: a large man, balding, perhaps in his late fifties. He wore a dark suit and a striped shirt and an air of deliberate charm. "I'm sorry, I didn't know who you were. I gather you're a friend of Molly's father? Please come in."

I hesitated for a moment. "Is he in?" I asked. "Mr Brouard, I mean?"

From behind the stranger I saw Mr Brouard approach, smiling, neat as always. He was wearing navy cord trousers and an open-necked blue shirt with a lemon yellow sweater, as if he could still see colours, and preferred them to be vivid. I stepped forward, took his outstretched hands and kissed his cheek, which was roughened with age and the trimmed beard. At my side Penny was suddenly shy, but she took his hand and said hello, and he smiled at her and said: "so this is your daughter. It is a pleasure to meet you, Penelope." Then he turned to the man who had opened the door for us. "I'm sorry – you won't know David. David Drummond-Hay. You won't know, of course, that Molly recently became engaged."

"Engaged? Molly?"

"Yes," said David Drummond-Hay. "You know Molly?"

"Well – not really – we've met once or twice – "

"Come along in, both of you," said Mr Brouard. "Let me get you a cup of tea. Or a drink, perhaps?"

"Tea would be lovely," I said.

We followed them into a central hall with a beige carpet, mahogany furniture, a lot of china in a cabinet, a small chandelier:

then into an airy sitting room carpeted in the green I thought was called celadon, matching some pale green plates hung on wires on the pale pink damask walls. There were two unsquashed pink sofas and a lot of cushions and Mr Brouard clashed with everything. He told us to sit down while he made the tea, but Penny offered to help, and he did not refuse the offer. I sat down on one of the pink sofas and David Drummond-Hay glanced at his watch.

"When are you getting married?" I asked him at last.

"September, we think," he answered. He must have been a good deal older than Molly, and I had an impression that he had been married before – something in his attitude towards me, as if he was accustomed to women, and did not think a great deal of them. Yet he was marrying Molly. I wanted to ask him why; instead I said: "have you known Molly long?"

"A year, perhaps."

"How did you meet?"

He did not much like being questioned but he replied "we both sing in a church choir."

"St Asaph's?"

"Yes, that's right." He glanced at me with a slight thawing of his faint antagonism. "Do you know it?"

"Not really. I've been there once. A beautiful little church."

"Yes," he said.

"Are you – in the civil service?" I enquired then, suspecting that he was not, although perhaps civil servants now wore expensive suits and striped shirts with white collars.

"No, an accountant. A fund manager," he said. Then he asked me if I had known Molly's father for a long time, and I explained that I had, although we had not seen each other much over the past forty years.

"Forty years?" he said in surprise. "You must have been a child."

"I was," I said.

Mr Brouard returned then with a tray of tea and Penny. I noticed, with amusement, that he was treating her with the same courtesy with which he had treated me at the age of ten, and that she was responding by losing her shyness.

"We just happened to be in London," I said. I was still flummoxed by the revelation of Molly's engagement. "We just thought – well, as we were going to the Science Museum – and we're staying with a friend of mine not far from here – we might as well call in and say hello."

"I am delighted to see you."

"I did try and phone, but I couldn't get a reply, so I thought I'd just take a chance – "

"I'm glad you did. I have been away a good deal. And Molly and I went on a cruise last month, in the Mediterranean."

"Oh. Lovely."

He smiled at me with his old humour. "I don't think I'm cut out for cruising myself, but she enjoys it... And Turkey is fascinating. We were able to visit the Institute of Nautical Archaeology at Bodrum, where they have the finds from the Uluburun shipwreck. But tell me, how is Tom? And Al? And the dog Whim?"

I began to tell him about these domestic things, and then we all heard the sound of a key in the lock of the front door, and sat suddenly silent, even furtive. We listened with increasing awkwardness to the sound of Molly dropping her briefcase on to a chair, looking through the letters on the hall table, crossing the hall to the open door of the sitting room. She stopped in the doorway. She said:

"What is going on?"

She was wearing a dark suit with a pink blouse. I thought she had lost some weight. Her hair was longer, curly. Under her freckles her face was very pale.

David Drummond-Hay, who had not sat down at all but was standing by the window, walked across and kissed her cheek, took her hand and led her into the room. "Unexpected callers," he said.

"Hello, Molly," I said. "It really was just a spur of the moment thing – we were in Harrods – oh, this is Penny, my daughter. Penny, this is Mr Brouard's daughter."

"I see," said Molly, ignoring Penny. Then she turned to Mr Brouard and said: "Daddy, did you know they were coming?"

"Of course not," he said. "It's a very unexpected pleasure. We've just made some tea – I'll get you a cup."

"I will," said Penny quickly.

"Thank you," said Mr Brouard.

"Why are you here?" she asked me abruptly.

I explained about our visit to London, and how it had occurred to us to call. I could hear my calm voice, the simple ordinary words, and yet I was aware that to her I was no ordinary visitor. I glanced across at her fiancee. Why did I seem to represent some kind of threat to her? I said how pleased I was to hear of her engagement. She looked at David Drummond-Hay and for a moment I saw her expression soften. I thought she must really be in love with him.

Penny brought a fifth cup and said she would pour. I was quite surprised and rather proud of her poise. David Drummond-Hay said abruptly: "how old are you?"

"Fourteen," said Penny.

"Bit younger than my daughter," he said.

"You have a family?" I asked.

"Three sons and a daughter. All grown up now. Well, almost. Joss – my daughter – is just eighteen."

"David is a widower," Molly said.

"Oh," I said, intrigued. So she was taking on four grown up children? I wondered what they thought of her.

"They're very fond of Molly," David Drummond-Hay said, as if divining my speculation.

"And I of them," said Molly.

"I am – really pleased for you," I said. I smiled across at her, for it seemed to me that she must have no reason for her hostility now, and I was quite genuinely very happy that she should have found someone.

"Thank you," she replied.

Then I asked: "will you be staying in London?"

"Of course," she said, as if no one could think of living anywhere else. "I have quite a senior position – and David has a house in Highgate. We'll be living there."

"Highgate?" I looked across at Mr Brouard. "Bit further for you to get to the British Library."

"Daddy won't be living with us," Molly said.

"Oh?"

"I'm actually moving into a flat," he said. "Not far from Molly."

"A flat? On your own?"

"Not exactly. I suppose you would call it an apartment."

"It's a lovely place," said Molly. "A conversion of a beautiful Georgian house into sheltered accommodation. There's a warden always on call, and care assistants – it really will suit Daddy very well. You like it, don't you?" she smiled at him.

"It's very comfortable," he said.

Penny said: "what – a sort of old people's home?"

"Not at all," said Mr Brouard. "I shall have all my independence, but just a little more help."

There was a small silence. Then I asked: "when do you go there?"

"Next month," he said.

"You're not old, though," said Penny. "I mean – you are, I suppose, but you don't seem old."

"I'm seventy-four," he said. "And almost blind. It makes life a little difficult. This is undoubtedly the best solution."

"We were very lucky to get him in," said Molly. "David was able to help, of course, because he's on the board of Hope End – "

"Hope End?" I queried.

"Yes," said Mr Brouard, looking at me in amusement. "They didn't change the name... Hope End House."

I did not know what to say. I thought of him at Boury, with Jean-Claude and Freddie, and his own study with the french windows opening on to the sunny garden. I could not picture him in a flat in a Georgian house. Was it on the ground floor? How could he share with the sort of people who live in such homes? Would he have to play bridge and watch television? Except of course he wouldn't be able to see to do any of those things...He could listen to music, Radio Four, read braille. What would happen to him? My wise, vigorous, unique Mr Brouard? Quite suddenly he had become just somebody's elderly relative, to be put away in a home. For that was what it was, surely. And David Drummond-Hay was on the board? I stood up and looked at Penny. "Darling, I think we must be going. We told Nicky we'd be back by seven."

Mr Brouard rose to his feet, as did Molly. David Drummond-Hay remained standing by the window. I looked across at him and said how nice it had been to meet him, and how glad I was that he and Molly were to be married.

Molly said suddenly: "Hope End is a lovely place. Really it is. Twenty-five acres of parkland and gardens and everyone has their own sitting room..."

Mr Brouard saw us to the door. "How much can you see now?" I asked him.

"Not very much," he said.

I turned to him then and said fiercely: "you can't go into a home."

"It isn't a home. Seriously. I am very happy for Molly – she's done so much for me over the years. I know that for some reason she has always been jealous of my friendship for you, but I hope that will change now. I think she is in love with David, and he – well, I can't say I like the chap, but he's got plenty of money, which will help. Please – don't worry. I've almost finished my work. All that is left is to look at the latest research, the most recent discoveries, and see how they fit into the hypothesis. I can complete that even in Hope End House. So don't worry about me. I am glad that you do, but there is no need."

"Molly said – something about angina?"

"Oh, that. Nothing serious at all. I need to take more exercise, cut down on the pipe."

"Well – all right. Let me know your new address and telephone number."

"I will. It's been such a pleasure to see you – and to meet Penelope."

"It's been lovely to meet you, too," said Penny warmly, and kissed him on the cheek.

We left him then, standing in the doorway, watching us descend the dark stairs into the cool grey evening.

A tear ran down my cheek and Penny squeezed my hand. "Don't cry, Mummy. He'll be all right."

"I hope so," I said.

The following week Yolande came up to Bristol to go shopping for an outfit for the wedding of her youngest daughter, Melanie. For someone who spent most of her life on a smallholding in Cornwall she was astonishingly elegant. We went to Bath and she bought a cream and red linen dress and a scarlet straw hat. When she mentioned that she and John had had a cancellation for one of their holiday cottages, I hatched my plan.

Mr Brouard moved into Hope End House, Muswell Hill, at the beginning of August, and sent me a short tape giving his new address and telephone number. He did not say much about what the place was like but I knew he was not happy there. I sent a tape back inviting him to come to Cornwall with us for the last week of August, before Tom and Penny went back to school. "Short notice, I know, but we'd love you to come – please do."

He did not reply at once so I telephoned him.

"Please," I said.

He said he would come, but insisted on taking the train by himself from London to Bristol before travelling to Cornwall with us. I met him at Temple Meads. He looked suddenly quite frail as he fumbled his way off the train, carrying an old hold-all and his white stick, which at least encouraged strangers to offer assistance. In fact there was a small group of people around him. None of them left him until I came to claim him, and then there was some intense questioning as to whether I could manage.

"People are incredibly kind," he said.

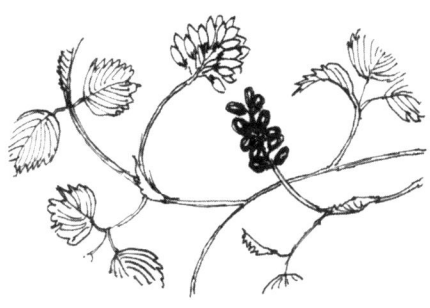

40

Medes and Persians

The gods smiled on us in Cornwall. The air was like warm silk and smelled of dry grass, the sea was diamond-bright, the lanes full of cushiony blue hydrangeas and sprays of orange montbretia. Sand martins scissored over the cliffs and violet spears of viper's bugloss studded the rabbit-nibbled turf.

We took one of John and Yolande's holiday cottages, and it was arranged that as so many of their children had come home for summer and for Melanie's forthcoming wedding Mr Brouard would have one of the two small spare rooms in the farmhouse. It suited him, being small and simple, with an adjoining bathroom. It was next to the larger room occupied by John and Yolande's eldest daughter, her husband and their two small children. Altogether there were fifteen of us, plus Whim, and a number of other assorted dogs. Yolande was in her element, spoiling her grandchildren, cooking vast meals, frequently wearing her red wedding hat as she supervised the next meal to appear on the long wooden table under the apple trees. "I'm wearing it in, darling..."

Tom and Penny disappeared to the beach almost as soon as we arrived and together with some of the Drayson offspring decided to sleep out on the cliffs, so that Al and I found ourselves in the unfamiliar situation of being more than usually both together and on our own. That took a little adjustment, so used had we both become to somewhat separate lives save when united by the children, and our slight unease was emphasised both by the closeness of John and Yolande's relationship, and the presence of Mr Brouard. Everyone, save me, called him Bill from the moment we arrived, and Yolande said one could not possibly continue to call him Mr Brouard. I had not seen him in such a context – not in any context, really. To me he was simply Mr Brouard, and I was still ten. Although when I had been ten, I had felt quite grown up...

His blindness was something they had all been a little apprehensive about, but at the outset he declared that although he was grateful for help – he did not want to fall over a step or into the pond – he was quite capable of finding his way about. He pointed out that he could still discern light and dark and within a very small area could actually see objects, at least in daylight. I heard him once talking to Yolande in the kitchen:

"The trouble with them is that they don't seem to understand how the overcoming of these trivial obstacles takes on a perhaps disproportionate significance. They want to make life easy and comfortable, but that way lies disintegration. I want to have to negotiate the stairs, to try to read, to get a bus or do my own shopping. And because they try to stop me, I find I am fighting a series of humiliating skirmishes in some protracted guerilla war..."

And I knew he was talking about Hope End House.

He did not impose upon anyone, either physically or with the force of his personality, but seemed to enjoy simply being there. He wore khaki shorts that I thought might have dated back to Hong Kong, a series of very bright shirts and a denim hat to cover his balding head. Yolande's grandchildren, who were nine and seven, often commandeered him to play cricket or boules on the beach, giggling when he lost them. Curiously, bright sunlight made him almost as blind as darkness. Once the children persuaded him to join them in the Mirror dinghy they kept hauled up on the sand above the high tide mark.

"Wonderful," he said, scarlet with sun and wind and the effort of obeying shrieked orders to duck every time the mainsail boom swung over, as Al and I stood in the surf to help them in on the breeze and a turning tide.   As he clambered out of the little boat, shorts flapping in decidedly indecorous fashion round his bony knees, he grinned across at me and said: "Remember the difficulty of getting papyrus boats to land to windward or an ebb tide?   Just like this!"

He did not seek to talk about his work, but I could tell by such moments that it rarely left his mind.   Once, when we all went up to load bales on the tractor and trailer after John had taken a second cut of hay, there was another.   We had finished the final swaying load and collapsed in the dark shade of an oak tree, quenching our thirst with a bottle of water and listening to the simmering oven of summer beyond the canopy of leaves.   Tom lifted a handful of spilled hay and said curiously, "it isn't just grass, is it?"

"Well, mostly," John said.   "But several kinds. Cocksfoot, Timothy, rye, meadow grass. The scent comes from sweet vernal grass."

"But there are wild flowers and things," Tom said.

"Well, yes – of course buttercups, clover, scabious.   That's yarrow," he added, as Tom picked out a flat composite flowerhead.

"Woundwort, they call it," Yolande put in.

Mr Brouard leaned over and Tom put the dry flower in his hand.   "Strange," Mr Brouard said.   "Achilles is said to have used yarrow to cure wounds.   But specifically wounds made by iron weapons."

"Not bronze," I aid.

"No.   Iron was very different."

"All right," said Tom. "What about this?"   And he lifted a handful of stringy green plant with leaves like tiny shamrocks and small black seed pods.

"Horrid stuff," said Yolande.   "Smothers everything."

"But good for the cows," said John.   "Now, even I know something about this one. Black medick. Nothing to do with doctors or medicine.   Do you know what the name means, Bill?"

"Well, no," Mr Brouard said. "I have to admit to never having heard of it before."

"Well, it means 'plant of the Medes'," John said. "But all I know about the Medes is that they're mentioned somewhere in the Bible, along with the Persians."

"Come on, Bill," said Al suddenly. "You must know about the Medes."

"Well, yes – they were an ancient people from what is now north west Iran, part of Azerbaijan and Kurdistan. Famous for their horses. They were to become part of the vast Achaemenid empire of Persia, which stretched from Egypt to the Indus valley in the sixth century BC. But you say this plant is named after them?"

"Apparently," said John. "But I don't know why."

"How very odd," said Yolande.

"It probably goes back to the Romans," said Mr Brouard. "So many things do. They took what they wanted from every source. Although even then, such plants may go back much further."

"Sixty-five million years back?" Al remarked. He sat up, taking a gulp of water from the Vittel bottle. "Isn't that where we all began, Bill?" He did not look at me, but I looked across at this lean bony face, the glint of his dark eyes, and knew that he knew I knew this was not directed simply at Mr Brouard, but at me.

"Well – I think that might well be true," Mr Brouard said. His face was shadowed by his floppy denim hat but I could see the silver shine of his beard.

"Despite all the scientific evidence."

"Scientific evidence?"

"Well, I would have thought it was pretty much proved that we actually originated with tree-dwelling apes who gradually learned to walk upright on two legs about seven million years ago, and subsequently developed into Homo sapiens sapiens comparatively recently – something like fifty, a hundred thousand years ago. All the evidence from Africa surely confirms that."

Mr Brouard said thoughtfully, "I suppose it has always seemed to me that the evidence from Africa was curiously unscientific. The topography of the Great Rift Valley, for instance, has a very particular feature, in that it brings ancient fossil remains to the surface. And why should some apes have decided to endure the very difficult and painful process of walking on the ground – while of course others did not – rather than the other way round? The ability to walk on two legs is not something that could have evolved over a short space of time. It depends on a much older physiology."

"Sixty-five milion years older."

"Well, that's my idea. The concept of an upright, bipedal egg-collecting mammal seems to me rather less outlandish than an ape who one day decided to drop off a branch and try to walk, grew a big brain and walked into Europe. Then he went on to conquer the primitive northern Neanderthals, become a skilled hunter and fine artist, and finally proceeded to walk all over the world about twenty-seven thousand years ago during a peak in the Ice Age, when sea levels were low and he could trudge through the mud to remote islands. Now, it seems to me curious that this early man, or woman, reproduced and diversified into many races, but retained the same specific characteristics. Some, of course, like the inhabitants of Tierra del Fuego that Darwin thought such barbarians, and those hunted to extinction in Tasmania, apparently ended up rather more primitive than the initial emigrants from Africa. I find this logic – unscientific. Particularly as the evidence is extrapolated purely from those artefacts durable enough to survive, the flint tools, ornaments, pottery shards, paintings. That there may be evidence which has not survived is somehow not taken into account. And some evidence which might seem to undermine the basic ideology of evolution, the idea of the upward progress of mankind, is quietly removed."

"But from what I understand, you take this theory of yours into the realms of real fantasy. Fred Hoyle land. Aquatic ape theories, Atlantis, all that stuff."

"No, he doesn't," I said fiercely. "It isn't like that. I've challenged him all the way through – it's not a matter of crazy theories, it's just looking at the evidence – all the evidence, that is, not just the archaeological or – or the – oh, you know, the word I can't say – "

"Paleontology," said Mr Brouard carefully.

"Yes – well, not just that, but everything." I said.

John, conscious of tension in the air, said: "it is true, isn't it, that scientific disciplines today have become so complex, each so specialised and separate from another, that we might be in danger of not seeing where they overlap, where they might touch?"

"Who said 'only connect'?" said Yolande.

"E. M. Forster," I said. "In *Howard's End.* But things didn't."

Mr Brouard said: "I wouldn't deny the scientific realities. Genetics, natural selection, cultural change, communications. I would simply ask that every archaeologist, palaeontologist, ethnologist, might include in their thinking such things as mathematics, mineralogy, botany, zoology and astronomy."

"I think you underestimate the way science works," said Al. "With all due respect, I don't think you realise the rigour of the experimental hypothesis, the testing of ideas, the discipline that must underpin them."

"Darwin once said that to make new discoveries one has to have a theory, an experimental hypothesis, so that one has something to look for. I agree with him. That's all I am doing. Perhaps it is the looking for that is important, since without it we are unlikely to find anything."

Tom, uneasily, said: "come on, Dad. You wouldn't say that no one but a trained scientist can have a theory about something."

"No, but I would expect even an amateur to discriminate between that which can be proved, and that which is simply the product of the imagination."

"Without imagination," said Mr Brouard, "there is nothing to prove."

Yolande scrambled to her feet and said "well, now, I think that's enough debating."

And John, smiling across at her, added: "yes...let's get this last load down to the barn. Then it really will be the end of summer."

41

The Blind Poet

With the hay in the barn there was a scent of autumn in the air. A cooler night, a vaporous new moon, dew on the grass in the morning.

"The last chance, I think, to have a barbecue on the beach," said John.

John and his sons' idea of a barbecue was neither modest nor refined. Great logs were hauled down to the beach in the sun, dragged across the wild thyme and the cloudy clump of lime-green alexanders that had colonised the place where we descended from the low cliff to the dunes and the sand below.

"Alexanders - a herb from Macedonia," said John - "is that right, Bill?"

And Mr Brouard grinned as he watched the progress of the logs, and said "you must be right, John. Probably named after Alexander the Great".

Once the logs were piled high, together with old pallets and anything else flammable and not too noxious, the old iron barbecue, like some strange detached jetty on stilts, was stuck in the sand just below the high tide mark. We put nightlights in jam jars around the base of the cliffs, in the mouth of the two big caves, on ledges in the blue-grey and pink limestone. In the Yolande's kitchen we women, as ever, prepared the food, salads, pitta bread, sausages and trays of lamb. Plastic bottles of red wine and water were transported in boxes. Lingerers on the great ribbed sweep of sand watched us, as they were walking dogs, carrying children home. The late sun glittered on pools, on the blue estuary and the bleached cut wheatfields beyond. Trawlers were beginning to come in on the evening tide, flagged with seagull bunting, the steady beat of their engines rising and falling behind the rustling murmur of the incoming waves. Boats under sail caught the last of the fickle wind as it fell away from the cooling shore.

When all was set we left John and Al and the boys to light the bonfire while we returned for the last of the food. Mr Brouard came with us. I forebore to take his arm as we climbed up to the edge of the lowest part of the cliff, although the shelving sand took some effort to negotiate. Yolande suddenly said, looking across at the rock that rose above us on the western side, "look – there's some samphire. Shall we pick some to go with the meat? Penny – look, take the carrier bag and pick some. We might as well. It really is delicious. A bit like asparagus, only a little tougher."

We reached the welcome path between the brambles – bearing blackberries now – where the worn turf was as slippery and brown as rush matting, and sat down to rest while Penny scrambled lightly over the cliff ledges towards the drift of samphire. Its bluey-grey stems were covered in yellow-green flower heads and seemed to grow – indeed, did grow – out of the very striations of the rock. We watched as Penny filled the carrier bag, and returned triumphant with her haul.

"You know what this is," she said, pink with success: "it's the same as in King Lear – you know, when Gloucester and Edgar are on the cliff, and they see the man gathering samphire below – we did it last year: 'Halfway down hangs one that gathers samphire – dreadful trade!'"

"I remember," said Mr Brouard. "And Gloucester falls, and believes he has thrown himself off the cliff that Edgar described so vividly. But he hasn't."

Penny looked at him, her small face suddenly scarlet. Then she said slowly: "Because he was blind. 'Alack, I have no eyes – ' "

He smiled, but he continued the quotation: "'Is wretchedness deprived that benefit, To end itself by death?'"

And for a few minutes we sat silent there on the cliff, while the gulls wheeled and cried around us, and the scent of the burning wood rose from the shore below.

Penny brought her guitar with her when we carried the last of the food and drink down to the beach, chiefly, I think, because she then had no other duty but to sit on a ledge and play background music while various young men plied her with red wine.

"She's only fourteen," I said once.

"I've watered it," said the young man.

"I hate it anyway," said Penny from above.

The sun slipped behind the angle of the cliff, and then into the sea. The lights in the jam jars twinkled like stars and the wind had dropped completely. The sky was a vast illumined bowl of violet and palest cerulean, pink and gold in the west, and white-winged fleets of gulls rested in the skeins of the tide. Silently, almost imperceptibly, it came ever nearer the black metal legs of the long, rickety barbecue. John, standing back from a slow drift of smoke, found his bare feet in water. We sat on the rocks and at the cave's mouth, leaning against the dinghy drawn up under the cliff, ate and drank, and watched the light ebb from the air.

I looked across at Mr Brouard. He was sitting at the mouth of the cave leaning back against the flat strata of the rock, talking to Al – or at least Al was talking to him. As I watched, Al refilled their glasses with red wine. Above them on her ledge Penny sat with some of the young men, giggling over home-made karaoke with her guitar. The logs of the fire rustled, charred now, concealing the red embers within.

Had it been like this, I wondered, for the people of the Island, as they had watched the darkness come? Perhaps they too had lingered on the shore beside a low burning fire, contemplating their departure from the home they had known to some unknown landfall beyond the sea.   And was it like this for silver-footed Thetis, who had felt that first sensation of satisfaction when she built her reed nest on an even earlier shore?

It was now so dark that we were all shadows, ill-defined, part of the very sound of the sea, the licking waves, the occasional cry of a distant bird. A yacht was coming home, only its lights visible, catching the turn of the tide, the low drumming of its engine carrying across the dark water.

On such a night, I thought, did the horseshoe crabs come out of the sea. Perhaps even now their shining helmets were emerging from some faraway ocean and moving up the sand to lay their eggs, as they had done for six hundred million years. Only it was September, not summer... I thought of Rhea, on such a calm, warm night as this, the last night of the world before the cataclysm, sixty-five million years ago. Through my mind, in that suspension of time before the tide turned again, went all those people I had met and briefly touched: the Neanderthals of the cold northern seas and icy rivers, the swift brown seafarers who shared the southern seas with the dolphins and the shoals of flying fish, whose reed rafts spun upon the currents. I thought of Don Marcelino de Sautuola in the cave at Altamira, Aesop in the dusty market place telling his stories. Henry Rawlinson on his cliff face. Joshua Slocum navigating by the stars and a tin clock.

A sound broke into my reverie. A raised voice. Al's voice.

"I wouldn't dispute that there is a lot we don't know about the past, but some unknown ancient civilisation – come on. If what you're saying is that *Homo sapiens* – that is, us – developed much earlier than is generally accepted, on an island in the Indian Ocean, then there surely would be more evidence of their existence, once they'd left the island about three hundred thousand years ago."

Mr Brouard answered: "there is a great deal of evidence, both in artefacts, fossil remains and the very existence of people today across the globe.   But the link with the sea, with the required technology to build nest, rafts, boats, to travel across oceans, to understand the winds and currents and navigate by the stars – I would agree, of that there can be little evidence, because by its very nature it is ephemeral, quite literally perishable."

"All right, but you're talking about a degree of civilisation that surely would make its mark – "

"What would we know of Homer if *The Odyssey* had not been written on papyrus and stored not in Greece, but in Egypt? We don't even know who Homer was."

"Don't we?" said Yolande, from where she sat near the fire, leaning against John, who had abandoned the barbecue. A faint glow from its cooling charcoal, a black skeleton against the sucking sea, was all that could be discerned. "I thought he was a blind singer. I always imagined him with a beard – you know, rather noble."

"It's possible," said Mr Brouard, "but not certain. The Greeks themselves argued about where he came from. He wrote down these epics of mingled history and myth, of gods and men, in about the eighth century. It was a time when Greece as a nation was emerging from a dark age, an age of natural disaster and war, into the beginnings of what we think of as its classical period over centuries to come. The past golden epoch of Minoan and Mycenean civilisation, the glory of the seafaring Bronze Age, was not forgotten. It was still alive in the memories handed down by the bards – of whom we must suppose Homer was one."

"So he would have been a singer?" said Penny curiously. "I mean – could you sing the whole of *The Odyssey*?"

"It's a good question. We do know that there was a brilliant singer at about that time, called Homeros – which actually means 'hostage' – but no one knows if he was our Homer, as it were. There does seem to be agreement, though, that Homer was a singer, and that he was blind. He writes of such a man in *The Odyssey*. Demodocus was the favourite bard of King Alcinous. Homer said the Muse loved him above all others – 'though she had mingled good and evil in her gifts, robbing him of his eyes but granting him the gift of sweet song.'

"Like you," I said. I thought I said it to myself, but for a little while no one spoke.

Mr Brouard lit his pipe. I saw his face briefly illuminated by the flare of the match, his silvery beard catching the light.

"What we do not know for sure," he said, between puffs, "is whether it was actually Homer who wrote down these great poems. They were undoubtedly sung, and they are part of a very ancient oral tradition, but they are also literature – they were written in a literary form. Did he dictate, perhaps, to scribes? Or did he do it himself? But there is one curious paradox in this. Writing had virtually been lost before Greece began to renew itself in the eighth and seventh centuries, and it was only at this time, in the eighth century, that the ancient Phoenician alphabet was rediscovered and adopted by the Greeks. With this new writing, Homer could turn the oral epics into true poems, refining the words, cross-referencing, adding shades of depth and meaning. And perhaps it was such literature, and the spread of literacy, that saw the end of the old sung tradition."

Penny, on her ledge, more discernible now that our eyes were accustomed to the darkness, and illumined by the occasional glow of a cigarette beside her, threaded the hushing of the sea with liquid notes on her guitar. It was like the sound of the lyre to which the blind poet sang.

"On such small things do civilisations, empires turn," said Mr Brouard. "Trace the alphabet back to the Phoenicians, those peoples of the sea, and since nothing comes of nothing, trace it back again...And then we are with the seafarers who first made marks upon the sand, who interpreted the stars, and found a way to pass on their knowledge. Go forward, and we are with Shakespeare, Jane Austen, the mobile phone. The greatest genius who ever lived could not dream up something out of thin air. He could only combine ideas based on the objects of his personal experience. It is a principle that applies equally to the technology of communication, from the first bundle of reeds used to float down a river - to the internet."

I saw Al ease himself on the sand, change an elbow, reach for the wine. He said: "I still find your thesis elusive...But tell me this, then, Bill: why do you pursue your ideas about the ancient origins of *Homo sapiens sapiens*? What has made you send these tapes of your research to my wife for nearly forty years?"

Mr Brouard drew on his pipe, saying nothing for perhaps a minute, while we sat in silence. I thought that perhaps I should some time ago have gone to sit beside Al, that our physical separation might signify something more. But then, could he not have come to sit beside me?

Then Mr Brouard said: "I think...I think perhaps an awareness of what we have lost, and are still losing, for we don't always know it exists until too late. You talk of evidence: well, if we go back to the Greeks, perhaps it is worth remembering that only one work of Aristotle survives in its entirety. All his other works are edited versions of notes made by his students. We speak of Socrates, but he may never have written a line. All we know of him is through Plato, and of Plato we have only what he considered his popular writing, because all his serious and scientific work has been lost. Of the tragedies of Aseschylus, Sophocles and Euripides we have left about ten per cent. Even Shakespeare's plays were only collected together in a single folio seven years after his death, for he himself considered them much less important than his poetry. Originally they were written down only in separate parts for each player to learn his lines, and kept in a box by the players' company – the Lord Chamberlain's box might well have been consumed by the fire at the Globe, had not someone thought to save it. In our time we are losing not only man-made treasures but landscapes, forests, the plants and animals with whom we share the earth."

"Well, I can't disagree with that. But why should you think it worth pursuing your particular hypothesis?"

"Because I believe the truth matters, I suppose. I don't know whether I've found a part of the truth of our origins. But the idea that we are always climbing the staircase of human evolution just doesn't add up. Evolution isn't progress. Civilisations come and go, empires rise and fall. There is a kind of theological arrogance about some of the assumptions of archaeology that I enjoy challenging. I don't believe we can ignore the seas, the rivers, the ice, which make up eighty per cent of the globe, or the part water has always played in the development of human technology."

Al replied: "I would like to say that the sea is simply water, a compound of hydrogen and oxygen. But water isn't simple. I acknowledge it. The structure of water, the properties of water, are fascinatingly complex. Even now it remains essentially an enigma.

To that extent I concede you have a point. We do tend to forget how integral it is to our lives."

"I think our future will depend increasingly on not forgetting it. Water is likely to be a cause for conflict in many parts of the world, just as it could also be a cause of peace, if we understood its importance."

"Well, I'd agree with that. Certainly the sea could be the key to energy in the future, especially if we succeed in developing fusion power, since it depends on sea water. And we'll need energy if we are to exploit the sea, if only in desalinating it for drinking water."

"But perhaps it's more than that," Mr Brouard said. "There is something about the sea, about water, that seems to be linked to the human spirit, and if we deny that then we lose something valuable. There's a passage in Melville's *Moby Dick* which expresses it. He wrote:

'Why did the old Persians hold the sea holy? Why did the Greeks give it a separate deity, and own brother of Jove? Surely all this is not without meaning. And still deeper the meaning of that story of Narcissus, who because he could not grasp the tormenting, mild image he saw in the fountain, plunged into it and was drowned. But that same image we ourselves see in all rivers and oceans. It is the image of the ungraspable phantom of life; and this is the key to it all.'

"And now, perhaps, a libation. To Poseidon, God of the Sea."

And so we poured our wine on to the sand.

42

Beyond the Sunset

The weather broke. As we started packing to go home the soft Cornish rain drifted in from the sea.

Mr Brouard found me in the farmhouse kitchen, making sandwiches.

"John and Yolande have suggested that I stay on in one of the cottages," he said.

"Have they? Well, I knew they'd like you. And that you'd like it here."

"They mean, I think, that I could rent the cottage on a permanent basis."

"And not go back to Hope End?"

"No. Well, only to collect my belongings, such as they are, and settle up."

"What about Molly?"

"Molly has the wedding to think about. And I don't think she'll mind too much. Not now. If she does – well, so be it. It is my life."

"So it is."

Whim came and put her grey muzzle on his knee as he sat at the table.

"I thought I might try and get a guide dog," he said.

I sat down opposite him. "Would you manage, down here? Cornwall is a long way from anywhere. At least, from places like the British Library and the Festival Hall - and The Royal Geographical Society..."

"I can always go up to London. In any case, I don't think I'll miss them too much now. I think I have finished my project. No doubt I shall continue to read the new research, to write – but in essence, I have finished."

"So the Roman Empire was the end of the story, then?"

"I suppose it was. By then the people of the sea had become subsumed into their essentially land-based culture. Even before then the old freedoms of the sea had become corrupted by the tides of history. The power of the Roman Empire laid the foundations for the next millennium."

"Like that Monty Python film – *A Life of Brian*. 'What did the Romans ever do for us?...'"

"Yes, I remember it. Law, new roads, sanitation...And it's true, the Roman Empire even changed our perceptions, ordering the way we began to think as well as how we ordered society in our western civilisation. And through us of course it has touched the whole globe. Of course there were empires before, conquest, destruction: but this was the beginning of an *administrative* conquest, a desire for order. That spiritual dimension you see in previous cultures became essentially practical and utilitarian. Beauty, nature, imagination, were not part of the mainspring of life. Not that the Romans were without imagination or creativity, but perhaps they lost touch with the things that refresh the spirit, that could have regenerated a decaying civilisation. There are parallels with our own society today that don't give me much optimism for the future."

"No more tapes, then."

"I don't think so. And you have your own work to do. And I don't just mean your writing."

I smiled at him. "Well. I'll miss them."

"So will I."

"Will you do something with all those transcriptions?"

"Well, I shall take great pleasure in reading them all, in going through them, checking what we knew then and what we know now. Perhaps at the end of it I shall come to some final conclusion, something to add to the sum of human knowledge – perhaps not."

"Thank you, anyway," I said, "for telling me the story."

"Thank you, for listening to me for so many years."

He put his hand on mine, and we sat in silence, because suddenly there seemed nothing to say that we could put into words.

He did stay in Cornwall. He was given a guide dog, a golden labrador called Oscar, and walked a great deal, but his angina troubled him, according to Yolande, and he seldom left. John and Yolande became very fond of him, as did their children and grandchildren. I always intended to go down and see him, but somehow life was very full and I only managed it twice. Al was seconded to LIGO – the Laser Interferometer Gravitational Wave Observatory project in Glasgow, which delighted him. I remained in Bristol while Tom went on to A levels and Penny did her GCSEs. Perhaps the separation helped our marriage. We all took the opportunity to explore Scotland. Al took Tom and Penny skiing in the winter holidays while I walked and worked on another novel. The news was full of dire predictions about the Millennium Bug which Al said were ridiculous, but I bought lots of tinned food.

In November I had a telephone call from Yolande. Mr Brouard had died, apparently in his sleep. He had been fine, she said, the day before – they had eaten together the previous evening and he had not mentioned any discomfort. They had been alerted by his dog whining in the early morning. I remembered how we had walked in the park on the eve of my wedding and I had told him about my hamster. How stupid, I thought, to think of that now, and him saying that going from a death-like sleep into death was a good way to go.

He left a will, leaving his estate – such as it was, which was not much – to Molly. A separate bequest was to me. It consisted of a cardboard box of all the transcriptions of the tapes he had sent me over the years, tied together with treasury tags, in rough chronological order. There were eleven further boxes of books, magazines, maps, yellowing photographs, letters and various objects. Among this evidence of his years of research was the shell of a horseshoe crab, mounted on a piece of wood, long ago painted blue. The paint was beginning to peel. I searched through my old Hong Kong wicker baskets to find his drawing of the horseshoe crab clock and put them together, and some time later I set them both in a frame made of driftwood and put it on the wall in the kitchen. It was not comforting to see how brief a span of time mankind had lived upon the earth, compared to the horseshoe crab. My family found it distinctly disturbing. But perhaps it made us all try to make the most of what time was left.

Mr Brouard also left instructions that he should be cremated, and that his ashes should be scattered on the sea, just as he had told me.

I told Molly that he had wanted them scattered off the coast of Antarctica, but she thought I was being silly, and what difference did it make as long as it was the sea? It was her decision. However she did agree to the sea off the Cornish coast. Jean-Claude and Freddie both said they would come over for this small ceremony, as did Roger Laurent, the cider-maker who so long ago had been Mr Brouard's amanuensis in Boury. And I asked Geraint. It made for quite a lot of people in John's small fishing boat.

We crossed the bar on a bright winter's afternoon, out of the estuary and on to the ocean swell.

"Look," said Tom – "Look, Mum. Dolphins."

They accompanied us all the way out to sea, just ahead of us, as if their shining grey curves were leading us to the right place, for after a little while they ceased their swift passage and seemed to circle round us, interleaving through the vast dark green waves. Perhaps it was just my imagination. Molly emptied the box and the ashes blew away on the wind. And when we turned back into the estuary the dolphins disappeared.

"What happened to all those tapes he used to send you?" Geraint asked me. He was not a good sailor and his face was even paler than usual, his beak of a nose pinched with cold although he was wearing his Murmansk greatcoat.

"I've got them all in a Hong Kong basket.   And now I've got the transcriptions, too."

"Why don't you try and publish them?"

So I did.